NO DAUGHTER
OF THE SOUTH

A Mystery by

Cynthia Webb

New Victoria Publishers

Published by New Victoria Publishers Inc., a feminist, literary, and cultural organization, PO Box 27, Norwich, VT 05055-0027.

Printed and Bound in Canada
1 2 3 4 5 6   2001   2000   1999   1998   1997

Library of Congress Cataloging-in-Publication-Data

Webb, Cynthia.
    No daughter of the South : a mystery / by Cynthia Webb.
        p.   cm.
    ISBN 0-934678-82-0
    I. Title.
PS3572.E1952N6   1997
813' . 54- - dc21   96-44569
                                                                         CIP

Chapter One

The first thing you have to know about me is that I'm no daughter of the South. People get the strangest ideas about me because of the way I talk. My accent gets even thicker when I've had too much to drink. Some people don't hesitate to make fun of me for it. They want to think it's cute or charming. Well, I'm not interested in being cute or charming. Men let me know, in what they think is a subtle way, that my particular accent is an indication that I'm not as smart or sophisticated as they are. One guy even gave me a brochure for a class called "Getting Rid of Your Regional Accent." You'd be surprised how many times it turns out that these are the same guys that revert to *dat dere* when they have had a few too many.

They can all fuck themselves for all I care.

Same thing applies when they assume that, just because I was born in the South, I'm automatically a racist. The South is full of bigots, they say. I ask them, "Like Bensonhurst and Howard Beach?" Again, these are the same people who have their own little supply of racist jokes. I've thought about it a lot, and what I've come up with is that when you come right down to it, I think some white guys are still afraid that black guys are sexually superior.

Unfortunately, I can't give you a comparison of black guys and white guys in bed. I've never gone to bed with a black man. It's not that I wasn't attracted to them, because I was. For one thing I've heard enough black women talk about the pain it causes them when they see a black man with a white woman. And for another, I used to be so tempted to sleep with a black man that I was sure it was something very deep-rooted and psychological. So if I ever did, I was certain that I'd be consumed with guilt, thinking that I did it just because he was black. Southern-white-liberal-guilt runs very deep and can be very confusing. To be absolutely honest here, I've got to tell you the third reason. No good opportunity has ever arisen.

And then there's my sweet Sammy. Ever since Sammy I've seen things differently. But first I just want you to know, before I tell you what happened, that I sure as hell don't believe that all the racism is in the South. The South. That's another problem. People hear "the

South," and they picture Tara, and magnolia blossoms. Or they think "new South" and picture Atlanta and Dallas and I don't know what else. If I tell them I'm from Florida, right away they think Miami or Daytona. That I grew up on a beach in a bikini. The truth is much more complicated than that. It almost always is.

My name is Laurie Marie Coldwater. Bad last name. It proves irresistible to a certain kind of man who considers himself a wit. He feels he has to make an original observation along the lines of "You sure are a long drink of cold water." Yeah, you got it. I'm tall. Very tall.

I've got blond hair and blue eyes, but I don't have the perky little nose to go with them. Helpful friends and relatives have suggested plastic surgery more times than I've been able to respond to politely.

I live in the Chelsea section of Manhattan, in an apartment over a French bakery. The apartment is rundown, but it smells good, and I feel safe. The bakery is open all night, baking bread for restaurants all over the city. There's no way someone could break in here without the guys downstairs noticing. For a woman living alone in the city, that makes up for a lot, including the crack dealers on the sidewalk outside.

I make my living with a little writing, and a little photography, and a lot of temporary work as a word-processor. I'm working hard to turn the percentages the other way around. Sometimes I think I'm actually going to do it. Sometimes I'm afraid I never will.

My family thinks I'm crazy living in New York City. I don't visit them often, but when I do, something goes wrong inside me. I feel clumsy, out-of-place, and, at the same time, I feel that I don't quite exist. I explained that to Sammy when she first asked me to find out about her father. I don't think Sammy realized what I meant.

On a brisk, spring afternoon, I was sitting at my desk working on a piece about tap-dancing classes in the city. It wasn't as exciting as the last piece I'd done, an account of my interviews with the married guys from the suburbs who cruise the meat market district for queens. They actually drive up in their station wagons or four-wheel drive jeeps. A lot of them have car seats strapped in the back and toys spread out over the floor.

I'm so tall that with over-done makeup, big hair, and uncomfortable shoes, I could pass as a transvestite prostitute. Until I was in the car anyway. Then after the initial shock, most of them were relieved to have a chance to talk. I promised not to reveal their names, or any identifying details. As insurance, I told them right away about Jerry, over on the sidewalk, who had already taken down the license plate number and who had his portable phone in hand. Once I got them talking, most of them couldn't shut up. They had things to say about love and passion and life and guilt. These guys, who left wives and children in safe, suburban homes to risk violence and disease for a chance to have sex with a man dressed like a woman, these were guys who knew a lot about two of my favorite subjects, longing and guilt. The series of articles that resulted from that project received the first real attention in my writing career. I accompanied each section with a photograph. One of a Volvo station wagon with a "Child On Board" sticker in the window, and a particularly flamboyant transvestite lounging against the side. Another photograph was taken from behind a man in a suit while he was negotiating with one of the ladies. There was something about the pathetic sag in his shoulders, the pleading way he held his hands, that tore at me every time I looked at it.

But now I was working on the silly tap-dancing article, because Jerry wanted it. He had this incredibly kinky fascination with tap dancing. Jerry paid me regularly and well for my stuff, and no one else was standing in line to do that. He also let me write about whatever I wanted. In return, when he got some crazy idea about something, I humored him. That's what I was doing with this tap-dancing stuff when Sammy interrupted me.

"Laurie? I've got a favor to ask. A big one."

I'd been wanting to do something for Sammy. Sometimes I felt like this big kid that Sammy took care of. This was my chance to give something back. After a moment, I said, "What is it?" As the words left my mouth, I wished I had said, "Anything you want."

She smiled that big, sweet smile of hers. "Next time you visit Port Mullet, will you do something for me?" And I was thinking, what could I possibly do for Sammy in Port Mullet? Port Mullet is where I'm from, where my mother and father and brothers still live. I'd left it behind me every which way I could. I knew Sammy's mother once lived near there. We'd talked about that the night we met. It was one of those weird coincidences the city specializes in. Like, you're walking around in a city of millions of people, but you get on an uptown bus, and who is sitting across from you but your college roommate's brother. Anyway, Sammy's mother had had the good fortune to leave Port Mullet before Sammy was born.

"I've been wondering about my father. I want to know if anybody there remembers him. Anything about him. What he looked like, if he liked to dance. You know. Just what he was like."

Sammy had barely mentioned her father to me before, but then I hadn't asked either. I wasn't interested in anybody's past, including my own. I liked to pretend I had been spontaneously generated, that

I really had no genetic ties with the people that I called my family. That Sammy didn't talk about her father was fine with me. She did talk about her mother, though, and how hard it had been on her, a young widow, raising two daughters alone.

Sammy continued. "My momma and my aunt and my grand-daddy never wanted to talk about him, so I figured there must have been something shameful about the way he died. I just let it it be. But Annie's starting to ask about him, and you know, I realized it's not right. I should face my past, whatever it is. I ought to know the truth. I owe it to my girls."

Face up to one's past? Now that was something that had never occurred to me before. I stood up, and walked over to the chaise lounge where Sammy was curled up, knitting.

She put her needles and wool down and patted the seat beside her. I sat down, feeling confused. She reached out her hand and stroked my hair.

"You did such a great job on that transvestite article, Laurie. It started me thinking. You can talk to anyone. You're not afraid to ask or look into anything. So, just ask around."

"But what could I do that a private detective couldn't do better? It's not that I don't want to do this for you, but your father was black, right? I don't know the black neighborhoods down there, Sammy. I never did." I could hear how weak and scared I sounded and I hated it. That's not the way I wanted to be with her.

Sammy was the sweetest lover any woman could wish for. Chocolate-brown, warm, generous, compassionate. Sometimes I wish that I could curl up inside her and stay there.

Years earlier I had made up mind that I was done with all that monogamy stuff. From then on I was going to take love every place I found it. I didn't care if my lovers were male or female; I didn't care about their marital status or creed. If they made my blood pulse and my heart beat, if they made me feel that all was right with me and the world, even for an hour or so every now and then, hey, that was more than enough.

But that was before Sammy. We'd been seeing each other a couple of months and I was still crazy about her. The painful truth was that I was afraid that I was falling in love with a grown-up woman who had a life full of responsibilities and commitments and that whole truckload of things I'd never wanted. Now that truck was bearing down on me, ready to run me over. Even if I found the courage to do something stupid like stay in the middle of the street and let it leave tire marks across my chest, I didn't know what I meant to Sammy. How could a woman like Sammy be serious about someone like me? Even I couldn't take me seriously.

Sammy wound a strand of my hair around her finger, then let it go. "I don't want to know things a detective would tell me. I want to know the things you could tell me. The years have gone by and pretty soon it will be too late. I can't ask my mother. She's old now, and my aunt, too. I don't want them to think I'm ungrateful after all they've done for me." She cupped her hand under my chin and turned my face towards hers. "It's not the bare facts of whatever it was he did. I want you to help me understand him. If he was drunk and drowned himself—well, I hope I won't despise him." She dropped her hand, but I couldn't look away. "You'd be good at this. And I can't go. I can't leave my practice or the girls. I want to feel that someone's tried, even if there's nothing left to find."

Here she was asking me to do something important, something that mattered to her. "Sure," I said with my best swagger. "Of course I'll do that for you." A trip out of town would give me time to think about truck avoidance procedures. Anyway, I've always been better with actions than words, when it comes to my love life.

We met at a party one night, and it was love at first sight. At that time I was a great believer in love at first sight, and I was on a campaign to experience it as often as possible. But after we danced and chatted, and I'd turned my charm up full blast, I suggested that we go somewhere for a cup of coffee. We did, and I sat across the table from her thinking about drowning in those eyes. Then I noticed her accent, which is much less obvious than mine. I asked her where she was from and she said the Upper West Side.

"Before that?"

"A lot of places." She'd been talkative and open all night, so I was intrigued by her reticence.

"Well, where did you grow up?"

"L.A."

"L.A.? With that accent?"

She stirred her coffee, which really didn't need it. I'd been watching and she hadn't added any sugar. "L.A. Lower Alabama."

I told her my life story then, with all the humor stuck in the right places. My spiel is pretty good. I've told it enough that I've got the timing down just right. I tried to get her to come home with me, but she wasn't buying it. She looked me over for awhile, though, and invited me to dinner at her place the next week.

She pulled her beeper out of her bag and showed it to me. "I'll be on call, though. I can't promise you that I won't have to leave."

So right away, I thought she was a doctor. It fit, because she had this quiet, confident way about her, and I could tell she had brains

7

to spare. But one thing bothered me. She was so warm, and open, not like any doctor I'd ever seen. I guessed that maybe she was a pediatrician. I asked her.

"Unh-uh." She shook her head. "Midwife. I've really got to go now, Laurie. I'll see you on Friday."

That week I finished my tap-dancing article, developed the pictures in my combination bathroom/darkroom, and turned it all in to Jerry. *The Rag* makes no money. It is in a severe deficit situation, and Jerry is the one who keeps funding it. His story is an old one: rich boy gone bad. He lives in utter poverty in the East Village, using his monthly trust fund check to make sure we keep the presses rolling for *The Rag*.

My heart belongs to *The Rag*, I guess, but my body belongs to the corporate world every working day between nine and five. I go to a boring law firm where I type boring legal briefs into the word processor, except for an hour off for lunch, when I get the hell out of there.

Yes, it is a waste, but no, it isn't so bad. While I'm typing, I'm thinking about the article I'm working on, and the photographs I've got to develop. That particular week, the week after I met Sammy, I spent a lot of time thinking about how nice Sammy looked in that short red dress. A midwife! I'd never even met a midwife before. If I had ever thought about midwives, which I hadn't, I would have thought about some little old lady with dirty fingernails in a primitive village.

The week went by like that, punctuated by my pretending to be respectful to the lawyers in the office and to the word processing manager, a woman not five years older than me who dressed and acted like she could be my mother. Then it was Friday, and after work I went home to change before heading up to Sammy's place.

I had a hard time figuring out what to wear, which is unusual for me. My theory about dressing is, if you keep enough outrageous items tossed around the apartment, you can throw one of them on with your jeans, and you're dressed. Throw one of them on with a black leather miniskirt and you're dressed to succeed in love. Something about Sammy, though, made me choose the jeans to go with my red leather, pointy-toed cowboy boots with the map of Texas embroidered on the side. I stopped on the way to the subway station and bought some flowers.

Sammy lived in a substantial pre-war apartment on West End Avenue. The doorman said she lived on the first floor, right up a flight of old marble steps, so worn that they sloped down in the middle. I raced up the stairs, trying to outrun my nervousness. The heels of my boots clattered against the marble, making an embarrassing racket. I rang the bell, and could not believe what I saw when the door opened.

It was a kid! She was a sharp, New York kind of kid, though, in black leggings and an enormous black t-shirt with a picture of Bob Marley on it. She looked like an even tinier version of Sammy. She said, "Hi, you must be Laurie. I'm Annie. Come on in. Momma's in the kitchen." Then she turned around and went back into the apartment, leaving me standing at the open door.

I stepped into this pleasant apartment. High ceilings, good woodwork, cream-colored walls, big windows, lots of light. A few bright rugs, a few big, comfortable pieces of furniture, lots of bookshelves, a couple of cats. And more kids. For a moment I panicked and thought there were dozens of them. I took a deep breath and counted. Including Annie, there were three. I wondered if I should add in the number of cats. Then I wondered exactly what it was I was doing.

Annie was already back at a coffee table with an even younger girl playing Parcheesi, a game I hadn't thought about in…I found myself counting again…twenty-eight years. When did I get so old? And why was it just dawning on me just then?

There was a baby on the floor in a diaper and a t-shirt. At least it looked like a diaper, but it wasn't plastic, it was some kind of fuzzy cloth. The baby was chewing on some wooden blocks.

I stood there, my knapsack over one shoulder and my paper cone of flowers in the other, feeling like a visitor to another planet. Sammy came walking out of the kitchen. She had on jeans and a brown sweatshirt, and one of those aprons that cover up most of a person. She was wiping her hands on the apron, and she was looking at me. She didn't have on the bright red lipstick she was wearing at the party, or any make-up at all. She looked nice enough, in a quiet way, but I was a little disappointed. She had looked fabulous that first night! Spectacular!

She said, "Have you met my girls?"

"Sorry, Mom," said Annie, looking up. "I forgot. I'm too busy trying to keep Sarah from cheating."

Sarah started a whining moan. "Ooh-ooh-ooh. I do not cheat, you liar. You're the one that always cheats!"

Sammy stepped in and calmed the girls down, but I was in too much shock to catch the details. I was trying to figure out how I was going to get through dinner and how soon I could leave afterwards. I was wondering how I could have been so wrong about Sammy.

How could she have missed that I had been putting the make on her. Had it all been just a misunderstanding on my part? But damn it, there had been no mistaking the way she danced with me. Or had there been?

Then Sammy was taking my flowers and thanking me, and saying I should come in the kitchen while she found a vase and finished up dinner. She turned and went ahead of me. I followed, eyes fixed on her sweet, high, round ass covered with tight, faded denim and topped with the string bow from her apron.

The kitchen smelled good and it was pleasantly cluttered. I got a funny feeling when I saw the refrigerator covered with school papers and crayon drawings and notes, all of it stuck up with magnets. That kind of thing still existed? Here, in New York City, at the tail end of the twentieth century? When I calmed down a little and thought about it, of course, I had to have known that this kind of thing still happened. I'm going to tell you the truth, even though I can see now that it doesn't reflect well on me. I thought it was the not-quite-hip girls, the not-smart-enough ones—the boring ones, O.K.?—who ended up with a refrigerator looking like this. Not someone like Sammy, who looked like a fire in that red dress and danced like a flame and made me hot, hot, hot. What the hell was going on here?

I ended up helping Annie set the table. She unfolded a blue-checked tablecloth and Sammy put my flowers in a pitcher in the middle, with candles on either side. While we were working, Sammy called out, "Elena, supper's almost ready."

A door off the kitchen that I thought led to a closet opened and out came this young woman with long dark-blond hair and pale skin and cat's-eye glasses. She looked in her early twenties. The other girls, Annie and Sarah, and Rachel, the baby, all looked to one degree or another, black. But Elena's complexion was fairer than mine, and her hair was perfectly straight and silky. How old must Sammy be, if she was the mother of this woman? I tried to conduct a discreet surveillance to determine whether more children were popping out of closets, drawers, wherever. I didn't see any, but I was nervous.

Sammy picked up a tureen with pot holders and carried it towards the table, saying, "Elena, would you please make sure that Rachel has a dry diaper and that Sarah washes her hands?"

And then we were all seated at the table, and they all held hands and said "Blessings on the mealtime." We started eating split pea soup and salad and whole-wheat dinner rolls. The kids told knock-knock jokes, which made me laugh, and demonstrated terrible manners, which I thought was even funnier, but Sammy didn't. Annie got sent to her room awhile for telling Sarah that the soup was made of frog guts. No amount of persuasion was sufficient to convince Sarah to try the soup after that.

Annie was back in time for dessert, though, which was baked apples with cream. Somewhere during the course of this, I realized that Elena was not Sammy's daughter, but a graduate student at Columbia. She was from Czechoslovakia and helped with the children in return for room and board. She lived in the small room off the kitchen. After dinner, the girls showed me the room that they shared. It was tiny, and filled with three beds, and all kinds of art supplies and toys and dolls and clothes and Annie's CDs.

Annie said, "You wanna see Momma's room? It's right here." I knew I shouldn't. I should wait for some time when Sammy wanted to show me. But I really wanted to see it, so I went in anyway. I was looking for clues. If a guy has a jumbo size box of condoms next to his bed, that tells me something. If a woman has black leather underwear and handcuffs strewn across the floor, that gives me an idea of what to expect.

Sammy's room was also small, and absolutely crammed with books. The bed was stripped to the bare mattress. A quilt and some pillows were stacked on a worn armchair that was crammed into the space between the bed and the window.

Elena appeared behind us and looked over my shoulder into the room. "Oh no, I forgot the sheets in the dryer. I will scream should the swine from the third floor have thrown them on the filthy floor." It sounded funny in her soft, elegant accent. She ran down the hall and a moment later I heard the front door of the apartment slam shut behind her.

Annie sighed. "We have to do Momma's sheets every night. Elena and Momma and me take turns, because it's such a pain. Rachel gets out of bed every night and crawls in with Momma. Her diapers leak. We've tried everything. Come on, you want to play Parcheesi?"

I was mesmerized, fascinated, and horrified by the life in this strange place. It paralyzed me. I stayed on, through an endless game of Parcheesi, Annie's violin practice, Sarah's good-night story, Rachel's good-night story. Eventually, Annie announced she was retiring for the evening to read. Elena supervised the little ones' baths, while Sammy made a pot of coffee.

I stood beside her watching her pour it, feeling comfortable, and that made me nervous. I'd spent over a decade in the big city living the life of an emotional transient. I knew why I had come to

Sammy's apartment, but I didn't know why I'd stayed once I knew the score, once I'd seen the hotbed it was of fertility and stability and all those related anti-aphrodisiacs. The warm, full smell of coffee rose as she turned to me, holding out a chipped mug by its handle. I looked at the curve of her forearm and her sweetly plump wrist. Her fingers were surprisingly thin and elegant. I reached out and held the mug in both hands although the coffee was hot.

Just then Elena brought in the little girls, clean and sweet-smelling from their bath. Sarah kissed her mother good night and Elena led her off to bed.

I tried to calm myself by focusing on the reason I had come here. I watched little Rachel crawl onto her mother's rocker and I wondered what final ritual of good night would be necessary before I would be alone with Sammy. Rachel settled comfortable in Sammy's lap and placed her fat little hands on Sammy's sweatshirt. Then Sammy pulled up the bottom of her sweat shirt, revealing her left breast, round and plump in a red lace bra. She unsnapped the front closure with one hand. In response, her breasts hopped slightly apart. She peeled off the left cup, revealing her brown breast and her large, brownish-pink nipple.

Rachel wasted no time in fixing her baby lips on Sammy's nipple. At first, she made little gulping noises, and then she slowed down, so the only evidence of her swallowing was the rhythmical movement of her throat muscles. Her little fat hand stroked the top of Sammy's breast to the same beat.

I hadn't ever considered a prospective lover's breasts as baby food production before. I glanced down at my own flat chest as if it were an enemy in my camp. When I looked up again I saw Sammy watching me with amusement. She'd been watching me all night, now that I thought about it. I felt set-up and angry but as I watched the baby suckle, I felt the emotion fade, replaced by desire or even something deeper. I was aware of a terrible longing, a pull towards something I'd never known I wanted. I'd been a lot of places, done a lot of things. I'd lived as if I was afraid to leave any sensation unexplored, miss any experience. And I tell you this: I hadn't let many chances go by. But I knew then I'd never felt what they were feeling.

I drank my coffee.

Sammy rubbed Rachel's little hand for a moment, and then she looked up at me. "Before we go any further, I wanted you to see what you're getting into."

I had seen plenty.

Chapter Two

In spite of my misgivings that first night at Sammy's apartment, or maybe because of them, I was fascinated with her. I tried hard not to be too obvious: I tried to be cool. And actually, it wasn't that hard, because, between her patients and family, Sammy didn't have a lot of free time to spend alone with me.

She invited me over for a rerun of the whole-damn-family show fairly often. The first few times I refused, would only see her if she could get away for a party or a movie, with me for dessert, of course. I made up some pretty good excuses, but I was also sure she knew what my problem was. I ran out of excuses after awhile, and began accepting her invitations. Or maybe I couldn't get enough of her.

The first few weeks, we made love only at my apartment. She wouldn't sleep over; she wanted to be home when the girls woke up. She didn't ask me to stay at her place until the girls knew me pretty well and then I refused to stay the first time she asked—a retaliatory gesture. Sammy just smiled at me, this irritating, knowing, beautiful smile. That made me so angry that I jumped out of bed and walked all the way to my apartment at two o'clock in the morning, fuming the whole way.

By the time I left for Florida, I'd stayed over maybe a half-dozen times. The lovemaking was great—with me in bed, how could it be otherwise? But it wasn't as terrific as at my place. She was preoccupied. Or maybe she was just listening out for the girls, but I suspected it was more than that. She wasn't just listening for them...they were taking up space inside her. My pain surprised me, because, to say the least, I've never been the jealous type. I've never felt I owned a lover's body, let alone his or her heart and soul. All I've asked for has been the moments we were together. With Sammy, I felt that even that wasn't all mine.

After we made love, she'd made me put on a t-shirt to sleep in. Sometimes during the night, Rachel would slip into bed between us. Then I'd wake up, the early morning light would be bathing my lover, and Rachel would be nursing. I'd give Rachel a dirty look that was meant to say, "Why don't you give us a break, kid?" She seemed to understand, because she'd nestle even closer to Sammy and suck harder. What was I to do, just lie there full of jealousy towards a baby? Anyway, there was usually that ammonia smell in bed which I had learned was a bad omen. In the end, I was a woman who knew she'd be beaten. That's when I'd get up and make coffee.

So we had never slept late together. Never. We hadn't had any luscious mornings in bed with some sleepy, good-morning sex, and then breakfast in bed, and more sex, and maybe a nap. I don't know, maybe I thought that if I pulled off this quest for her, she'd think she owed me a weekend away together.

Her 'big favor' had become a quest for me. Something I had to do. Should I have questioned myself more closely about my motives, made sure what it was I hoped to obtain before I left? Hell, yes, but then I would have been someone else if I thought before jumping into an act of love, wouldn't I?

When Sammy realized I was planning to head off for Port Mullet right away, she insisted she hadn't meant for me to make a special trip of it. What she had in mind, she said, was for me to work it in to my next visit to my folks. She hadn't yet grasped how rare my family visits were, mainly because I never spoke of them. But now that I had agreed to do it, I wanted to get going. The distance might give me time to ask what I was doing with a family woman when I was allergic to families.

Besides, something occurred to me. Sammy, who overflowed with self-sufficiency, mental health, and clear thinking had this one chink to her carefully constructed life—her unresolved feelings about her father. She wasn't in the habit of asking favors of anyone, but she'd asked this of me. My growing need for Sammy was making me nervous. Well, now she needed me. It might be my only chance to even up the score.

Before I left, Sammy told me the little she did know about her father, Elijah Wilson. She had never seen him; he drowned before she was born. At the time of his death, Sammy's mother was living near Port Mullet. Not in it, of course. No blacks lived in Port Mullet back then. Her mother lived out somewhere in the unincorporated part of the county. After Sammy's father died, her mother went back to Alabama to live with her own father, Sammy's grandfather.

As a child in Port Mullet, I didn't even know black people lived anywhere in the county. Only the few well-off families had their "colored help." It never occurred to me to wonder where they lived.

It wasn't until I was in the sixth grade that someone announced that the colored school was closing and the children were coming to our school. Until then, I hadn't ever heard of the colored school. By that time some folks were beginning to say "negro," while for others saying "colored" was already making a point not to say nigger, so a lot of people didn't see the need to make any further effort. I wished my own parents had stuck with "colored," because "negro," in their Florida woods accent, came out "negra", perilously close to the epithet to be avoided.

When I asked where all those children I hadn't even known about had been all this time, I was told they had had their own school, Booker T. Washington School, over by where they lived. Out in the quarters, they said, you know, Piney Woods Road.

The following September, a handful of scared black children showed up. Two of them were in my class. None of their teachers came, though, and I remember wondering what had happened to them.

Sammy grew up in the red clay hills of Alabama. She claims she remembers with a certain perverse fondness the bathrooms and drinking fountains marked "colored." At least in that time and place, she says, it was clear what she was up against.

I told Jerry I'd figure some way to get a good article out of the trip, but he was doubtful.

"Tampa? Who cares about Tampa? Why don't you go to Miami? Things are happening in Miami."

"Unh-uh. Tampa."

"So, what's there? Night clubs, fashion, big money, culture?"

"Unh-uh. But there is something..."

"What?"

"Hot dog vendors."

"Laurie, love, you want to write a piece on hot dog vendors, go to the corner out there. Abdul. Northeast corner. Tell him I sent you."

"These are very young women, you know, with firm thighs and nice tans and aerobicized muscles. They set their stands out beside the highway, and they all wear those thong bathing suits."

"I'm beginning to get the picture."

"Yeah, and they stand with their backsides to the cars. Seems that it is often necessary for them to bend way over their carts to reach things, and..."

"Hmmm. Maybe I better go check this story out myself."

"No way, Jerry."

I left my apartment very early and dropped by Sammy's on my way to the airport. I knew she wouldn't be home. She was off at The Birthing Place delivering a baby. I'd spoken to her earlier on the phone and we'd whispered some things that would serve to keep me perking along nice and warm until I got back to her.

So, why was I stopping to say goodbye to her *apartment*? A few rooms in a building? I was accustomed to following my impulses, but up until I met Sammy, I'd understood them better. Up until then, they'd been pretty simple, dealing mainly with food, drink, and sex.

Elena answered the door. She had a textbook in one hand and Rachel tucked under her other arm. She smiled when she saw me. "Laurie!" I liked the soft, slightly foreign way she pronounced my name. It made me feel European and mysterious. "You go to airport station soon, yes? I am so pleased you visit before your journey."

She dropped the book face down on the table in the hall, careful not to lose her place. She headed back into the apartment, with Rachel still under her arm. She obviously assumed I meant to come in and stay awhile.

I stood in the entrance for a moment, not ready to go all the way in. Annie was alternately practicing the violin and arguing with Sarah. Elena was trying to finish cooking dinner with Rachel on her hip. Sarah was whining that she needed help with her puzzle, and Elena called from the kitchen, "Get Laurie to help you." I felt a sour pang in my stomach.

But I stepped in. I'm doing this for Sammy, I told myself. It's just one of those good manners things. You're nice to your lover's family.

I sat on the floor beside Sarah and helped her fit the pieces of her puzzle together. I wanted to be bored by it, to be doing it just for Sarah, and, by extension, for Sammy. Actually, it was fun. I didn't do many puzzles as a child, and none as an adult. I sat there with the smell of dinner cooking, and Annie squeaking and scratching away on her violin. I picked up pieces that didn't look like they belonged together at all. I didn't really think about it; I just held them in my hand. Something about the weight and feel of each piece in my hand told me where to put it. Each time I was rewarded with that nice little snap as I fitted each piece into its place. It was immensely relaxing, satisfying. Something like I imagined the practice of meditation to be, although that's one thing I've never gotten around to trying.

Sarah and I worked in companionable silence. She's a striking child, with golden skin and startling green eyes. Both Annie and Rachel are a warm brown, like Sammy. They all three have different fathers. I studied the girls out of the corner of my eyes, and kept working on the puzzle. I thought, I'll never figure out all the pieces of Sammy. The woman who carefully constructed the life going on around me, with the comfortable apartment and the good meals and the music lessons and all those books, bore these three children to three different men. Men who apparently have no place in Sammy's life now, because I've never heard any of them mentioned. By Sammy, anyway; I'd not been above asking Sarah one evening when we were alone together, only to find out they each had a different father whom they knew but didn't see much. I was afraid to ask more, afraid that she'd realize how interested I was and mention it to Sammy who had managed to avoid giving anything away. Not a clue. As if it isn't important.

Of course, I blindly dismissed the possibility that she still saw the girls' fathers. On the nights I wasn't there, maybe they visited their daughters, and chatted with Sammy, and who knows, maybe even slept with her. Maybe they were better lovers than I was. Maybe one of them was the true love of her life. Still, I refused to consider it. Because if this were all true, would I have had cause to complain? No. Sammy would not have betrayed me. She would not have broken any promises, explicit or otherwise.

She had not told me a thing about these men. Not a thing. This is the same Sammy who is wild in bed with me, the best lover I ever had, who makes me feel that there are no limits, no boundaries, ever, anywhere. But I was afraid she could take away my fairy dust and dump me back on earth. Dump me hard.

When we finished the puzzle, Annie and I set the table. It had sort of become my regular chore. Sarah put the napkins around, but Annie claimed she put them on the wrong side, and Sarah said she didn't, and Annie said Sarah was stupid. Elena said that name calling wasn't allowed and sent Annie to her room. When Annie came back she apologized, and Rachel spilt her milk. Around all this, we were eating a casserole that Sammy had put together that morning, when one of her patients had called to report mild, irregular contractions. Sammy had had a feeling that the woman would be in hard labor by the afternoon. She'd started cooking and she had called me to let me know that she wouldn't be able to say goodbye in person. She'd be midwifing.

I can't compete with the commencement of a new life on earth, either.

After we ate, I looked at my watch and said I had to go. They all said goodbye, and have a safe trip and come back soon. I felt really nervous and started backing towards the door, still awkward about initiating hugs. Then Rachel started after me and threw her arms around my knees, crying "Up-ee, up-ee." I picked her up and hugged her. I saw too late that she had tomato sauce on her hands and now it was smeared all over the front of my shirt, a tight, gold-colored, Lycra body shirt. I kissed her dark, crinkly hair, and hugged her and put her down. Then I got the hell out of there, while the getting was good.

The flight down was uneventful enough. I had brought some books stuffed in my shoulder bag, but I didn't read them. It doesn't seem right to me to read too much on a plane. Oh, the in-flight magazine would be all right, if you could stand it, or maybe a *People* purchased from the magazine shop in the airport specifically for the occasion. But how could it be safe to concentrate on something good, to really get into reading something, when you're in a little cylinder of metal hurtling through the air? Flight is a form of levitation, after all. Seems like all that concentration might interfere with the pilot's, or maybe it's the navigator's, brain waves. I bought a couple of drinks instead, just to slow down my brain waves and do my part toward cooperating with the flight crew's vibrations.

I stared out the window at the cotton-candy clouds beneath us, and thought about what I was doing. At first, it was mainly profound thoughts like "What the hell am I doing?" Then, after a while, without meaning to, I started organizing it all in my head, everything I knew, and what Sammy had told me. I started to get a picture, or more like a feeling, for what I was doing. It was like one of my articles, a story I was investigating, and I knew that I wouldn't be satisfied until I had a tale worth telling about Elijah Wilson to take back to Sammy.

What else *could* I give Sammy. Except my body, of course, but, hey, I'd given that out like some cheap party favor in my time. I had a feeling that Sammy thought she was giving me a taste of family life, and stability, some kind of special warmth and love she thought emanated from the life she lived. Kind of like I was a stray she was taking in.

I got a lot of good meals at her place, but it's not like New York City isn't full of good restaurants. And even though I'm not much of a cook, I am an expert at city food. The best hot dog, the best knish, cheap Indian food, pain au chocolate, fresh bread in any of a hundred varieties—I knew where to find it all. So it's not like I was starving or eating out of cans when I met her.

But she did give me something, something that felt real good. I could tell she was happy about this, that was what she wanted to do. Problem was, we both knew I'd be moving on. When that happened, I'd be stuck with the memory of this feeling, and where in hell in the big city—or any other place on this earth, for that matter—was I going to find it again? For a moment I felt pure, intense anger directed towards Sammy. Hadn't she thought of that? What she was setting me up for?

Truth was, I felt like a visitor in her life. When we were alone, I'd give her what I thought was the best I had to give, my skills as a lover. But others had done that for her before, and three men had given her daughters. Even her patients gave her more than I did. They listened to her, and trusted her. Followed her advice. They labored and pushed out the babies she caught in her warm, competent hands. Pictures of babies she'd delivered were stuck all over the bulletin boards in her apartment hallway.

Sometimes I'd breeze in, with my latest article or photographs, to show her. I'd walk into her living room, and there she'd be watching Sarah draw with her crayons, or listening to Annie practice her violin. I'd stand there and think, I'm nothing but another one of her kids, an overgrown child she's nursing.

So I was looking out the window of the airplane and wondering, where do I start with this investigation? A black man fell off a bridge and drowned thirty-five years ago. I just wanted to find enough of the details of his life so that Sammy could put him to rest. She suspected there was something unsavory about him, but she was ready, she said, to face the truth about him.

I was born not long after it happened, a few miles from where Elijah Wilson had drowned. But black and white lives were so separate back then. Even after the schools were integrated, there was little connection between the communities. The black boys in our high school were well-respected for their football and basketball playing skills, but they didn't come to our parties. And I couldn't remember a single black cheerleader.

Even now, Port Mullet remained relentlessly white. How could that be? I remembered my American history teacher firmly assuring us that there was no longer a viable Ku Klux Klan in the South. Had not been for a long time. "The automobile did it," he explained. "And folks are more nosy today. Back then, a bunch of guys would ride on out in the country on horseback. These days, your neighbors would see guys getting out of their cars dressed in sheets and wonder what was going on. That's why there's no more Ku Klux Klan."

I don't know if I believed it at the time or not. The same teacher showed us the movie that claimed one puff of marijuana would lead us to becoming heroin addicts. My English teacher claimed that a woman who engaged in premarital sex would never achieve sexual satisfaction, even after her marriage. My Sunday School teacher told me the Pope was the anti-Christ.

At any rate, while I read enough to know the Klan did still exist, I'd never seen or heard any evidence of it around Port Mullet. I knew there were people who used racial slurs, but Momma said they were just tacky, like folks that kept old cars and plumbing fixtures in their front yards. My daddy made it clear, in his dinner table conversations with my brothers, that he didn't have any patience with folks who wasted time running negroes down. "Just shows that they don't think too highly of their own selves," he'd say. "Folks who are worried about their own position on the totem pole, they're the ones that have to make sure somebody else is lower than they are. Besides, some of those negro boys are mighty fine football players."

So, to make a long story short, I didn't know any black people around Port Mullet. My first problem was finding someone who had known Elijah Wilson.

It wasn't likely that my own family would be much help. I was pretty certain they would consider the whole thing just another one of my crazy ideas. I decided I would start off by talking to Forrest Miller, the father of my childhood friend, Susan. The Millers were an old family, had lived in Port Mullet for a long time. Mr. Miller had owned some groves and a citrus packing plant when I was a girl. He'd employed some black and Mexican men to work in his groves. Then, when the building boom started, he'd moved right into real estate development. He knew a lot of people, and was well-respected. Maybe he could give me some ideas about where to start.

I'd call him Mr. Miller, of course. There are those little things, indications that the South is still another part of the world. One of them is that a grown woman never calls her childhood friends' parents by their first names. When I'm fifty years old, I'd still be calling him Mr. Miller.

The plane landed and taxied to the terminal. I looked out the window at the clear blue sky, and the palm trees, the bright green shrubs and lush lawns. I shivered. Nothing could be as clean and easy as this place looked. I was sure of that.

Chapter Three

My brother Seth met me at the baggage claim. Six foot four inches, muscular, blue eyes and blond hair, wearing a pale aqua sleeveless t-shirt and raspberry sweat shorts with expensive-looking high-topped athletic shoes. Only thing was, I was the one who looked out of place. I like to think that I haven't forgotten a thing about life there, but, the truth is, I can never remember just how hot it really is, and how no one wears dark colors. I was the alien, sweating in my boots and black leather jacket.

He hugged me and insisted on carrying my bag. I tried to guess what sort of vehicle he would be driving. He usually alternated between low-slung sports cars and jacked-up, oversize pick-up trucks, complete with gun racks and bumper stickers.

It was a sports car, lean and red. I pushed my seat back as far as it would go to accommodate my long legs. It's a good thing nobody else was with us, because we were practically in the back seat. I could see how a year driving a car like that would make him long for a truck as big as a house.

He turned on the radio and ran one hand through his short blond hair. I noticed he had pierced one ear. Now I knew for sure that earrings for men were completely mainstream.

"So, what's up, Sis?"

We glided across the causeway. Palm trees swayed and the water sparkled. Ski boats bounced across the surface of the bay.

"Usual, Bro. What's up with you?"

"Don't give me that. You're down here. There's no wedding, no funeral. It isn't even Christmas. What gives?"

The dazzling sunlight hurt my eyes. The open horizon, the space, the cleanliness, it all oppressed me. I pretended to be looking out the window, but out of the corner of my eyes, I studied Seth. The same blood ran through our veins. We had shared our parents, our childhood home, thousands of childhood memories. And yet neither of us had a clue as to what the other was about. I had empathy to spare for the variety of life in the city. But I'd never aimed that sort of acceptance in the direction of my brothers. Maybe they deserved that. Certainly Seth did, because he had gone out of his way to try to connect with me. He'd even been to visit me a couple of times, and had been good-natured about the way I paraded him to my friends as an exotic species—the country boy in the big city.

We passed a couple of the female hotdog vendors in their thongs. I wondered whether they ever worried about skin cancer in some very delicate areas. I also figured that the local electrolysis clinics ought to be doing really well.

Then we passed a cart manned by a good-looking young guy in a tiny g-string. Seth shook his head. "There you go, Sis. A little something for you to look at."

"I don't know," I said. "From here it looks to be more than a *little* something."

Further down the highway, we stopped for a light opposite yet another hot dog stand. Beside it stood a scrawny old man with a long grey beard, also wearing a thong. His sagging, fish-flesh white buns glittered in the sunlight. When he moved, his cheeks jiggled like a pillowcase full of jello. Seth and I started laughing, and we didn't stop until we reached the place that used to be Cowboy Ranch.

For as long as I could remember, Cowboy Ranch had been the only landmark in the long, uninteresting ride from Tampa to Port Mullet. Miles of pine scrub, orange groves and cows, relieved only by the gigantic concrete cowboy boot at the front gates of the ranch. The last few years, subdivisions and strip malls had sprung up to line the road. It looked like the transformation was complete now, and not a single pasture, grove, or cow remained. The ranch and its boot were gone, too, replaced by yet another strip mall.

"Seth," I said. "I've got some things to ask you. I don't know exactly where to start."

"Shoot."

I looked nervously at the glove compartment. Knowing the men in my family the way I do, I thought it probably held a loaded pistol. Seth impatiently repeated, "Go ahead. Ask away."

That was true enough. I had four brothers, lots of male cousins, and I was the only girl in the family. Girls don't seem to run in the Coldwater family, nor the Monroe, my mother's side, either. My singularity only increased the familial dismay that I had turned out to be such an unsatisfactory representative of my gender, and this based only on the little bit they knew about my life. Which was certainly not the half of it.

"I'm going to tell you something, and I don't want you to tell anyone else."

Seth turned to look at me, his forehead lined in indication of his puzzlement, and then looked back at the road. He popped another CD in the player, to make it look like he wasn't too interested in what I had to say.

Seth is my oldest brother. He was plenty wild there for a while, but he has settled down some now. He is into real estate, just like every other person you meet in Florida these days.

The next one is Daniel, the biggest, the only one of us with Daddy's brown eyes. He's also the most dangerous. He seems quiet, and he often looks preoccupied. He isn't given to proclamations and loud talking, but when he's angry, there's no stopping him.

Paul is the third. In the shadow of the older ones, and not quite as big. He lacks a half-inch being six-foot, and his arms and legs are bony and long, instead of bulky. He has always tried harder than the others. That has meant, among other things, that he drinks and fights more.

Walter is the baby and it's still hard for me to think about him with any sort of objectivity. I came along just a year later, and I think that the long-running hostility between us comes from the fact that I just about stole the show. After a few years it dawned on them that I wasn't going to play the sweet baby sister role they all had in mind for me. But to show you how persistent they are, to show you how they haven't given up, how deep their dreams are of what I ought to be, most of the time they still call me "Baby Sister."

Three of them have been married, two of them twice, but they're all single again at the moment. None of them have any kids that they've told us about. Can't any of them figure out the cause of their matrimonial problems. They don't do anything different than Daddy does, and he's stayed married all those years, right?

Seth can put up the same act as the rest of them, but while he may call me "Sis," he never calls me "Baby Sister." That is as good a reason as I can give you as to why I thought I'd trust him. I told him, very briefly, why I had really come to visit, "A dear friend of mine, no, actually my best friend has asked me to look into her father's death. He died a long time ago in Port Mullet."

He smiled, ever so slightly. "Well, don't tell Momma and them I told you this, but there has been a lot of speculating going on. Paul is sure you've come home because you're pregnant. Momma hopes that you've finally decided to come back where you belong, and live among your own people. That's about what Daddy thinks, too, but Paul has him a little nervous. Walter thinks that you're broke, and you're here to borrow money. But," and as he said this his smile widened, "don't forget, Sis, how happy we all are to see you."

We both chuckled there for a minute, but I sure as hell don't know what we were really laughing at.

"As to the other thing, first of all I don't think you're going to be able to find much—or anything—after all these years. Second, if there is anything to find out, you're probably getting in over your head. Some things should just be left alone, you know? And I don't think much of your friend for trying to get a secretary to do a private investigator's work. If it's so important to her, why doesn't she get her butt on a plane and come do it herself?"

I knew he didn't mean anything by calling me a secretary. There was no social stigma in Port Mullet to doing honest, wage-earning work. But what hurt me was that he knew so little of me, they all knew so little of me, that they didn't know the most basic, crucial fact about me. I paid my bills with my day job, but in my heart, I was a writer and a photographer. I took it as a slight, and then I did what I often tend to do when I'm put on edge. I spoke without thinking. Or rather, I spoke with only one thought: to shock.

"I want to do this for her. She's my lover. And she's black too, if that matters to you."

I was rewarded by a bright red flush that spread from the neck of his t-shirt, up his own muscular neck, from his chin to the roots of his hair. The tips of his ears glowed an especially deep crimson. We rode past more fast food joints and banks and furniture stores in a strained silence.

After a while I started recognizing the houses, because they were older, built in the seventies, instead of last week. And then, just before we turned onto the street where my parents lived, where I grew up, Seth said to me, his throat tight, "You don't have to tell that to Momma and Daddy. I know you think we're all just a bunch of hicks and it's your job to bring us enlightenment from the big city. But you're not the one that stays here and looks after them. You don't sit at Momma's table for Sunday dinners, which is what the woman wants more than anything else on earth. How do you think she feels, you going a thousand miles away to do a job you could do right here in Port Mullet? You could buy a nice little house here on what secretaries make, and have a decent life, instead of living in that run-down apartment, surrounded by criminals and filth. How do you think she feels, knowing that's how bad you wanted to get way from all of us?"

Long speeches weren't much of a male art in Port Mullet, so I thought he must be finished. Long stories, yes, about drinking and hunting and the one that got away, the kind that swims and the kind that wears a skirt, not speeches about emotions or feelings. But he wasn't even done yet. "If you tell anyone this, Momma will think you are degrading yourself just to spite her. To spite that sweet woman. I don't care what people will think of you, as long as you don't. Just don't do this to Momma."

I was stunned into silence, a pretty unusual state for me. They thought I left to get away from them. They thought living in the city was a torture I endured just to be away from them. I would have left anywhere, fled from paradise even, to live in the city. But even so, what did they think there was to hold me here—fast food joints, dredged beaches, nylon pastel running suits? How about the little retirement houses with tiny lawns and home state license plates on the mailbox? The Lincoln Continentals with bumper stickers that said "Out Spending Our Children's Inheritance"?

Well, yes, it's true, I left my family. And I came back only for state occasions, and then I left again as soon as possible. I loved them, God did I love them, and I never meant to cause them pain. But, hell, it couldn't be an accident, could it, that everything I wanted to do, everything I had to do, everything that made my life worth living, gave them pain? Was I a thirty-five year old adolescent rebel? Was there any cure for this condition that wasn't worse than the disease?

We pulled into my parents' driveway. Seth parked the car, took off his seat belt, and swung his car door open. Before he ducked his head to swing his big body out of the little car, he said, "I'm not forgetting you're my little sister. I love you no matter what you do. Just stay out of trouble while you're home. You hear me?" He was pulling my backpack out of the dinky little trunk when he added, like an afterthought, "Momma will kill me if I let anything happen to you."

By then Momma had come in the yard to greet me. Three or four tiny lizards darted into the bushes before her approach. Wiry and thin, she moves like she means business, which she always does. Surrounded by an armor of perfume, she gave me a big hug that made me feel like a small child, even though I'm nearly a foot taller. Her hair was in a careful set from the hairdressers. She was wearing a baby blue jogging suit with white fringe and rhinestones across the chest, her earrings had fringe and rhinestones hanging from them, and so did her white leather sneakers.

"Baby Sister, I'm so glad you're home!" I could have told you what she was going to say next. I could have lip-synced the words along with her. "You must be hungry. Come in, sit down, I'll fix you a plate of something." She turned to Seth, "You, too, Seth, I made the lady peas the way you like them."

"Aw, Momma," he said, "I surely appreciate that, but can't I come by later? I really have to drop by the office."

"Just let me make you a plate to take with you. It won't take me a minute. Just some fried chicken, and biscuits, and a little gravy, and some of the fried okra that Baby Sister loves so, and a big helping of the lady peas."

"I can't carry all that to the office, Momma. I'll come in and eat, but I've got to hurry."

Momma hustled us in the back door. Nobody ever used the front door. The kitchen, which looked smaller every time I saw it, was cluttered on every surface. It smelled like a sweet dream of my childhood, like everything good I remembered about home.

Seth and I sat in the breezeway, at the formica-covered "breakfast table" (actually, every meal was consumed there, with the sole exception of Christmas dinner). Momma heaped plates for us of the greasy, cholesterol-ridden, wonderful food, and then brought us gigantic glasses of sweet iced tea.

The table looked smaller than I remembered. It was hard to imagine all seven of us eating supper here every night for so many years. Momma didn't sit down; she never did. Every time either Seth or I finished a serving, Momma ran into the kitchen and brought back more okra, or biscuits, or whatever. I kept eating a long time after I should have stopped. I was filling myself up with everything I had missed. I love fried okra. There's nothing like it. It isn't the same frozen, and you can't even find it in most grocery stores in the city. I saw some once in an Indian market in the city, and bought a big bag and brought it home to my apartment. When I dumped it out on the tiny surface in my kitchen that calls itself a counter, I saw that the pods were big and tough. Momma always used small, soft, fuzzy little ones.

I had watched Momma many times at the kitchen sink, cutting the okra into thin, even pieces with a small, sharp knife. She did it with incredible speed, slicing them against her thumb, never nicking herself.

I had a hell of a time hacking my dry old okra into uneven pieces, then I rolled the prickly, dry things in flour and fried them in oil. They turned out hard and tasteless except for the burned grease coating, and the oily smell had hung in my kitchen for days. Nothing like the tender nuggets in front of me.

Finally Momma brought us bowls of banana pudding, with sliced bananas and vanilla wafers and whipped cream on top. She poured herself a cup of coffee, and sat down at the table beside us. Seth said he had to go change and get to the office. He thanked Momma for the food, and went out the back door, leaving his dishes on the table. She carried them into the kitchen, and then came back and put artificial sweetener in her coffee from the little bowl in the middle of the table that held the tiny pink envelopes.

It was kind of nice, for a moment there, Momma with her coffee and me with my banana pudding. I'm sure there must have been moments like that when I was growing up, of peace and contentment between us, but that's not the way I remember it.

Momma looked at me, full in the face. I had her attention for once, and, in spite of myself, I was enjoying it. She reached out and stroked my hair thoughtfully. "I can make an appointment with Reginald for you. He's booked up ahead for weeks, but I know he'd work you in right away for me."

"Reginald?"

"My new hairdresser." She delicately patted the blond structure on top of her own head. It reminded me of those "floral arrangements" advertised on television. The ones you can order by number from a book of photographs anywhere in the country. Within twenty-four hours, your designated recipient will be delivered an exact replica, each flower and piece of greenery standing stiffly in its assigned spot.

"You don't go to Bobby Ann's anymore?"

"Why no, honey, she closed down her shop and sells real estate. Everybody gets done at the mall now."

For as long as I could remember, my mother had had a standing appointment at Bobby Ann's House of Beauty, every Thursday morning. The "House" was actually what used to be the garage of Bobby Ann's small, concrete-block house. Her construction worker husband had converted it to a beauty shop. I had been forcibly compelled to accompany my mother there on many occasions. The fumes of hair spray and permanent solution and nail polish remover burned my nose and throat while I flipped through the exotic magazines: *Today's Hair Styles; Soap Opera News; The Star*. I half-listened to the women's gossip. Their facial expressions and voices were entirely bright and cheerful, and yet there was something terribly sad underneath it all. The talk was about who was pregnant (Again! Already? They're not Catholic, are they?) Whose husband had left her. Whose husband was drinking bad again. These were hard-working women, for whom this was a rare opportunity for female companionship and conversation. I think it took the strong combination of community grooming standards and the purifying effect of the pain inflicted (the pulling of strands of hair with a crochet needle through tiny holes in a plastic cap looked excessively sadistic to me) for them to allow themselves this luxury.

Although I had submitted to Bobby's arts on very few occasions, and then only under the most extreme compulsion, I felt a strange sense of loss. The rituals of Bobby Ann's House of Beauty, which had appeared to me to be at least as sustaining to my mother as those of her church, were no more.

I pulled back from my mother's reach. "No, Momma, I like my hair just fine the way it is."

The puzzlement on her face was obvious. She couldn't understand why her only daughter wanted to look so tacky, her hair hanging down all wild and witchy like that. What had she ever done, except sacrifice her own life to her children, that would cause her daughter to ruin her own looks just to spite her mother? Shit, I thought. My plane had landed less than two hours earlier, and already I was stuck in that mess again. To save myself, to keep from getting sucked into the quicksands of my complicated family currents, I had to keep my focus on why I'd come.

"Momma, did you ever know anyone named Elijah Wilson?"

She frowned. "I don't think so. Should I? Is he one of the Grove Hill Wilsons?"

"No." I hesitated, then plunged in. "Momma, did you know any of the black people who lived around here? Back when I was little, and even before that, before I was born?"

"What a question! Let me think. Well, you know, you just did not see many black people around here in those days. Not like in some cities or towns. There just weren't any around. When I was a child in Selma, well, everybody had their colored help. But, by the time I got married and moved here with your father, only the best-off did. And I didn't know any of them personally, if that's what you meant."

"When they integrated the schools, where did the black children come from?"

"Oh, them. They lived way out over by Piney Woods Road. A few families, not many. I don't know where they did their shopping, because we never saw them in town. Some of the men were grove workers for your Uncle Billy, and Miller's Groves, but I don't know any more about it than that."

"Do they still live out there?"

"I really don't know. I haven't been out that way in quite some time. It was all country back then, you remember, between here and there, but you wouldn't recognize it anymore, the way it's built up."

You wouldn't recognize it anymore. I had heard that phrase so often, whenever I came back to Port Mullet. I was finally beginning to realize the fundamental truth of it. I wouldn't recognize anything. What had made me think that I was any more qualified than a Californian or Texan or hell, a Japanese, for that matter, to come waltzing into town and start researching the life of a man who had drowned thirty-five years ago? I hadn't really been here even back when I lived here.

Momma picked up my glass and took it into the kitchen, then returned with it refilled with ice and tea. "Now, Baby Sister, I don't want to upset you…" I held my breath as she continued, "…but I saw Johnny the other day."

"Johnny who?"

Tears welled up in her eyes, messing up her blue eyeliner and matching eye shadow. "You've got no business talking to me like that, young lady."

I sighed. "All right. I'm sorry. How is he doing, Momma?"

She wiped under her eyes. "He still hasn't remarried. I think he still holds a candle for you. He always worshiped the ground you walked on. You know, I always thought that if you'd gone for counseling from the Reverend Andrews…"

I tuned her out for a few minutes. I knew she could go on indefinitely about my ex-husband, Johnny Berry, and I couldn't bear to listen. I tuned back in again when I thought I'd let her ramble enough.

"…you know, if you got your hair fixed, Mary Sue down at the Clothes Carousel could help you pick out some nice clothes, and you'd be a fine police chief's wife."

"Police chief's wife? Me? Who's the chief of police?"

"Why Johnny, of course. Your daddy and I did a lot of politicking for the new mayor in the last election. So did Johnny's folks. After the election, old Billy Thompson retired, and, why, Johnny got promoted."

I felt certain now that this was an alternate universe, and one where the air mixture didn't suit my breathing, and the gravity had strange effects on my limbs. In New York, I was a happy person, a funny, bright-colored fish on a coral reef full of other bright, exotic creatures. I fit right in, and had a great time swimming around. But here, in this dark and dangerous world, I'd just discovered that my ex-husband was the god-damned *chief of police* of all things. I had a funny feeling that meant, among other things, he wouldn't like me going around telling the story of how I taught him to smoke pot. Or the time we drove through the night at a hundred miles an hour, all the way to Key West, just to steal the sign that says "The Southernmost Point in the US." And then drove back, singing songs and drinking Tequila Sunrises out of a gallon thermos.

Why did I have to go and think about that? Why did I ever

have to think about Johnny again? Now, it's Johnny my family feels sorry for. But here's the god-awful truth. I got hurt mighty bad there, too. I haven't really ever gotten over it, and I don't think I ever will.

By the time I was twenty-two, I'd been married and divorced, so I wasn't being arbitrary when I said that I wasn't cut out for any kind of long-term monogamy. It was what you might call a field-tested proposition.

Momma said that Daddy was out in the Gulf, fishing. I knew I wasn't supposed to take it as an insult that he wasn't there to greet me. *Everyone* knew that when the fish were biting or the hunting was good, the men would be gone, business or family be damned. There was even a nightly fishing report on the local news station, ending with the slogan, "Remember, if you're too busy to go fishing, you're just too busy."

My own Daddy wasn't the worst, not by a long shot. We knew some families where the men left for their hunting camps before Thanksgiving and didn't return until after New Years. Other men, "real good family men," drove up to their own houses in the late afternoon on December 24th, in their bloody, dirty, camouflaged shirts and pants, with muddy boots, reeking of whiskey. Good sports, they tried to be patient with the childish Christmas rituals. Their patience lasted until about 9:30 Christmas morning. They'd be sitting in their recliners, surrounded by ripped-open boxes, and messy piles of wrapping paper. Noisy, over-excited children begging for batteries and for help in putting together their new plastic toys. The women were busy in the kitchen, but the comforts of dinner were hours away. It was too early for a beer or a bourbon.

Sometimes the well-meaning patriarch would let it slip that "Hell, Christmas would mean a lot more to me if it didn't come right in the middle of hunting season." My father once said something like that. It didn't seem to bother my brothers, intent on their presents from Santa. They had G I Joes at first, and toy guns. Later there were b.b. guns, and not long after that real shot guns. I'm still bitter that the boys each got mini-bikes on their thirteenth Christmas, while I got a pink bicycle with a white wicker basket on the front.

When I realized I was sitting there, filled with rage for Christmases of twenty years past, I decided to get up and get started. Momma refused my offer of help with the dishes, a pleasant switch in our relationship from the days when I lived at home.

She was willing enough to loan me her car, but uneasy about

letting me drive: "If I call Seth, I'm sure he'll come right over and drive you where you want to go. He'd be happy to do that for me."

"I can drive, Momma. I had a job delivering groceries when I was in high school, remember?"

She looked like she was going to cry again. "Of course I remember. It's just you've lived so long in that city, without a car. I worry about you up there, walking alone at night."

I tried a sweet, conciliatory voice. "Really, Momma, I appreciate your concern. But I'll be fine. I promise I'll drive real careful."

"You just watch these old people. I don't think you realize what terrible drivers they are."

I doubted that it would be more dangerous than taking a cab through midtown Manhattan at rush hour, but I knew enough to let the conversation end there.

I took the keys off the hook near the door. Momma stood there, looking forlorn. It's not like I was leaving her without a car. Daddy had taken his truck and both his Buick and her Oldsmobile sat in the driveway. What I really wanted to do was rent a car, but I didn't know a way to do that without Momma taking it as an insult.

In Manhattan, I was properly contemptuous of Florida's bull-dozed lots, rows of identical houses with tiny windows, and central air in every house, blasting all day and night, every single day and night—except, of course, the two cool, breezy days a year. The lawns were seeded with scraggly St. Augustine grass, which required extensive watering to keep its appearance from imitating well-done bacon. From Manhattan, the use of electricity and water had seemed heedlessly extravagant. But when I tried to slide into the car, the seats were so hot that it felt like my legs were blistering through my jeans. The metal ignition and the turn indicator burned my hand. I felt like I couldn't breath in the thoroughly-stewed air. Sweat ran down the back of my neck. Air conditioning seemed an inspired idea. I turned it on full blast

I was a little rusty in my driving skills, but my main problem was the big car. It felt like I was steering a yacht. I was also unfamiliar with power brakes, electric windows and locks. Even the control to move back the front seat was electric and complicated.

I drove through the downtown proper, and was amazed yet again at how right Momma and Seth were about one thing. I almost didn't recognize the place. New houses everywhere. More people moved here all the time. My God, what did all these people think they would find here? What was it that they hadn't found wherever it was they came from?

Every year I'd been in school here, my classes grew larger. I'd been born into a small Southern town, surrounded by orange groves, and open countryside. But I had left a homogenized Sunbelt blight of development after development. I was maybe nine or ten when building really took off. People retired to Port Mullet for the low taxes and the warm weather. Construction workers were brought down from up north to build retirement villages for retired firemen and teachers and insurance salesmen from Ohio and Michigan and Maryland. When the masons and carpenters and roofers saw the nice weather, and the low cost of living, they sent for their families and settled them in little concrete block houses. Their cousins moved in next and opened pizza parlors. (Up until then, we'd thought of pizza as an exotic foreign food.) Then suddenly there were miniature golf courses and drive-in movies and bowling alleys, fast food restaurants and car dealerships. It wasn't too long before as many kids in school talked Yankee as talked right. And yet the development continued. Each time I visited Port Mullet I thought, that's enough, there's no more room, but the next time, more tacky little buildings were crammed in.

Along with the new, there were a couple of things I found disconcertingly familiar. The names on the signs on the law offices, doctor's offices, real estate offices. I recognized a lot of them. They were the names of the boys I'd gone to school with. In the city, most of my friends my own age or older were still struggling to become what we wanted to be when we 'grew up.' But while I'd been gone, my male classmates had had families and now they were fathers and husbands. They were grown-ups. It made me feel old, and, at the same time, unformed.

When I got past the old downtown, with the Baptist Church, and the bank and the post office and the old hotel, I noticed something else. The place had certainly gotten raunchier!—I cheered up at the sight of a tattoo parlor, and a boutique of leather wear. I was surprised to see a restaurant named Cantaloupes. It had the glossy, prefabricated look of a franchise operation. The sign pictured an impossibly curvy woman in a bikini holding a cantaloupe in each hand at chest level. Under it was the caption: "Guaranteed ripe and juicy." Some things had loosened up, definitely.

I drove through a few miles of subdivisions, each house looking just like every other. Then the houses thinned out, I passed some scraggly fields, and turned right at the sign that said Piney Woods Road. There were maybe two dozen houses huddled together. There were a handful of unfinished houses, the weeds and bushes growing through the foundations, indicating that work had been abandoned long ago. Some of the others, obviously inhabited, could not really be called "finished." Jagged plywood patched holes and covered empty spaces surely meant to be windows. A few houses were neat, with tidy lawns, but most had yards of sand, weeds, and trash. Kids, almost all of them dark-skinned, wearing shorts or underpants and not much else played in the discarded lumber, or under the rusting cars up on blocks.

I wondered which had been the house where Sammy's parents had lived. And why any residents from that time would still live here in this depressing place. Surely whatever the case may have been twenty or thirty years before, they could now find better housing somewhere else. I was still reeling from my drive over, from all the brand new buildings and the signs offering new houses for thirty thousand dollars. Accustomed to the outrageous housing prices in the city, that seemed almost as good as free.

I'd had this idea that I'd just stop and talk to the residents. Ask around and see if I could find anyone who remembered Elijah Wilson. It struck me then what a stupid idea that had been. With my pale skin and city clothes, and driving my Momma's big car, why would anyone tell me anything?

I tried knocking on a few doors anyway. The harried black women who answered the doors just shook their heads, said they'd never heard of Elijah Wilson and looked at me as if I were very lost.

I was ready to give up. My last try was going to be an old man I saw sitting in a tattered old armchair in the middle of a junk-strewn front yard. I introduced myself, tried to make small talk. That failed. So I just came out and asked him if he had known Elijah Wilson. He said no, he sure didn't remember that, but then he was an old man, he said, and he had forgotten a lot of things. He was polite enough. I was polite, too; I turned and left. But I could have sworn I'd seen something like fear in that old man's face when I mentioned the name. I was sure of it. Almost.

Whatever it was I was looking for, I hadn't found it on Piney Woods Road. I turned the car around, and headed east on Night Lake Road. I figured that the farther inland I went, the fewer new developments I'd encounter. I hoped something was left of the countryside I remembered: quiet scrub, shaded springs and slow rivers.

I did find some new developments and a few strip malls, but my hunch had been right. It didn't measure up to the chaos of the Gulf coast. I sometimes got the feeling that developers had a deep, pervasive fear that one lot would be left undeveloped when it could be the site of a fast food joint, a bar, or a mall. Such a fear seemed to me totally unwarranted by the evidence.

The highway department had straightened out the sharp curve around a hardwood hammock. As a teenager, I had loved to take that curve as fast as my car could handle. Now the trees were all gone. Now I missed the hammock and the curve, although I had not thought about them in all the years I'd been gone.

I was thinking about that when I noticed a sign. I'd seen a couple before: "This section of roadway has been adopted by the Kiwanis," one read. There were a few more. Adopted by the Jaycees and the Lions Club, or something like that. I hadn't paid much attention. But the one I passed there, right past where the highway used to curve, shocked me so that I nearly ran off the road.

"This Section of Highway 14 has been adopted by the Ku Klux Klan." My heart started to beat faster, I felt sick to my stomach. Then suddenly I had to laugh. I laughed convulsively, uncontrollably, tears running down my cheeks. I pulled over onto the grassy shoulder and shut off the car. Hugging the steering wheel tight against my chest, I laughed for a long time, until my eyes burned and snot ran down my lips. Then I sat up, and wiped my nose against the shoulder of my shirt. I dug at my eyes with the heels of both hands.

Sammy and Annie and Sarah and Rachel. Anger burned in me as I thought how I would feel—and worse yet, how they would feel—if they were beside me. I had grown accustomed to the city abounding in every shade of skin, with every style of clothing, with dreadlocks and veils and turbans and saris, pierced noses and navels. And when I thought of the way Sammy and the girls looked, I saw them and myself as part of that bright mix. But I'd been fooling myself, had been believing what I wanted to believe, and that sign in front of me made that absolutely clear. I was angry for Sammy, and towards the girls I felt something strong and unfamiliar, an emotion so powerful that I was surprised my body could contain it. A vengeful protectiveness. I thought of Rachel jumping into my arms before I left, of Annie's sweet self-consciousness, of Sarah's stubbornness, and in that moment, I felt I could kill anyone who hurt them. I dropped my hands back to the steering wheel and opened my eyes. Enough of this shit, I thought. I've got work to do.

Chapter Four

The day had been clear, but clouds were gathering at the horizon, and soon it would be dark. I suddenly felt a desire to watch the sunset at Deer Key. When I was a kid, Momma used to take us there after supper in the summertime. As I started the car, pulled across the road, and headed back toward the coast, the thought of not finding it didn't even occur to me. I did make all the turns, but I had to look hard, and I almost missed a couple.

But once I turned onto the narrow spit of land that led out to the Key, it was lonely and desolate, and I knew where I was. When I pulled up to the beach, I saw that some improvements had been made: bathrooms installed, the parking lot paved. But it still looked pretty much the same. The beach was gray sand, with clumps of seaweed everywhere, and covered with tiny holes made by fiddler crabs. I took off my boots and socks and walked carefully along the sand. Hundreds of tiny crabs scurried to their holes far ahead of me. Small birds stood in the water, while the grey and white sea gulls circled and cried up above. Brown pelicans stood farther out. Large, dark, long-legged birds swooped down in the water and came up with struggling fish.

On one side of the small, cleared beach area was a marsh, and the other was wooded, with crooked, grotesque trees stooping over the water. I saw two large horseshoe crabs in the shallow water. I had always thought them ridiculous with their heavy armor, but I was happy to see them. It had been a long time.

There was the constant drone of insects, and the cries and splashes of the birds. I rolled up my jeans and waded in the warm water, breathing in the smells— salt, of course, but also the fertile, sexy smell of low tide, the decay and rot, the dead fish and the live eggs, and the seaweed. I could just make out the weathered, gray stilt houses clustered out in the Gulf, unlikely veterans of dozens of hurricanes. I couldn't see, but could never completely forget, the nuclear power plant five miles up the coast.

The sun was dropping into the Gulf. I left the water and walked up to where the sand was dry, and sat down to watch the show. It looked to be a perfect, postcard sunset. A few cars had pulled up while I was wading. An old couple walked hand in hand along the beach. A young couple reclined on a blanket covering the hood of their car, facing the west. They leaned back against the windshield, sharing a can of beer. An old man and a young boy ignored the sun, and fished off the northern point. I was grateful that the wind had picked up, because it kept the mosquitoes just bearable.

I watched the oranges and reds to the end, hungrily, almost passionately. I had missed Florida, all right, but I had not known how to say it, even to myself. If I had said it to anyone I knew in Manhattan, they would have heard me saying I missed long afternoons on a white sand beach, rubbing myself with oil, or else going water skiing. But it was something else. It was partly the natural beauty—not the bland beaches, the perfect blue of sea and sky in travel ads, but the messier reality of snakes, alligators and sawgrass, the fishy smell of the marsh. And the way the Key had remained, miraculously, while almost everything else was bulldozed or paved over. There was something, too, about the lack of pretension. I mean my brothers and their girlfriends could actually wear polyester without shame or irony. People in Port Mullet didn't seem to grub so hard at life. My friends in the city demanded so much out of their lives that life recoiled, withdrew, all generosity drying up.

Sometimes I told myself it was the destruction of paradise that I had left, that the coming of the malls and highways and the subdivisions had driven me away. But I couldn't let myself think that kind of sentimental junk. After all, I'd moved from Florida to an island completely paved over in concrete. Sometimes I think I just moved away so I could misbehave in a place where no one knew my momma and my daddy. And what does that do for my vision of myself as a fearless rebel?

This realization reminded me of the time I'd been parking out on Deer Key in Jethro Agee's Mustang. We were rudely interrupted by a police officer knocking on the window. He trained his super flashlight on us right when we were experiencing the simple form of ecstasy that comes from the raw newness of sensations and not with the sophistication of the technique. Anyway, this officer demanded identification. He didn't ask the question I was expecting, the stupidest of all possible inquiries: "What are you doing out here?" But he did ask the first runner-up. He asked, "Does your daddy know you're out here?"

Meanwhile I had to get to work. I walked back over to the car, brushed sand off my feet, and started towards home. Or my parents' home. Or the place I grew up. Anyway, I was on River Road when I had an idea. The Pirate's Den used to be on River Road. And a lot of people I once knew used to spend time there. One of those people might still be hanging around, and that same person might be very useful to me. And even if that person wasn't there, or didn't want to be useful, I still appreciated the value of a little something to drink before my next encounter with my beloved family.

The parking lot was heavy on motorcycles, pick-up trucks, and those cars that appear to be a material manifestation of pure testosterone.

A few moments passed before my eyes became adjusted to the dark interior of the bar. The first thing that took shape for me was a man standing up at the bar—losing his hair, tall, in fairly good shape, but with that little paunch around the belt line men get as they approach middle age. His features were boyish and good-natured while his skin was lined and leathery.

I walked up to the bar, placed my order, and told the barkeeper, who looked vaguely familiar, to give the man another beer.

The bartender did as he was told and, right on cue, the man looked over at me.

I sat on the barstool as he made his way over. He set his beer bottle on the bar and took the stool next to me without a word.

The barkeeper was back, wiping the bar with a cloth. "Lucky guy," he said. "Not so often a lady buys a gentlemen a drink around here."

The man grinned.

"So happens," I said, "that I'm not a lady. Furthermore, this is no gentleman, this is my ex-husband."

The barkeeper suddenly found something he had to do at the other end of the bar.

Johnny laughed until he nearly choked. I took a long swig out of my bottle, and then I thought, what the hell, and I laughed too.

I got control of myself first. Johnny was winding down when he got the hiccups. Grabbing his beer, he took a long swallow, then said, "Your momma told me you were coming back for a visit, but I didn't dream I'd be lucky enough to run into you."

You have to love a man like that. After what we did to each other, you'd think he'd act like he didn't care, that he wasn't affected by me. I looked around the crowded bar, filled with guys I considered rednecks. Most of them wouldn't let a woman know he appreciated her if she was down on her knees in front of him. And Johnny wasn't ashamed to let me know he still cared about me, right off, before I even said a word. Damn. What was I doing in this place, this bar, this town, this state, this state of mind? What was I doing here, anyway?

Unwanted images filled my head. Johnny and me in bed, Johnny and me screwing in a rowboat, Johnny and me in a cow pasture searching for psilocybin mushrooms. My heart beat and my skin tingled. Then something in me clicked and my mind filled with a completely different set of pictures. Johnny yelling at me for not doing the dishes, me heaving a greasy frying pan in his direction, and it hitting the wall instead of him, leaving a ragged hole with splashes of dirty bacon grease all over. Johnny choking me the same night he called me a dyke the first time, and then Johnny sitting in the bathtub with all his clothes on, crying for days. That was the day I called his father, told him to come see about his son, then packed up and left town.

There sure as hell ain't no place like home. And sometimes I feel that there aren't any mistakes like the ones I make. Right then, looking up Johnny felt like the last in a long series of mistakes.

"Places to go," I said, "things to see, people to do." I got up off the stool. "Not leaving angry, Johnny, just leaving." I turned away, and Johnny reached out his hand and touched my arm, gently, carefully. The contact reminded me of Sammy somehow. I stopped for a moment, completely still. Everything between me and Johnny was in the past. But me and Sammy, that was now, and I had promised her I'd do my best to find some answers. Just because I'd screwed up and broken promises before, that was no reason to let Sammy down now.

I turned around and faced him. "I'm gonna tell you something a long time overdue, Johnny. I'm sorry. I'm as sorry as a person can be about what happened between us, and I am fully aware that I behaved about as bad as person can, and a little worse than that, too. Which isn't to say you didn't do some pretty nasty stuff yourself. And you and I are never gonna really get over it."

Johnny had dropped his hand from my arm. He just stood there, staring at me like I had grown another head or something.

I took his arm and led him over to a tiny table in the corner. He followed like a well-trained puppy dog. After I sat down, I looked at him and he seemed a little pale. "Are you okay, Johnny?"

"Am I okay? Are you crazy? You just go tearing up an old wound like that and you ask me if I am okay? Hell, no, I'm not okay."

Well, I felt like a real jerk. Here I was thinking about Sammy, and I'd gone and made things worse for Johnny, like the two of us hadn't suffered enough.

I sagged back in my chair, stumped. We sat that way in silence for awhile. I was barely aware of our surroundings, of the time, of anything. I was just tired, and overwhelmed by the futility of it all.

Then Johnny said, in this voice so weary that it scared me, "You think you were just being honest and generous with me, don't you? Well, you weren't. The way to do this, you know, was to have a nice, polite conversation between us here tonight. And maybe a phone call tomorrow. And we go out to coffee now and then and send each other Christmas cards, and we just act civil, good manners, you know, talking about nothing for years, maybe. And gradually, we'd get comfortable around each other. And little by little, we'd forget the bad stuff, and we'd be something like old friends, maybe, and that might help neutralize the pain a little bit."

I tried to break in, but he just kept talking.

"But that's too slow for you, right, Laurie? So you just cut to the chase. Remind me of things I've spent all my time and energy for years—it's thirteen years, Laurie, thirteen years—trying to forget. Well, fuck you. Just fuck you." He stopped and sat back in this chair and looked at me. In a soft voice, he said, "God, would I love to fuck you."

"I need a drink," I said. He didn't say anything, so I walked up to the bar, ordered and drained a shot glass right there, and then walked back to the table with a pair of beer bottles. I put one down next to Johnny's head, which he had down on the table, cradled in his arms. From that angle, I could see how his neatly cut, short hair was thinning on top. When I first met Johnny, he had long golden curls. Believe it or not, I'd called him my "angel of love."

I sat there, nursing my beer, listening to the god-awful music and watching the locals. Finally, Johnny sat up. "Okay," he said. "What is it you want? You sure as hell want something. That's what this is all about, right?"

He stared at me and I felt my face redden with shame. "What is it?" he insisted. "What do you want from me?"

"I'm sorry, Johnny." How many times could I keep apologizing? "I was wrong to do this. I don't want anything from you, I really don't. Let's just forget everything." I stood up to leave. Johnny grabbed my wrist. Hard.

"Dammit, Laurie. Let me do something for you. Don't make me go on remembering that the last months between us were so bad. You're right, I did some awful things, and that's all I can remember when I think of you, and I can't quit thinking of you. So let me do something for you. Come on. Please?"

I felt like I'd been hit upside the head with something hard. All those years we'd been apart, he'd been blaming *himself*? Part of my self-righteous rage every time I thought about our marriage had been my certainty that he blamed me. Not that there wasn't enough blame for both of us, with a good helping left over.

"Okay," I said, and we sat back down, and I told him why it was that I'd come back to Port Mullet. I figured he wouldn't be surprised about the relationship between Sammy and me, given some of the things that happened during our short, but very eventful, marriage. I'd always been grateful that certain allegations hadn't turned up in his divorce papers among all the other charges he'd made against me. And if he had told anyone else, not a word of it had gotten back to my brothers or my parents, or I was sure that I would have heard of it.

He listened, breaking in only to ask good questions. When I was finished, he sat back in his chair and drained the last of his bottle, then set it back on the table.

He looked calm, authoritative, in control. He didn't look like a man who had been eating his heart out for twelve years anymore. "We can do it," he announced.

"Who's we, white man?"

"You can't do it by yourself. You've been out of touch around here too long. And besides, you've got a reputation. Me, I'm the law around here. I can talk to the old-timers, find stuff out. No problem."

He made it sound easy. Too easy. He said "I" as though he was my partner. He thought I needed him. Or his protection. He was taking over already. I might as well go home and deal with my family if I wanted this kind of grief.

"Forget it, Johnny. I don't need you. I don't know what I was thinking. Police Chief in a town where the Klan adopts a highway. That sounds like someone I sure as hell don't need."

He started to say something, but I was already on my way out. I was nearly to the door when I heard the wolf whistle. I turned, smiling, warmed by the thought that the locals had finally come to appreciate my charms. Then I saw who my admirer was. The years had not changed the smug grin, nor improved the mean features of Wallace Montgomery's face. I'd gone parking with the asshole out of pure pity one Friday night in tenth grade, and he'd paid me back by informing the whole homeroom on Monday morning that I wore a padded bra.

I whirled around, stuck out my backside and wiggled it for him, then shot him a bird over my shoulder. When I pushed open the door and left, it was to the sound of raucous laughter, this time directed at old Wallace.

Chapter Five

When I got home and walked into the kitchen, Momma was standing at the counter fixing a tray of sandwiches. She looked up just long enough to penetrate me with the hurt in her eyes. Those baby blues were saying that it was my first day home, and already I was taking off for hours at a time, Lord knows where, doing Lord knows what. What she said was, "The boys are watching the ball game in the front room. You ought to say hello to your father. He's been waiting for you. He was worried sick about you."

I couldn't decide which message to respond to, so I said nothing. I walked on to the livingroom. Six examples of Southern manhood were sprawled around the room, watching some sort of game involving a ball on the large-screen TV. All four of my brothers were accounted for, across the couches and chairs, along with a man I'd never seen before. And, of course, Daddy, tilted back in his Sears recliner, holding a beer can and looking mighty well for someone who was worried sick. All of them were staring intently at the screen. Empty beer cans and peanut shells littered the coffee table.

When the exertions in pursuit of the spherical object were interrupted by a commercial, my father looked up at me. "Well, look who's here. Come give me a hug round the neck, Baby Sister."

My brothers looked up then. "Hi, Baby Sister. Good to see you." "Howya doin', Baby Sis." "Look who finally paid us a visit." "Baby Sister, meet my good ol' pal here, Josh Livingston."

I was surprised that Josh stood up. He was tall and fit and dark. He offered his hand. We shook. He was wearing a baseball cap, like most of the others.

Walter said to Josh in his most artificial southern accent, "According to Seth, Baby Sister Laurie is here *investigating* something, but he won't say what." He drawled the sentence out for everything it was worth giving it the full measure of ridicule.

Josh looked interested. "Investigating what? Are you a c...a police woman?"

My brothers all howled with laughter. "A cop? Laurie? She hates guns, don't even get her started on that. The only way she could get a criminal to surrender would be to argue him into submission. And believe me, once she got started talking, it's the criminal I'd feel sorry for."

My father chuckled. "Sounds about right."

The commercial was over, and their attention was immediately focused on the screen. Momma sailed in with her tray, handing out sandwiches, careful not to get in their line of vision. They grunted acknowledgements.

Next commercial, Josh asked me what it was I was investigating.

Before I could answer, Walter spoke for me. "She writes something for some little newspaper. I bet maybe its drugs, right? The Florida-New York drug pipeline?"

My father said, "They wouldn't send a secretary down on something like that."

I forced myself to let it pass, and turned to Walter. "What made you think of drugs? Guilty conscience?"

"See, we warned you about her," he said to Josh. Then he said to me, "There's been a whole lot of stuff in the papers about all these drug investigations lately. We've just had a couple of big-time busts around here, too."

"You mean to tell me people are still doing drugs around here?" Somehow I thought the flourishing drug trade had been limited to my own high school and college years.

"You thought you were the entire market, Baby? Sure. The coastline is still here, and law enforcement can't keep their eyes on every single fishing boat. And we've still got all that flat pasture land a few miles inland, perfect for landing small planes. And there's not the federal presence here that there is over in Miami."

Daniel broke in, "What, you think New York has a monopoly on everything, Baby Sister? Anything you got up there, we got better right here. Am I right, Seth?"

Seth was the only member of my family who had ever been to visit me in the city. He gave a good-natured grin. "I don't know, boys. I told you about that Halloween parade she took me to. In Green-witch Village. Don't think we've got anything that can compete with that."

The others laughed. Daniel jumped right in. "Ooo-wee. That's right. That's one thing they got up there in the big city that we don't. All them queers. I don't know how you could walk around up there with them all around, Seth. Weren't you afraid you'd get raped or something? Goddamned perverts. Be afraid to bend over and tie your shoe, place like that."

Seth gave me a look that meant he was sorry he'd brought it up. I shrugged. In another moment, the commercial was over and they were all staring again, transfixed, at the screen.

Having thoroughly reacquainted myself with the male side of my family, I stood up to leave. As I walked out, Daddy said, without taking his eyes off the screen, "You know, Baby Sister, we've got a fishing trip leaving out of here about daybreak tomorrow morning." For a moment I thought he was going to invite me to go fishing with him. There was a time when my brothers got old enough to enjoy sleeping late more than fishing, that Daddy would take me with him on his Sunday morning fishing trips. We'd leave the house before dawn, come back a few hours later with a stringer full of fish, have fried fish and grits for breakfast. Instead, he said, "Your momma, bless her little heart, is gonna be up early fixing us breakfast and sandwiches to take along. You know, that woman works so hard I worry about her. I'd sure appreciate it if you could get up and give her a little help. Your momma would love it if you'd spend a little time with her."

He didn't seem to be waiting for an answer, so I kept walking.

In the kitchen, Momma was pouring Crown and Coke over ice into highball glasses and putting them on a tray. I made myself a sandwich and got a beer out of the refrigerator, and took them both to the breakfast table. I like a drink or so now and then; occasionally I like a whole lot of them. But I haven't overindulged on what you'd call a regular basis in a long time. No, I'd done that mistake up the way I like my mistakes: good and outrageous, and then put it behind me. Which is all to say that I no longer relied on alcohol as a part of my daily routine. But there's something about being home that makes me keep reaching for the booze.

I ate, and tried to figure out what my next move should be. One thing I knew for sure was that I was starting to drift. My so-called quest was starting to seem silly, even to me.

I chewed my food, not tasting it, thinking hard. I had scratched Johnny Berry off my list, that was certain. I might as well try visiting Mr. Miller. He had lived in Port Mullet since way back, knew everybody who was anybody. He was on every important committee, his support was essential in every local election.

Susan Miller had been my best friend from kindergarten to high school graduation. My parents had been happy about that, always hoping that one day her sweet normality would rub off on me. She was as wholesome and practical and law-abiding a girl as a family could wish. I personally had believed that she was the one who would profit from our association. I had hoped it would loosen her up. And for a while there it seemed to. She had been my companion on a couple of adventures that I remembered fondly. But in the end she had gotten in trouble and married Tom, one of the most insubstantial and boring of the football, sock-hop, and steady job types. What had really amazed me was not what happened to her. Getting knocked up could happen to anyone, I figured, and, once it did, a girl's options were limited. No, what took me by surprise was that she had seemed really happy that it had happened. She had been glad that she was getting married, she had actually looked forward to being a mommy.

Her father, Forrest Miller, was a tall, thin man. Faintly aristocratic-looking. I thought he was the only man in Port Mullet with any sense of style. He dressed elegantly. Around the house, he would wear a cashmere cardigan sweater over a beautiful shirt, instead of a t-shirt and a cap. You would never catch him in a recliner, wearing his undershirt and drinking from a can of beer. He would sit in his study and listen to music. I never knew any other person in Port Mullet, male or female, to sit absolutely still and listen to music. Outside of church, of course, where you didn't have any choice. Mr. Miller had been demanding of his wife and daughter. Even then I saw that his insistence on standards in dress, behavior, and demeanor were a burden to Mrs. Miller, and to Susan. But he wanted life to be something beautiful, something more than the shoddy, tacky affair everyone else was content with. And I thought that a man who played such music would understand passion, and longing, and desire. All the things I had struggled with while my classmates had been tortured over which class would win the spirit trophy.

How Susan felt about the way I worshiped her father was something I was never clear about. I didn't want her to think I was friends with her just because of her father and her house. Still, I'm sure she couldn't help noticing how much I envied what she had. The ballet lessons, the piano lessons, the charm school. Susan was more popular at school than I was. But I was the only friend she invited home regularly. I had never thought to wonder about the reasons for that.

My own father was pretty important around town, too, in a different way. He was the football coach at Port Mullet High School. If you don't know how important it was to the citizens of Port Mullet to have a winning football team every year, then you still don't have a clue about Port Mullet. Daddy coached winning teams for nearly forty years. He could have pressed for promotion to athletic director, and then later to the county school administration. Momma would have liked that, him having a job that didn't keep him out nights so much. But that wasn't what he wanted to do. He wanted to keep right on coaching high school football. And, if you can't tell by now, then you need to hear it flat out. My daddy did just about whatever it was he wanted to do. So I guess he and Forrest Miller did have something in common.

Sometimes Daddy would wonder out loud how his own daughter had turned out so contrary, so set in her ways. I wondered how he could miss the fact that I had inherited his own stubbornness, his own wretched addiction to independence.

Not that I don't have some fond memories of Daddy from early in my childhood. It's just that they didn't feel like memories. They're more like scenes from someone else's childhood. My father had teased and flirted and fawned over his pretty peaches-and-cream baby daughter with the curly blond hair. He had shown me off to everyone who would stand for it. He had doted on me to the point of provoking my mother's jealousy, something I had sensed, but had been too young to understand.

I had been both proud and ashamed of his favoritism, and its shadow has remained between me and my mother ever since. Even her fretting over my developing flaws—the button nose growing big, and the eventual refusal to wear pink—had something in it of gloating. As to my relationship with Daddy, I was never sure what had come first, his failure as a father, or my own as a daughter.

It happened just about the time Daddy and them realized just how willful I was fixing to be. There's a type of Southern girl, the apple of her daddy's eye, who's indulged and petted. That type can get away with murder, and they do. But they don't get away with flouting certain rules of Southern womanhood, and certainly not with flaunting their sexual freedom. Oh, there's a subtext of sexuality in everything they say and do, and in all that flirting with their daddies, too. But everything about them—their clothes and hair and make-up and mannerisms—says they are buying into the rules. They know they have a privileged position, but it's still playing by the rules that gets them their rewards.

Sitting alone there at that table where I had eaten thousands of meals with my family, I finally saw it. Those rules were what made the flirting safe, what allowed the father and daughter to carry on that way, him showering her with gifts and attention, her giggling and batting her eyes. But if she was to throw the whole thing over, if she was the kind of girl, just to take an example, who felt herself free to screw whomever she wanted, just because she felt like it, well then nothing was safe with her. I thought about that for a while.

I wasn't even sure Daddy saw that what we had was a failed relationship. Maybe this was exactly what he thought a father-daughter relationship should be, if the daughter happened to be a wanton hussy.

I was thinking about this, hunched over the table, biting my bottom lip, when I felt my skin crawl the way it does when I'm being watched. I looked up.

Josh was standing in the doorway, staring at me without a smile. He didn't betray any embarrassment at being caught. "Working hard on your investigation? I hope you're getting paid time-and-a-half for overtime."

I didn't answer, just stared back, hard, directly into his eyes.

He didn't look away and he didn't say anything. He was letting me see that there was a whole other side to him than that good old boy act I'd seen in the other room. He wanted me to see it. It was a threat of some kind.

I kept staring at him, and licked my lips. I ran one hand through my hair, and arched my back slightly. Acting like I thought he was there to admire me, hoping to hell I was bugging him. When I have to react fast, I tend to rely on my old habits; sex as a shield and a weapon is a deeply ingrained one. I guess it's something I need to work on.

We could hear the heavy steps of one of my brothers walking into the kitchen, and then Walter's voice, "What's going on out here?"

"I'm watching your sister investigate." Now Josh's drawl was exaggerated.

"Damn right," I said. "And I'm watching him watch me." Just so he had that straight.

Later, when the television was finally turned off, and the house silent, I snuck into the kitchen to call Sammy. It was late; I was afraid I'd wake her up because she usually went to bed pretty early, to save her energy for catching babies. But I needed to talk to her. I *had* to talk to her.

Her voice, while sleepy, was as warm and comforting to me as cinnamon toast on a cold morning. As I sank into that feeling, I knew my emotional balance had moved, some weight inside me had shifted. I had had an inkling of this when I found myself on the plane headed south on my quest for Sammy's sake, but now I felt the true consequences of that change. Sammy wasn't just my partner in fun and carnal pleasures, I knew that now. She was becoming part of my life. But that didn't quite cover it, that made her sound like a job or an apartment, something easily exchanged. She was becoming more like a part of *me*, like my voice, or my eyes, or my heart.

I described my visit out to Piney Woods Road. Pleased with my own bravery and ingenuity, I tried to seem modest, while also seeking to ensure that she recognized my stellar qualities. In her reply to me, I recognized the technique she used when reviewing Annie's homework. First, she praised me, "Laurie, I really appreciate what you're doing for me." Then she moved on to the next stage, "You know, Laurie, I wonder about the rest of the black community in Port Mullet." She was pointing out what I could have done better. She was being tactful, but I got the point. Only a handful of the most pathetically poor lived on Piney Woods Road. I'd acted like the entire black population of Port Mullet was clustered in what Momma had called "the quarters." I was ashamed to admit that I didn't know a thing about the lives of the rest of the black community. I didn't even know what had happened to the black kids I'd gone to school with. I knew, basically, nothing.

I felt stupid, but I still had to tell her about the sign out on Night Lake Road. I heard her audible intake of breath across the telephone line. And then silence.

"Sammy?" I said, wondering if I should have kept my mouth shut, wondering if she thought less of me, now that she knew the truth about the kind of place I'd grown up in.

"I'm here," she answered. "I just can't believe I was so stupid. So involved with my missing father complex. Knowing Momma the way I do, I should have stayed out of anything she doesn't want me to know. But what did I do?—I ask you to go asking questions about a dead black man in a place where the Klan is so powerful they go around adopting highways. My god, just like any other civic organization! I hate to even think about it. Laurie, just forget it. Have a nice visit with your folks, and hop on that plane and come on back to me."

Well, *I* was offended then. She didn't think I could handle it. Truth is, I was feeling a bit foolish for my oversight about the black community in Port Mullet. I hated feeling that way and was looking for something to get touchy about. I thought I had my bravery to prove, and I thought it was Sammy I had to prove it to. It was me, of course, that needed the proof. Over the following days, I found myself giving in to my impulsiveness, leaping into hell first and worrying about the devil later. I think my behavior had its start there, in that chip on my shoulder. That's just a partial explanation, though, and sure as hell not a good excuse.

Four-thirty a.m. came just as early as I had dreaded it would. I woke on the double bed in my childhood bedroom, a pink-flowered shrine to the kind of girl I'd never been, cursing the fates. I could smell bacon cooking, and heard noises from the direction of the kitchen, so that I knew my mother was up. She hadn't asked me to help. I could just go back to sleep. But I didn't want her to have to make this big meal all by herself for all those men. On the other hand, I didn't want her to think she was right to serve them this way. I could be selfish, or I could aid and abet my mother in her doormathood. Some choice.

I got up and brushed my teeth. I don't own a bathrobe, so I pulled one out of my mother's closet. It was lavender quilted polyester with a chiffon ruffle around the neck and down the front. The effect it had over my red union suit, which I had worn due to the air-conditioning, almost scared me when I went past the hall mirror. I mean, I'm partial to outrageous, but this even frightened me.

In the kitchen, Momma was neat in a flowered gown, matching robe and slippers. She had a skillet of bacon browning, another of sausage frying, a boiler of grits going, and she was scrambling eggs. I smelled biscuits in the oven, and the coffee was brewing. I heard men's voices in the yard and in the garage. They were loading the fishing equipment into the boats. Under Momma's instructions, I set the table for six.

The men came in the kitchen door. Some of them weren't quite as tall as me, but the situation made me feel small. Real small. Almost invisible. There were nods in our direction, but the men were intent on their talk. They were jovial and expansive. They sat down without removing their caps and started right in on the food. I was busy just keeping the platters filled. More biscuits, more eggs, more bacon, another jar of Momma's fig preserves. One of them, a guy I went to high school with—he'd been a football player—thrust his coffee mug in my direction. "Can I have a refill on that fine-tasting java your Momma makes, Sweet Thing?" I wasn't sure if I was going to get him more coffee or pour the hot coffee on his lap. In the kitchen, filling his mug, I thought about spitting in his cup.

Momma never sat down, of course, and I didn't have the stomach to sit with these men. They left, finally, carrying out the coolers Momma had filled, one with sandwiches, the other with beer and soft drinks. They complimented Momma's cooking, and made jokes about all the fish they were going to catch and how she was going to fix them.

When they were gone, I stood in the doorway to the kitchen, looking at the table. The plates were covered with cold bacon grease, congealed eggs, and sticky fig preserves. Momma looked at me with surprise when I started carrying the dishes off the table into the kitchen. We cleaned up in silence, the sky lightening outside the window as we worked.

She went out to get the paper and I filled two cups with coffee and sat them on the table. I thought for a moment, then went back in the kitchen and filled two glasses with orange juice. I was adding a good measure of vodka to one of them when Momma came back in.

She saw what I was doing, but she didn't say anything. We sat down across from each other, drinking our coffee. In the harsh light, I could see how old Momma was, and how tired.

Momma went back into the kitchen and put some cold biscuits on a plate for us and stuck it in the microwave. While they were nuking, she picked up the vodka bottle I'd left on the counter, and carefully poured a few drops into her own juice. I had never known Momma to drink, aside from a rare whiskey sour on those occasions when we had been far enough away from Port Mullet to make it extremely unlikely that she would run into someone from her Sunday School class. And here she was, drinking vodka before eight in the morning. "Us ladies do deserve a treat now and then," she said. I laughed, and she kinda grinned, and then she sat down and opened the paper to Ann Landers.

It was a nice moment between us, but it wasn't like we had resolved all our differences. Not by a long shot. When I borrowed the car again to go visit Mr. Miller, she gave me that kicked puppy look again. I tried to ignore it.

The route to the Miller's house was completely familiar, but everything—streets and trees and houses—seemed smaller. I was seeing the physical surroundings of my childhood shrunk to dollsize.

I got there sooner that I'd expected, and was surprised when I saw the house. I remembered it as grand. It was bigger than any other house around, but now the fake plantation style struck me as, well, tacky. I know it sounds funny to hear me say that, because I'm usually tacky's biggest fan. But, thing was, a lot of things looked different to me. If I was wrong earlier, I was afraid I could be wrong again, that I couldn't trust my own judgments. And since I've made it my business not to depend on anyone else's, where did that leave me?

Mrs. Miller opened the door. Another funny thing. I'd almost forgotten her existence. She was quiet, without presence. Whenever I had thought about her, she always reminded me of a little brown bird. She invited me in, exclaimed over how long it had been since she had seen me, and led me back to the Florida room. I sat down on the white wicker couch with floral, peach pillows. Mrs. Miller hurried away to get Mr. Miller and bring us some iced tea. While I was alone, I studied the framed photographs on the table by the wall. There was a formal studio pose of Mr. Miller, and several of Susan, including her wedding portrait. There was a small one near the back of the table, in a heavy, old-fashioned, silver frame. It was almost hidden behind the others, so I got up and walked over to get a better look at it. A pretty girl in a velvet dress with a sweetheart neckline. From the hairstyle and the dress, it looked to be from the late fifties or early sixties. I thought she must be Belinda, Susan's older sister. I had never met her, and had heard very little about her. I vaguely remembered that she was much older than Susan, maybe fifteen years, and I thought she had been institutionalized somewhere. I hadn't thought much about her, but if I had, I would have guessed she was mentally retarded, or something like that. One of those private family tragedies—you don't ask, and they don't volunteer. A shame, I thought, she looked so lovely, so alive, in her portrait.

Mr. Miller was just as I remembered him: courtly, polite, discreetly flirtatious. He asked me about my life, and managed to make all my responses to his questions sound fascinating. Mrs. Miller brought the tea, and cookies, and excused herself to do some sewing. After she left, Mr. Miller took the initiative.

"So, Laurie, tell me what it is I can do for you."

I did tell him, as simply as I could, what I was there for. I didn't lie, but I was reasonably sure that my words led him to believe that Sammy was a pal of mine. As I chose the words to give him that impression, I realized that it was even more important to me that Mr. Miller approve of me than my mother and father.

"I am certainly honored and pleased that you have come to visit me today, Laurie. And this is a most interesting project you have here. I am curious, however, as to why you have come to me with this."

I was at a loss. Of course he didn't know the role he'd played in my life, in my imagination. He had always listened to me, and talked to me, and found time for me when I was a guest in his house. At a time when my own family had found me uninteresting at best, and often unbearable, he had seemed to take me seriously.

While I was struggling to think of how to say this, Mr. Miller reached over and put his hand on my knee. The touch was warm, intimate, comforting. I couldn't remember the last time my own father had touched me like that. "It doesn't matter," he said. "You did the right thing coming to me. I will see what I can find out for you. We've missed you, Laurie, and it's good to have you home."

He bent his head close to me in a confidential way. As he did, his hand moved farther up my knee. "I'll ask around, and see what I can find out. You know, you don't look a day older than the last time I saw you, dear. You've certainly kept your lovely figure." And his hand moved up farther.

Or did it? I wasn't sure, because I'd stood up suddenly, in the grip of a sudden panic. As I so gracelessly leapt to my feet, his hand accidentally brushed my crotch. I didn't know where the sudden panic had come from. Yes, I was embarrassed that I'd remembered him as sophisticated and subtle in his appreciation of me, when he now revealed himself as clumsy and transparent. But he was a small town man trying to be kind to his daughter's best friend whom he hadn't seen since she was a teenager. I tried to convince myself that there was nothing sinister in his touch or his compliments.

I had jumped because his touch had opened up another fact about myself I'd been refusing to recognize. I'd had a crush on the man. That was one of the reasons why I'd spent so much time at the Millers' house. That was one of the reasons why Susan had been my best friend. I had basked in his compliments and attention. I had craved the proof of my attractiveness, my desirability. I had not thought it out consciously, but my feelings were something like this: My father doesn't find me interesting, but Forrest Miller, with his infinitely more refined taste, does.

But that was no reason to leap away from an innocent touch. Just because I'd been a girl desperate for adult male attention, and Susan's father, whose style and sophistication I had overrated, had been kind to me. I did see that there was a good chance I'd overrated his importance, too. I had to quit looking for people to bail me out here, to do my work. I had to do this myself.

Mrs. Miller appeared suddenly and quietly in the room, and I remembered she had always had a way of doing that. I felt guilty when I saw her, though I didn't know why the hell I should. She walked me out of the house that I had known so well, past the hallway that led to Susan's room. I wondered if they had changed Susan's room, or if it was the same. The canopy bed, the ruffled curtains, the pom-poms on the wall.

Mrs. Miller and I made the usual small talk on the way out. She sent her best to my parents. Then, just I was stepping out of the door, I realized something. Mrs. Miller stood there, as bland and hidden as a person could be. For all the hour, days and nights I'd spent in her house, I knew nothing about what she thought, nothing about what was important to her. And until that moment, I'd never cared.

Chapter Six

I stepped out onto the front porch and was nearly knocked over by the heat again. I wondered how long it was going to take for me to get used to it. It felt like I was crawling through waves of soggy air to the car. I kept thinking about the way Mr. Miller had touched me. It left me feeling funny, and I wasn't sure why. I wasn't normally a prissy person, to understate outrageously. I wanted to believe that his gesture meant to be warm and fatherly, and that my sudden movement had ruined it. Maybe my uneasiness had been caused by my Electra complex gone haywire. Still, something far back in my mind was nagging at me. There was something I was forgetting, or something I wasn't paying attention to, but whatever it was, it wouldn't let me be.

I started the car and turned up the air conditioning. Okay, so I had been disappointed with Mr. Miller's response. That was a good thing, I thought, because it reminded me of the first and last, and primary rule of the universe: that when it comes down to it, I'm all alone in this.

I even knew my next move. I'd seen The *Port Mullet News* on the coffee table at the Miller's, and it had reminded me to go read up on *The News* for the week Elijah Wilson had died.

As I was backing out of the Miller's driveway, a cop car turned the corner. It followed me slowly. Gave me the creeps, although I didn't have anything to hide.

I kept glancing in the rear view window, and it just kept following me.

Then I looked back and saw the cop had turned his lights on. No siren, just the lights. I pulled over to the side of Main Street, rolled down the window and started pawing through my backpack on the seat beside me, searching for my driver's license. I wasn't sure I was carrying it; all the years in the city has gotten me out of the habit.

I felt rather than saw the officer approach my window. I had just found my license when I heard a throat clearing and a tentative "Ma'am?" I looked up and was instantly relieved. It was Tony Gardner, the little brother of one of my high school pals, Marla.

The idea that he'd gotten old enough to be a cop, let alone that Marla—one of my pot-smoking, beer-drinking, skinny-dipping pals—had a brother in law enforcement blew me away.

"Miss Coldwater, Ma'am, I'm sorry to disturb you like this, but I've got a message for you from the Chief. Chief Berry, Ma'am."

Now I was pissed. "Yeah? Doesn't the mighty sheriff believe in the telephone?" And how the hell did he know where to find me? The answer to that takes just one word, of course: Momma. The two of them had me under surveillance.

"I wouldn't know anything about that, Ma'am, but Chief Berry would like you to meet him at Bobby D's Restaurant for lunch. Around eleven-thirty, if that's all right with you, Ma'am."

I'd forgotten there were grown-ups who really ate lunch at that ridiculous hour.

Tony was looking at me nervously, as if he was considering the possibility that he was going to have to call for back-up to deal with the crazy woman in front of him.

"Don't mind me, Tony."

"Yes, Ma'am."

"And don't call me 'Ma'am'. Or Miss Coldwater." I took a slow, deliberate look up the length of his body. "You've grown up awful cute, you know that, Tony?"

He had. He was lean and even that horrible uniform couldn't hide a fine set of buns. But he wasn't as young as he looked, even though he was blushing up to the tips of his ears. He leaned down towards my car window and said softly, "You're looking pretty cute yourself, Laurie Marie. But then you always were. Good dancer, too."

I almost blushed myself, I was so surprised. I had completely forgotten those dance sessions in Marla's bedroom. Marla and me stripped down to our bras and panties, dancing away. And little Tony, the irritating little brother we were always stuck with, watching. We had just ignored him. Figured he didn't count.

Ah, what the hell. I winked at him, started the car, and hit the gas, pulling off with a squeal of tires, speeding down Main Street.

I slowed down as soon as I saw he wasn't following me. I turned down a side street right before I reached the main intersection in town. There it was, the tiny, ancient office of *The Port Mullet News*. I pulled into the parking lot.

When I walked in the front door, I was surprised to see the woman behind the long reception counter. Well, actually, I wasn't surprised to see her. It was Mrs. Pannell. She'd worked there as long as I could remember. Of course, I'd expected to see her.

What surprised me was how she looked. She'd always been interchangeable with all the others, as far as I was concerned. Small, neat. Pastel-flowered dresses for work and church, pastel "jogging outfits" for home and casual wear.

But here she was, standing behind the counter at the *Port Mullet News*, wearing a tight yellow dress, bright red earrings, and a big, floppy red bow in her brassy red hair (formerly dull brown). Her lips were shiny and red, carefully lined into a perfect kiss shape. Her eyes were lined with turquoise, and her eyelids up to her well-shaped, penciled brows were a work of art. Various shades of pink, from pale to deep rose, along with violet, and purple were symmetrically applied over and around her brown eyes in an intricate pattern.

The effect was hypnotic. I couldn't help but stare at her lips and eyes. I had to refocus and blink a couple of times before I could even see the rest of her face.

"Mrs. Pannell?" I asked.

"Well, my goodness gracious. If it isn't little Laurie Marie! Bless your little heart, child, you're a sight for sore eyes!" She tottered out from behind the counter on red patent leather spike heels and gave me a warm hug. Even with her heels, her head reached my chest level and I was pretty sure I was now wearing lipstick, mascara and eye-shadow over my boobs. It would take a hot water wash to remove the heavy floral scent she had imparted to my black scoop-neck bodysuit.

Momma had told me that Mr. Pannell had died two years ago, and that Mrs. Pannell had grown quite eccentric. This new look of hers was not what I had envisioned. I had pictured her growing stooped and sad, wearing her loss like one of those white cardigans old ladies throw over their shoulders. Instead, she was glowing with a strange light, just like a neon sign for a good-time bar. I was having a hell of a time keeping back what I wanted to say, which was, "Widowhood certainly seems to agree with you, Mrs. Pannell."

Mr. Pannell had always seemed like a nice enough man. Why had thirty years of living with him suppressed so much in his wife? Because only many years of serious containment could have caused an explosion like the one I saw in front of me.

I couldn't just ask her right out for what I wanted, of course. I had to inquire after her grown children, and her cats, and her garden. And she had to exclaim over how I'd grown up, and what lovely people my parents were, and how they all missed me so, and wasn't I just the bravest thing anyone had ever heard of, living up there in that big city by myself? "I see your brother Paul quite regular, and I always ask after you, so I keep up a little with your doings that way," she said. But there was a little pause just then, and I looked at her funny. Surely Paul and Mrs. Pannell weren't...? No, I quickly decided, it just wasn't possible. Finally I got a chance to tell her the dates of the back issues I wanted to look at. She brought me file boxes of those years and sat me down in a quiet table in the back next to the photocopier.

I found the short piece easily enough. The body of an Elijah Wilson of Piney Wood Road was recovered from under Deadman's Bridge. He'd fallen off the bridge and drowned. That was it. It wasn't going to do me much good. Still, it was all I had, and I copied it, stuck it in my backpack as I went to thank Mrs. Pannell for her help.

As I walked out towards my car. I glanced at my watch. It was eleven-forty. Bobby D's was a two-block walk. It wouldn't hurt just to talk to Johnny, to see if he'd asked around, if he had any information for me. This was Sammy's quest I was on, and I couldn't let the fact that I'd once been stupid enough to marry the guy who eventually became the chief of police in this God Forsaken place interfere. If he tried to take over, I'd just put him in his place.

I stopped myself just as I was putting the key in the lock of my car door. That was one of the things I hated about this place. Nobody ever walked. Everybody drove even the shortest distance. Well, I wasn't one of them anymore, and I was walking. That would show them.

My bodysuit was glued to me and sweat was running down my sides, down the back of my neck, and dripping between my breasts by the time I reached Bobby D's. My hair was plastered to the top of my head. I felt weak and I was seeing spots dancing over my field of vision. I understood what sun stroke was all about.

I forced myself up the steps to the restaurant and opened the front glass door. A wave of cold air hit me; the shock of it on my wet body made me shiver. I stood still for a moment, trying to regain my equilibrium.

Bobby himself came from behind the cash register. "Chief Berry's waiting for you over here, Laurie Marie," he said. He was clearly anxious. I'd kept the chief of police waiting right there in Bobby's place.

He led me to a booth next to a window overlooking Main Street. Johnny was sitting across from another man in uniform who I didn't recognize. When they saw me, they finished their conversation quickly, and then the young officer slid out of his booth. He put on his hat, touched the brim, said "Ma'am," in my direction, and left.

Johnny looked at me. He didn't stand up. I slid in across from him.

"Have a good morning?" Johnny inquired in an even tone.

I shrugged, looking through the menu. The waitress arrived. I ordered chicken-fried steak, and mashed potatoes, and gravy, and biscuits, and fried okra, and black-eyed peas. If I had to be here, I figured, I might as well enjoy myself. I also ordered a large iced tea.

Then I turned my attention to Johnny. I looked at him a minute, trying to decide. Sometimes you have to do business with the devil, I decided. He wasn't saying anything, and I wanted to show him that I'd been busy. I pulled my copy of the newspaper article out of my backpack and pushed it across the table in Johnny's direction.

The waitress arrived just then with my tea. I nearly gagged at the sight of what she put down in front of me. A gigantic, fake mason jar with a handle, full of ice and tea and lemon. "Shit," I said. "What the hell has happened to Bobby? What did he do with all the normal iced tea glasses?"

Johnny didn't answer. He was looking at the copy of the newspaper clipping in his hand. When he finished, he handed it back to me and took a sip of his coffee. He looked preoccupied. "Okay," he said. "I see what you mean."

"Great," I said. "I'm glad you're seeing things my way for once." I didn't have a clue what he was talking about.

Johnny looked at me funny. Then he said, "Ever been out to Deadman's Bridge?"

"I don't know," I answered. "Probably. I don't recall it in particular."

"I'm taking you there as soon as you finish eating," he said.

There he went again, trying to take charge. Big man in control. "Well, I have some things I want to do this afternoon. Maybe we can get together later in the week." The waitress put down a big platter with my chicken-fried steak, and then littered the table around it with little dishes. One for the potatoes, one for the gravy, a separate one for each side dish.

"The fiesta starts this weekend, Laurie. I don't have the time to be sitting here with you right now. I've got a lot to do to get ready. This town is going to be flooded with thousands of tourists. Keeping the order around here is my responsibility."

"Well, excuse me, Mr. Policeman, Sir. Don't let little ole' Laurie Marie get in your way."

Johnny's face turned red. He brought his fist down on the table just hard enough to jiggle his coffee cup. I watched a little slop over the edge. "Dammit, Laurie, don't you see a problem with the story? That he drowned in Deadman's Creek, under the bridge?"

I was surprised. "How come?"

"That's what I'm going to show you. Hurry up."

I was torn between the desire to drive Johnny nuts by eating as slowly as possible, and my intense curiosity.

The food didn't taste the way I'd remembered it at Bobby D's. The potatoes were instant. The gravy was floury and too salty. The black-eyed peas were oily, but tasteless. And the fried okra consisted of uniform puffed-up balls of batter, with tasteless gray vegetable matter inside. I took just one bite of each item. "What's wrong with Irene?" I asked, in disgust. Irene was Bobby's wife. She'd always been the cook, and she'd made good, plain food. This stuff was obviously pre-packaged and frozen.

"Irene? She and Bobby split years ago. He's married to Rosemarie, now, one of the aerobic instructors at the Cleopatra Spa."

"Three-hundred-and-fifty-pound Bobby, peddling all this high-cholesterol food, and he's married to an aerobic instructor?"

"Quit talking and eat."

"I can't eat this stuff. Let's go."

"Well, your's is the minority opinion," said Johnny. "Bobby has opened three more Bobby D's, and he's raking in the cash. Getting rid of Irene was great for business."

We argued over the check. Johnny wanted to pay for my lunch, of course, and I wasn't having any of it. When we got to the front steps of the restaurant, he said, "I think it will be better if we take your car."

"Fine."

"Well, where is it?" he asked, looking around the parking lot.

"Over at the *Port Mullet News*," I answered.

"How'd you get here, then?" he asked, sounding perplexed and irritated. Before I could answer, he said, "Come on, get in, we'll drive over there in mine then."

I started to argue, but thought better of it, and climbed in the patrol car.

We switched to my car—or rather, Momma's—in the parking lot of the newspaper office. I let him drive.

He knew the short cuts all right, and was still a zippy driver. It wasn't long before we were out in the sticks. We had gone inland, I knew, because the land wasn't as flat as the coast. Not that you could call it hilly. The tepid swells of land resembled hills about as much as my chest resemble Dolly Parton's. Which is to say, no comparison.

Anyway, the ride was peaceful. I took off my boots and propped my feet up on the dash board. Riding around with Johnny. Something I hadn't done in forever, but it felt so familiar. Like being on a bicycle again, after a long absence.

We were way out in the middle of nowhere when Johnny pulled over to the side. I didn't ask him what he was doing when he opened the door and got out. I just climbed out, too.

He walked through the live oak trees dripping with Spanish moss until we reached a shallow creek lined with weeds. He walked alongside the clear, gently flowing water. Less than half a foot deep. I followed him, carefully picking my way through the bushes and weeds, until we reached a ratty-looking wooden bridge, just wide enough for one car to cross. There were signs at both ends, forbidding trucks. We climbed up the short bank and sat on the edge of the bridge, our legs dangling over the side. Our feet didn't touch the water, but almost.

"Deadman's Bridge?" I asked finally.

Johnny nodded. I sure couldn't imagine anyone falling off this low bridge into that quiet, shallow water and drowning. Maybe if he was drunk. Maybe if the stream was swollen with heavy rain. But I didn't think so.

The heat, the insect noises, the soft sounds of the water all made me feel sleepy. I looked over at Johnny to see if he felt the same way. He was looking at me. But it wasn't sleep his eyes were lusting for.

I couldn't help remembering how good Johnny was in bed. Well, actually, he was pretty good in the backseat of a car, or the front seat of a car, or sometimes in the sand beside a car. Couldn't remember trying it under a car.

I also couldn't help wanting him at that moment, and I was determined not to give in to that wanting. That was a rare state for me. Was it Sammy that did that to me, or just late-blooming common sense?

I started back to the car, and he followed. We reached the car about the same time.

"How'd you ever miss coming out here before?" he asked, sliding in on the driver's side.

"Oh, I've been here before. I just didn't remember that it was called Deadman's Bridge. Good name for it," I added.

Johnny nodded and started the car.

My boots were damp and sandy. I slid out of them again and stuck my feet back up on the dash, where the air-conditioning could blow up my mini-skirt and cool things down a bit.

Johnny slowed down as we approached the bridge. I tried not to hold my breath. I didn't want him to notice how nervous I was as we began to bump-bump across the wooden planks.

About halfway across, Johnny put his hand between my legs. He just rested it there for a moment and then he gently undid the snap at the crotch of my body suit.

My body remembered Johnny inside me a thousand times. It remembered what it felt like the first time I came with Johnny inside me, when I thought that feeling was my secret and the secret of the universe, the thing that would save me, would save us all. My body was remembering all that, reading all that in the movements of his fingers. Then my brain was remembering the pain, and all the years I'd tried to forget him and all things I'd done trying to forget him.

Sammy was there, suddenly, inside me, as real as if she'd been there in the car with us. I felt shame, then, and I'd never felt that way about sex before. I knew—and was surprised by the depth and certainty in me of the knowledge—that the theme of my life was not sex of every sort, at every opportunity anymore. And that there were things and even people who were more important to me, and provided more satisfaction.

"We're not going to fuck," I said.

Johnny's hand left me. He said nothing. Not a muscle moved in his face.

"I'm not gonna fuck you," I repeated.

No answer.

Frustrated by his silence, I asked sarcastically, "You understand what I'm saying?"

"Yeah. I got it. You fuck everything else that moves, but you're not gonna fuck me."

"I guess you got it," I said.

The car was stopped in the middle of the bridge.

"Let me drive," I said.

Johnny shrugged, got out, and walked around to the passenger door, while I was scooting over to the driver's side.

We drove in silence for a long while until we pulled up to a stretch of grass by the side of the road.

Finally, Johnny said, "We're not going to fuck but were going to swim?"

"Yes," I said. "Monkey's Hole."

I got out, and ran through the grass to the woods. Then down a narrow path between the trees. I remembered the way, but the distance was shorter than I had thought, so I nearly ran right into the spring. It was a deep, clear pool of cold water. The white sand bottom glimmered as if through glass in some places, while dark green weeds swayed in the center, and fish darted.

I stripped off my clothes. That was easy enough, since I hadn't resnapped my body suit. Then I ran out into the cold, cold water, up to my shoulders.

Johnny took longer to get undressed. He had to untie his shoes. There were all those buttons on his shirt, and the buckle on this belt. But he was finally naked. The sight of his body in that harsh sunlight was a shock to me. It wasn't that I was repulsed. Actually, I found his pot belly, and all the little sags and imperfections of time, endearing. The boy I'd married, and left, and who was gone for good now, was not the same as the man he'd ripened into, this middle-aged small-town guy with love handles. I didn't even know this guy. Not really.

Johnny gave a familiar yell—our football team had been the Port Mullet Rebels—and plunged into the water, diving under and resurfacing at the other side.

"You have to be so noisy?" I asked.

"Sure do," he called back. "You want the water moccasins and the alligators to keep their distance, don't you?"

I'd be damned if I was going to give him the pleasure of seeing me act scared.

Johnny disappeared underwater again. I felt something brush against me. Then my legs were pulled out from under me, and I was going under.

After a moment's panic, I realized it was Johnny. I kicked him away, and swam out deeper, where I treaded water until he walked up to the sand at the edge of the spring and threw himself down.

He rolled onto his back, propped himself up on his elbows, his body half-in, half-out of the water. He looked comfortable, so I joined him, but at a distance just out of touching range.

"You have to be more careful of the alligators these days," Johnny said.

The part of me in the water was tingly cold, and the part of me out was baking in the sun. The combination was great.

"Hmmm?" I said.

"They've been protected so long, and the damned Yankees feed them marshmallows, believe it or not. A lot of the gators have lost their fear of man."

I turned over on my stomach and put my head down on my folded arms. The wet sand felt great against my breasts while the hot air was drying and warming my back.

Johnny turned over, too.

"Fear of man?" I asked. "Just men?"

"Well, I don't know about women in general," said Johnny, "but I bet even the meanest old gator is afraid of you."

I ignored him.

We lay that way, together and yet apart, for a nice long time. "What about the Klan?" I asked suddenly. I guess I hoped I was going to catch him off guard.

He waited a moment and then said, "You mentioned the Klan the other night, too, when you left me so abruptly at the Pirate's Den. What's this about?"

I still didn't turn my face towards him. I kept my cheek pressed against the sand. I couldn't bear to look at him, I was so afraid of what I was going to find out. "The Ku Klux Klan, Johnny. You know what I'm talking about. The sign out on Night Lake Road."

He sat up. I felt him looking at me.

"Hell of a note, them adopting a road, isn't it? The county didn't want to let them, but the lawyers said they had to. They pay to keep that stretch of road maintained. They filled out the forms. They wrote a check for the fee. Can't discriminate. The other clubs get to, have to let them. Free country, you know."

"Discrimination. Free country." I let all my bitterness show in my voice.

"I don't like the Klan anymore than you do. But one of the regional big-shots lives here, so the idiots from all over come here for the rallies. They've got good lawyers, fill out all their forms, even get bonfire permits from the fire department. What are we going to do?"

"How long has this been going on, Johnny?"

"Well, let's see. I think there was a Klan here when we were little kids, like in lots of places. Then it kind of disappeared for a while. No need for it. Small black population, and no trouble when the schools were integrated. All those Yankees moving down here, and all the tourists visiting. Until right recent, the economy here was booming. Guess no one saw the need, when times were good."

"Isn't that nice," I said, as sharply as I could.

"Why are you being mean to me about it?" he asked. "Just like the other night… Wait a minute! You're not blaming me for this, are you?"

I didn't answer.

"That doesn't make any sense, Laurie. Anymore than if I blamed you for those black kids getting beaten to death up in New York City! You can't blame all of us for what a few weirdos get involved in."

He was right. I had been blaming him, and yet I hated it when I met some ignorant Yankee who assumed I was a racist because I had a southern accent. I turned over, and sat up facing him. "Johnny, about me fucking everything that moves…"

"What a provocative opening. Do go on."

"I don't. Not really."

"You used to."

"I had to."

"You don't say. Nymphomania? Maybe I can sell my story to the *Enquirer*. 'I Was Married To A Nymphomaniac.'"

"You know how my Dad screws around. How most men around here screw around. How the wives hold on to their meal ticket by keeping their eyes and legs closed. I couldn't live like that. You know I couldn't. I had to prove to myself that I could screw around as much as the guys. And that it didn't make me a bad girl."

"I'm not like your father, Laurie. I was never like that. I just wanted you."

"What about Linda, and the waitress at the Golden Spur…"

"Linda doesn't count. You were sleeping with her first. And the other one didn't mean anything. You know that. I was just trying to get your attention. Jesus Christ, I was a twenty-two year-old kid, and I loved you to distraction, and you were sleeping with girls! I didn't know what the hell to do."

I was quiet for a while, picking up handfuls of warm, wet sand, and squeezing them through my fingers.

"Yeah, yeah. I know that. But it wouldn't matter if you did or not. I was the sweet little wifey and you were the man of the house, and it was my job to keep you home at night with home-cooked meals and…"

"You cooked maybe two meals for me. And those two weren't any good."

"That's not the point," I said.

"So, what is the point? I don't understand what you are getting at. Instead of shacking up with me, you're shacking up with some black woman. What's the difference? Just this. You think you have to be original. You have to be the center of attention. You have to be different. Things were super between us, Laurie, until you screwed them up. You threw it away because I'm a white guy in a small town, and the idea of that just isn't exciting enough for you."

"It was exciting, Johnny. But exciting wasn't enough."

"You're telling me you've had better sex?"

"I wasn't talking about sex."

"Just answer my question. Have you had better sex?"

I thought for a moment. "Different, yes. Better, no."

"See?"

"It's not enough, I'm telling you. I just wasn't cut out to be a wife." I stood up and walked back into the water.

He stood up and shouted to me from the shore, "What's the difference? You're her wife, aren't you? Or are you the husband? How does it work?"

I dove under the water.

When I came up, he was swimming towards me. He stopped about a yard away. "Tell me how it's different," he pleaded. "Just tell me. Why can you be with her and not me. If it's not different, you're going to end up leaving her, too, right? And where's it all going to end? With you alone and lonely some day?"

I shook my head and little drops of water sprayed into the air. I saw tiny rainbows dance around me. "I don't know how it's different. For one thing, we don't live together. Look, I don't know what will happen with me and Sammy. But I know you and me didn't work, could never work."

He turned and swam back to the sand, left the water and started pulling on his shirt. I got out of the water too, and started pulling on my sandy clothes. My body was damp, and the sand inside my tight clothes made me itchy.

We climbed into the hot car and onto the sticky seats, turned up the air conditioning and drove back to Port Mullet in silence.

Chapter Seven

I walked through the kitchen door, my hair frizzled from the swim, the rest of me sandy, my skirt wrinkled. Momma was at her usual place over the stove, and she just gave me another one of those looks.

I went directly to the cabinet over the refrigerator and poured myself three fingers of Daddy's bourbon. I swallowed a good-sized sip of it, and then started towards the back of the house.

Something occurred to me and I stopped, went back to the kitchen and got another glass. Then I poured a nice stiff one for Momma and sat it on the counter next to the stove.

She looked at me like I was crazy and shook her head "no." I shrugged my shoulders and left it where it was. I carried my own glass back to the bathroom, ran a hot, hot bath, and climbed in. I leaned my head against the back of the tub, and kept one foot under the stream of hot water from the faucet. My bourbon was on the side of the tub, within easy reach, when it wasn't being administered in large doses. The hot water soothed my sand-scraped skin, and sharpened my memory of the cold spring water.

I got to thinking about Sammy, and the old claw-footed bathtub in her apartment. I would love to take a good long soak in it, with Sammy, lots of bubbles, and some fooling around. Unfortunately, that bathroom was only slightly less busy than Grand Central Station. I couldn't even take a quick shower without stepping on plastic ducks and boats and wind-up scuba divers, and without someone banging on the door. If I ignored the banging, Sammy would pick the lock with a coat hanger so one of the girls could rush in to pee.

Definitely not the sort of adventure I usually like to star in. I reached out for another sip of bourbon. There was this pattern in my life with Sammy, and I was beginning to make it out. Sammy had made no demands on me of any sort. She was just there, offering herself, and a warm place in that crowded life. And slowly, by tiny increments, I'd shifted more of my life there. Once Sammy left in the middle of the night to deliver a baby, and the next morning I'd stepped right into the task of running out for Saturday morning bagels, cream cheese, and lox. But it had been so gradual that I hadn't noticed the full extent of the change in my life, in me, until I had gotten away and gotten some perspective. The view from the tub was that I was more connected to Sammy and the girls than I had ever admitted to myself.

The water ran lukewarm after a while. My glass was empty. Even a hot bath and bourbon is only a temporary refuge. I climbed out and wrapped a towel around my body and another around my hair.

When I opened the bathroom door and stepped out, I encountered my father in the narrow hallway. He looked at me and said, "You mind putting on some clothes, Baby Sister?"

I went to my room, got dressed, and headed back to the kitchen. It struck me as another sign of an emerging maturity that I was actually feeling something between obligation and desire which was compelling me to help Momma in the kitchen. I wondered if it was something in the water. Or maybe a drastically delayed effect of being brought up a Southern female.

The glass I'd left for Momma was nowhere in sight, but her mood was definitely elevated. Singing to herself, she broke into little dance steps as she set the table. She put her arm around my waist and we did a little kick-step like a chorus line. She showed me how to mix biscuits, something she had tried to do many times before. Believe it or not, it took this time. I got it. I figured maybe I would surprise Sammy and make them for dinner one night.

Daddy was watching the local news in the other room. Momma was just about ready to call him in to eat when the back door opened and Walter came in, followed by Josh. I quit dancing. Momma hurried to set two more places.

We all sat down, and Momma kept shoveling out the food. My father, my brother, and Josh kept eating.

I tried to make conversation. "Walter, Daddy, have you two heard about the Ku Klux Klan?"

They looked up from their plates and stared at me.

Finally Walter spoke up. "Just how dumb do you think we are down here, Baby Sister? We do have newspaper deliveries and TV reception. Of course we've heard of the Ku Klux Klan." He took two more biscuits and slathered them with margarine.

"What I meant was, have you ever heard of it around here?"

My father's face was red, and I knew without looking at her that my Momma would be angry at me for riling everybody up at the dinner table.

Walter said, "There you go again. You really are a piece of work.

You think everybody south of the Mason Dixon line is a dues-paying member of the Klan." He helped himself to more gravy.

I glanced at Josh. He didn't say anything, just kept putting away Momma's good food.

"I didn't mean to imply anything about any of you," I said, waving my arms to indicate those of us at the table, "or Southerners in general, either. Don't you know that some of the biggest Klan organizations are in the Midwest? I'm sure that I read that somewhere. I just want to know what's going on right here in this town, damn it. Don't tell me you haven't seen the sign out on Night Lake Road."

Walter sighed. "Sure, I see the sign every time I drive out there. And the light from the rallies if I happen to drive down Highway 17 some Friday nights. That's all I know. What, you think I'm Grand Dragon, or something? Watch out, Momma, I might start stealing sheets outa your linen closet."

"What about the rallies?"

Walter took a big bite of biscuit. Then he squeezed more lemon into his iced tea.

"Go watch one if you're so interested. You can see the bonfire from the road. Last Friday night of the month."

"Who goes? Who are these people?"

Walter shrugged. I looked around the table, and everyone else shrugged, too.

"Do you know anyone who's a member?"

Momma said, "I'm sure I don't know anyone silly enough to get involved in such foolishness."

"What about you, Walter?" I demanded.

"I think they're all a bunch of jerks," he answered promptly, to my relief. "But," he drew his words out slowly, and my heart sank, "a lot of people think things have gone too far in the other direction."

"Who thinks what has gone too far?"

"Well, this affirmative action stuff. All the jobs are going to the blacks and women and other minorities, and us white guys are getting the short end of the stick. Reverse discrimination."

"What are you talking about? What jobs haven't you gotten because you're white? How many blacks and women work in your office? None, I bet you." I was waving my arms around passionately, dripping melted butter from my biscuit.

"Just because it hasn't happened to me doesn't mean it doesn't happen. There's this big preference for the minorities these days. Now, that's prejudice too, in my book, but you don't hear anyone screaming about that."

I bit the insides of my cheeks to keep from screaming. Looking around the table, I saw Daddy's place was empty. He had apparently finished his dinner and left while we were arguing. I hadn't even noticed. From the sounds of it, he was back watching TV in the front room.

Walter pushed back his chair and stood up. "But that don't mean I'm a Klan member, because I ain't. Understand, Baby Sister?"

The "ain't" had been chosen for my benefit. I ignored him.

He stalked out the kitchen door into the night, followed by Josh, who didn't look at me. Josh did pause in front of Momma to say, "Thank you for the fine dinner, Mrs. Coldwater." Then he was gone.

Momma and I were left alone once more at a table full of dirty dishes. She sighed, and said, "Well, Baby, I always did say you would argue with a signpost," and then she started clearing the dishes off the table.

I knew she was right. I would.

When we finished in the kitchen, Momma went into the front room. Daddy was still watching TV. Any conversation would have to be during the commercials. I'd wait patiently—well, not so patiently, actually—for the breaks in the show, and then I'd try to get all the information I could. It was harder than I thought it would be, because the commercials were the only part that interested me, and sometimes I'd forget and watch them instead of talking to Daddy.

"Daddy, what do you think about the Klan?"

"I don't."

"Don't what?"

"Think about it."

Show was back on. I waited for another break.

"If you thought abut the Klan, what would you think?"

"I'm with your brother. A bunch of idiots with nothing better to do than run around in sheets." He snorted.

"Do you know anybody in the Klan?"

He finally turned his head and looked at me. "What are you up to, young lady? Why are you asking me all this?"

"I have to know."

"No, you don't. You've gotten along this long without knowing, you can just keep right on." He turned back towards the screen. "Now, hush up. I want to see if Burt's team is finally going to win a game."

At nine-thirty, Momma and Daddy headed for bed. I tried calling Sammy, but Elena answered and told me she was out. Elena didn't say if she was out delivering a baby or out having a good time. I had a flash of jealousy, picturing her dancing with someone at a party like the one where we'd met. I scolded myself for that. Then I wondered whether I should have asked Elena how her studies were going, if I should have asked to speak to the girls. I had treated Elena like an answering service.

I was afraid if I didn't get back soon, Sammy would slip away from me. If I didn't get in touch with my New York reality soon, I was afraid I was going to turn into… I didn't know what. Maybe my alternate self. The trapped, frustrated person I would have been if I had never left Port Mullet.

I went back to the telephone and dialed Sammy's number again.

"Hi, Elena. It's me again, Laurie. I meant to ask, how's school, how's your dissertation going? And the girls, how are they?"

I listened as she told me, filled me in on the details of their daily lives since I'd been gone. I realized for the first time that Elena, brilliant as she was and self-sufficient as she seemed, was lonely. Thousand of miles from home, unable even to call her family who had been on a waiting list for a telephone for years. Never hearing her native tongue, studying in a foreign language, knowing her family's hopes for the future all hinged on her.

I told Elena to tell the girls "hi" for me, and then I added, "Tell them I miss them." As soon as those words came out of my mouth, though, I felt uncomfortable. I had never been a hypocrite. I had always tried hard not to say things I didn't mean. Nice things, anyway.

Then I thought that maybe it was true. Maybe I did miss the girls, too, for their own sakes, and not just for Sammy's. I felt something in the pit of my stomach that might be that. Unless it was just a side effect of treating an attack of melancholia by consuming bourbon a thousand miles from one's lover.

I tried calling Jerry. I got his machine and left an obscene message. That cheered me up a little.

I wandered into the kitchen and looked at the clock. Ten-fifteen on a Friday night. I had absolutely nothing to do, nowhere to go.

I thought about what I'd have been doing if I were back in the city. Not that long ago at this time on a Friday night, I'd just be starting to think about getting ready to squeeze into something tight and obvious, and start my tour of the clubs. There I'd find excitement, and a good time and I'd think that was the same thing as life and freedom. But lately, I'd been spending a lot of my Friday nights with Sammy. Sometimes we'd go out to dinner and a movie, but most of the time we'd have dinner with the girls, and then watch a video.

Now and then, just to prove I could, I'd tell Sammy I was busy, and I'd go out with some friends, and do the clubs, or a party. It really pissed me off that Sammy didn't seem to mind. But the thing was, that wasn't what I was missing. I was missing the evenings home with Sammy and Elena and the girls, watching old movies and making popcorn. Not that I'd give up the dancing nights, don't get me wrong. But what scared me was, even a night at Sammy's when she kept having to send Annie to her room, and Rachel was crying with a fever so we never got to fool around, was a real night, a good night, an important night in my life.

I didn't fully understand it, but it went something like this. I knew about quick sex with guys, him going in and out, yelling "oh god" and collapsing on me. And then the guys who knew a bit about foreplay, maybe even variety and taking his time. That was sex. And then I've known some really great women who made me see that the dinner before sex, and the sitting in bed after, talking about what you looked like in the third grade, and how sad she was when her dog died—well that made the whole experience even better, deeper, more fun. I was beginning to think that the whole scene with Sammy, *everything*, from getting up in the morning to changing Rachel's diaper at two a.m, was part of what made me feel the way I did about her.

Then I said the words to myself. Friday night. The *last* Friday of the *month*!

I ran back to my room and put together the most respectable disguise I could find. Jeans and sneakers. Not great, but fairly innocuous. I considered borrowing something pastel and polyester from my mother, but I was sure nothing she owned would fit me.

Maybe I could borrow a white shirt from my father. I stood at their bedroom door listening. I really couldn't picture them "doing it," not any better than I could when I was a third grader and Timmy Pritchard acquainted me with that possibility. On the other hand, I didn't want to take any chances.

All I heard was my mother's quiet breathing and my father's irregular snores. I slipped quietly into the room, leaving the door ajar for a tiny shaft of light from the hall. After my eyes adjusted to the darkness, I found the closet door and moved carefully towards it.

I opened it and reached in. This wasn't as easy as I'd imagined it would be. Whenever I pictured my father, I thought of him wearing the starched white shirts he had worn when I was a kid. But nobody, my father included, dressed like that anymore. I was wading through a lot of short-sleeved, knit shirts.

I had finally found a long-sleeved, semi-cotton shirt from the feel of it when I heard a definite heavy movement from the bed. Then I heard a sliding noise, like a drawer being opened. The next thing I heard was a metallic click.

My father said, "Stand still and don't move or I'll blow your brains out."

I stood still, of course, frozen and paralyzed. While my body and my mouth wouldn't move, my brain was racing. I thought how appropriate it was that my relationship with my family was finally going to kill me. I had one last vision of Sammy in her red dress.

There was another louder click, and my eyes were blinded by a sudden light.

I shut my eyes tight, and then blinked them a few times. Finally I opened them wide. Meanwhile my father was saying, "Jesus Christ, I nearly shot Baby Sister."

Momma sat up, looked from me standing by the closet door to Daddy holding his pistol aimed at me. The first thing she said was, "What's she done now, Sydney?"

I started laughing, then realized that I had put my hands up in the air without realizing it somewhere during the course of this. I put my hands down.

"I need to borrow a shirt, Daddy, is that okay?"

"You could have got shot, Baby Sister. What kind of fool did I raise, walking in people's rooms in the middle of the night?"

"You just about shot your daughter, and I'm a fool? Thanks for the shirt."

I picked it up off the carpet where I'd dropped it.

Momma said, "Wait a minute. What do you need a shirt for in the middle of the night?"

"I'm going out."

"Do you have a date?" she asked, the hope painfully clear in her voice.

"No. I'm going all by myself."

Momma sat up straighter in bed. "What kind of woman goes out by herself in the middle of the night? You're up to no good. You're looking for trouble, Baby Sister."

I started for the door with the shirt clutched to my chest, still feeling shaky. "It's only ten-thirty," I said. "But you are definitely right about one thing. I am looking for trouble, and I aim to find it."

I'm not going to tell you I wasn't nervous driving through the night towards Highway 17. My stomach churned, and my palms were wet against the steering wheel. It's ironic, I thought. I'm fearless in the most infamous neighborhoods of New York, but this little visit to subtropical suburbia was turning me into a nervous wreck. But I kept going, because I wanted to know exactly what sort of people I'd grown up with. If I'd failed to notice something this big when I was growing up, I didn't want to miss it any longer.

I turned onto the highway. I really hoped that Walter had been putting me on. That the Klan didn't really have rallies within sight of a major highway. Or, if they did, that there wasn't one scheduled for this particular Friday night. But I hadn't gone far before I spotted the glow from the fire, off to the right, set back a ways from the road.

There was only one turn-off in that direction. I pulled off the highway onto a narrow, oyster-shell road which wound through the pine scrub and palmetto. There were no street lights. I could not see farther ahead than the next curve, which was never very far.

I belatedly thought what a good idea it would have been to tell someone—Momma, Daddy, Seth, even Johnny—where I was going. That way, if my body showed up floating in Matthew Bayou the next day, at least someone would know who to blame.

Then I turned another curve, and there was a fence, with a gate crossing the road, and two men in white robes and pointy white hats at either side of the road. Beyond the fence, I could see a big field filled with cars parked in rows. Beyond was the large bonfire, and hundreds of people milling around it, silhouetted against the flames.

My throat was itchy. I licked with my dry tongue at my lips which were coated with a thick, bubble-gum pink lipstick of Momma's I'd found in the bathroom. For some reason, I had thought it would help my disguise. I wondered if I could just pretend to the guards that I was lost, and get directions to nearest bar. And then follow those directions.

The gatekeepers came up to either side of the car. They both carried flashlights. I didn't see guns, but I strongly suspected they were carrying those, too.

The one on the driver's side shined his light in my face. "This is a private party, Miss. I'm gonna have to ask you to leave."

I was too scared to focus on his face under the silly white hat, but I got the menacing tone in his voice clear enough. I was about to launch into my story about how lost I was when the other one, on the passenger side, spoke.

"Wait a minute, George. I recognize this car. Belongs to Mr. Coldwater." He walked around the front of the car to the driver's side, bent down and peered at my face.

"Why I bet this is Coach Coldwater's little girl. The one that lives up north somewhere with all those Yankees. That right? You Sydney Coldwater's little girl?"

I sighed. One thing I truly appreciated about the impersonal streets of Manhattan was that I was never referred to as "Coach Coldwater's little girl."

"That right?" asked the first one. "Little Laurie Coldwater. How about that. You remember me, don't you, Laurie?"

I looked at the fat, ugly redneck in the white costume. I had that same sick feeling I get in my stomach when I'm watching an old movie and there is a close-up of a huge Nazi flag and then the camera pulls back to show a plaza full of booted soldiers goose stepping as foreboding music grows louder and louder. No, I didn't remember him. I could never have known this man.

"Greg Johnson. Now you remember me, right?" he smiled with an eagerness that made me sick.

I did remember a Greg Johnson, a sweet, shy football player. Country boy. We laughed at him when he wore high-topped sneakers with a suit to the athletic-award banquet.

"Been out of town quite a while, haven't you?" asked the other one. "Tell you what," he said. "I'll park her car. You two get reacquainted."

I got out of the car, moving as if in a dream. My movements just didn't seem to have weight. I realized I still had my car keys in my hand. I offered them awkwardly to the Klansman, trying not to touch his hand.

Greg walked me over to the fence. I could hear the voices of the crowd around the fire, but only vaguely, as if someone had the TV on in the next room.

Greg appeared to be thrilled to see me. He had married Greta Altman, he said. He took out his wallet to show me his children's pictures. There were three boys. Teenagers. They were photos of them in their football uniforms, their helmets tucked under their arms. They all had short hair, and heavy faces and necks, and all three of them had a variation of their father's sweet grin.

"I'm a lucky man. I'll tell you that right now," he said, with an ever shy pride.

I stretched my lips into a smile. It felt fake and nasty.

"Three good boys. All athletes. Not a one of them involved with drugs. Nothing like that. Fine boys."

I remembered seeing Greg enjoy at least a joint or two at one party or another. There had been so many parties, but looking back, they blended into one, long endless night, with drugs and booze and stupid jokes and the waiting, always, the waiting. There was always someone who was supposed to show up with more beer, or some really good pot. Something that would make it all worthwhile.

"Do they drink beer?" I asked.

Greg laughed. "Sure they do. Boys'll be boys you know. Long as they stay away from the drugs, I can't complain."

I thought of the boys Greg and I knew who had died in car accidents. I thought of the quarterback my junior year, a star with several impressive scholarship offers, who had lost an arm and his bright hopes after one particular drunken night.

But all I did was nod my head and try to focus on my investigation. So many things I felt I had to know. How long had this been going on? Why were they doing this? How much of the population of Port Mullet knew about it? I had to figure out a way to ask all these questions without making him suspicious.

The mosquitoes were biting pretty bad. I kept scratching at my wrists and neck. Greg noticed. "No mosquito trucks anymore," he said. "They ought to bring them back. Remember when we were kids and there used to be those great fog-trucks?"

Suddenly, I did remember. I had completely forgotten those hot summer nights. How thrilled we were to hear the heavy roar of the truck in the distance, and smell its approach. We'd be playing barefoot in the street.

When the truck passed down the street, the kids would run behind it, just for the thrill of breathing in the heavy, smelly "mosquito fog." Our skin would be coated with a layer of heavy oil.

Insecticide. Nobody ever called it that. But that's what it was. "Poison" is another word we didn't use. I didn't want to think too much about it. About the effect on our little bodies of breathing in that stuff, year after year.

"Mosquito control and air conditioning, that's what's made this place. You ever think about it, Laurie? I mean this little town was nothing, nothing, when we were born here. But every year, a few more people, then a few more, then by the time we were in high school, this place had become something. Some old timers complain about it, but hell, I say, most of those old timers got rich in real estate. If not for the newcomers, they'd still be mullet fishermen, living in shacks. It's mosquito control and air conditioning that made this place what it is today." Apparently the economic boom had been good to Greg. "Come on, Laurie, I'll show you around. Lots of folks here haven't seen you in a long, long time."

I followed him, almost numb from the shock that this was really happening. The atmosphere was like that of a big barbecue. There appeared to be a family section way on the other side of the field, where the wives and children were gathered. On the near side, it looked like any gathering of men, drinking beer, telling jokes. Greg said that the main event would be later, an inspirational speech by some Klan bigshot.

Greg showed me around. A lot of people knew me, or rather, knew of me. To some people, I was introduced as, "You know, Seth Coldwater's little sister." To more, it was, "This is Coach Coldwater's little girl." One of them answered, "Well, how about that, now. I didn't know Coach had a daughter. Those four boys, now everyone knows about them. Your daddy's a fine man," he said. "Fine man. We've had a winning team for more years than any school around here. We beat them all, even the big city schools from Tampa and St. Pete. Those teams full of those big nigger boys, not a white one in uniform. Coach Coldwater fields a winning team every year, and he does it with more white boys than black." There was a murmur of approval from all around.

I turned away, and, there in front of me, was Forrest Miller, Mr. Miller, the man I had once so admired.

Chapter Eight

Surprise and annoyance flickered across Forrest Miller's face. It was gone in a moment.

He greeted me warmly. The men around me quieted right down. Forrest and the younger, bigger man at his side appeared to be objects of reverence. After some greeting and remarks to the men, Forrest pulled the man with him to the side and spoke quietly in his ear. Then he turned back to the rest of us.

"George," he began, indicating the man with him, "why don't you buy this young lady a soda, and then see her to her car. Wouldn't do now, would it, for us to leave a pretty doe alone with a bunch of big-antlered bucks like this crew, would it?"

There were appreciative chuckles around the group. Greg said it sure was nice to see me again, and Greta would be calling me about a visit to their place. I smiled and waved as I left.

George walked behind me, but was clearly in control of my direction. His hand on my arm, gentle but firm, told me where to go. With that kind of style, I figured he'd be a hell of a slow dancer.

There was a grill set up, and a table where hamburgers and hot-dogs and fixings were sold. Beside that was another folding table holding soft drinks. He bought me a coke. Before I could drink any of it, he led me over to the parking lot.

We found Momma's car. I leaned back against the door on the driver's side, and sipped at my soda. I was feeling cramped and confused. I wanted to feel spunky and in-their-faces. I wanted to be free. I wanted Manhattan. I wanted Sammy. I wanted to go home. But I didn't want to be made to leave before I found what I had come for. I had to find out what I could about these people, my childhood neighbors. I'd always thought I was Port Mullet's most hostile critic, but I'd never, in my most vitriolic moments, imagined this. A thriving Klan.

Maybe I'd started a search for Sammy's past, but now I needed to find my own, too. I'd thought it didn't matter, not since I'd moved to the city, anyway. Every other person you run into in Manhattan has come there to make a complete break with the past. To be someone they couldn't be in their hometown.

I thought the only vestige I carried was my accent. But I had also carried with me the things I had been blind to, the things I had missed. It's like when you're at a party and you're smiling and having a good time and thinking, boy am I sexy. And the whole time you've got a big gob of spinach stuck in your teeth.

I had felt the flush of shame the minute I'd seen Forrest. Yeah, I knew what it said about me. I'd misjudged him, all right. Me, the self-proclaimed cynic and iconoclast, and rebel, so suspicious of authority and privilege. I'd let his money and taste pull the wool over my eyes. He had actually been my *fantasy father*, though. In the time it took to walk away from the crowd with George and settle against the car, I was over that. Lesson learned. I just hoped I could keep the moral firmly in mind.

George took out a cigar and went through an elaborate routine of lighting it. He didn't ask, "Mind if I smoke?" until it was lit.

"Not at all," I said. "Mind if I indulge, too?"

He smiled at me, a superior smile, and I reached into his inside jacket pocket, and took my time finding a cigar. As I pulled my hand out, I brushed it slowly across his shirt, right above his belt.

I mimicked his action in lighting the cigar as closely as I could, then drew on it. It was foul and nasty, and immediately made me slightly nauseated, and very light-headed. But I would be damned if I was going to let him see that.

"So," I said, trying not to cough.

"Yes," said George. "Exactly. So." It was clear that George fancied himself a Southerner along Forrest Miller's aristocratic lines, instead of the good old boy mode that appeared popular among most of the crowd at this event.

He didn't say anything else. Just stood there smoking his cigar, looking me up and down. We smoked our cigars in silence. I was trying to figure out how I could get a conversation going quick, so I would have an excuse to keep the cigar out of my mouth. Also, I was planning to get some information out of this guy.

I had an idea. I took my cigar and very deliberately placed it on the hood of the car, carefully balancing it so that the ash end hung over the edge. Then I reached out and took his cigar from him and put it in my mouth, trying not to gag. After a moment, I removed it slowly, and placed it back in his mouth.

I'll give him this. He didn't crack. Just raised his eyebrows. "Gee, I'm sorry," I said. "I'm afraid it might be a bit wet." I licked my lips.

Then I unbuttoned the top button of my father's shirt and rubbed my hand into my cleavage (such as it is). "These mosquitoes. I'm getting eaten alive."

He didn't make a move. I was impressed. "Would you like to go someplace quiet and…chat?" I asked finally.

"Why don't we get in your car?" he said. "Get away from the mosquitoes. You go ahead and get in. I'll be right back."

I was nervous getting into the car with him, but I figured nothing could happen that I couldn't handle, not with hundreds of people ten yards away. He wouldn't want to be embarrassed in front of this crowd.

I was hoping that I could distract him with his desire and get some answers from him. I had no intention of actually having sex with him, that's for sure.

He got in on the passenger side with a flask of bourbon. I smiled. He passed it to me. I drank, then handed it back.

"Come a little closer, sweet thing," he said.

Now I really smiled. "In a minute," I said. "First I want to talk."

"No, darling. You've been awful inviting, and it wasn't to a lecture."

"I want you to talk."

"You want me to tell you what I want to do to you?"

I sighed inwardly. Another jerk who thought his dirty thoughts were fascinating. I seriously doubted whether there was a single imaginative, creative, or original act on his list.

Outwardly I scooted a little closer, still keeping the parking brake between us. I reached over and rearranged my backpack, which was on the floor on the passenger side, between his feet.

"Should I call you George or Mister…?" I asked, trying to distract him from what I was doing.

"You can call me anything you want," he said.

Good. Finally. Between the booze and the come-ons, he was starting to melt.

"I was so surprised to run into a sophisticated guy like you here," I said.

"And we were surprised you came to visit us." He reached his arm around me and pulled me across the parking brake onto the bucket seat with him. Needless to say, it was crowded. "But very pleasantly surprised."

I thought I had him then. I could start asking him questions about the Klan and he'd answer them all, just in the hopes of getting to stick his little wee-wee in me. Then I'd figure out some way to get away before it came to that.

He tried to kiss me, and I thought for a moment I could go along with it. After all the things I've done, and all the people I've done them with, what's one more kiss?

But I couldn't. I couldn't bear it. I pulled my face away. He let me go. I was relieved, and was trying to figure out what to do next.

He was quick for such a large man. And I wasn't the only one who'd been planning ahead. He had pushed his seat back down and climbed on top of me before I realized what was happening.

I struggled against him and reached out one hand for the handle. It didn't open. He'd locked the door. I reached for the lock, and he grabbed my hand. He held it with the other one over my head. I tried to arch my back, but he was too heavy. I tried to kick, but my legs were pinned down.

He yanked open the shirt and ripped my bra. I tried to bite him. He slapped me hard across my face. I tasted blood.

He was working on my belt buckle. I took a deep breath and then started screaming. He put his hands around my throat and throttled me some, and then he hit my head against the seat back a few times. Just hard enough. He knew what he was doing.

"Shut up. You scream once more and I'll call Forrest. He'll hold you down while I fuck you and then I'll let him have sloppy seconds. If you just want to do this once, shut up."

The world was spinning around me. I'd done it. I'd seriously underestimated both George and Forrest.

George was struggling to raise himself up to unzip his pants. "Any man in there would love to help me fuck you senseless. Who the hell do you think you are? You think I don't know all about you? Walking your pussy around town half-undressed like that. You were a goddamned divorcee before you were twenty. Hell, you were a whore before you were sixteen. Only reason men don't jump you in the street is out of respect for your daddy and your momma."

"Okay," I said. "Don't hurt me. One more guy won't make any difference. I'll cooperate. Just don't hurt me."

"It'll make a difference. I'll fuck you like you've never been fucked before. You won't even know those tiny-dicked Yankees are there next time they stick it in you." He was yanking at my bluejeans. I lifted my hips to help him pull them down.

He had let his own pants fall, and I reached around with my left hand and squeezed his ass. Then I reached into my backpack with the other and pulled out my Swiss army knife. I fumbled with it for a moment, praying he wouldn't notice, sucked hard on his tongue to try to ensure he wouldn't.

I murmured, "Stick it in me now," and he pulled his body away from me to accomplish that task.

But I was quicker. I had the knife up, with the point against his testicles.

"Shit," he said.

"Not in my car, you don't. One move, and you're a eunuch."

I sat up and scooted back across parking brake into the driver's seat, still holding the knife against him. I pressed it gently against his purple, shriveled scrotum to let him know I was serious.

"I've seen chickens with bigger gizzards," I said.

He was staring at me wild-eyed, crazy with fear, fully dressed except for his pants around his knees. I was thrilled at his humiliation, and sick that I felt that way. I hated him, and I hated myself.

"Get out." He didn't move.

I pushed the tip of the knife a little harder. I didn't think I was cutting his flesh, but I wasn't sure. I wondered how it would feel if I did.

"Get out," I repeated.

"Just let me pull my pants up," he pleaded.

"No. Get out. " I applied a little more pressure with the knife. He started to turn to unlock the door.

"No. Back out," I said. "I'm with you all the way." I made circles on his flesh with the knife.

He reached his hand behind him and felt for the lock. He pulled it up, and then moved his hand down to the door handle.

"Now back out slowly. Real slowly." I scooted across the car seat with him, keeping my knife right where it frightened him most. When he was almost out, I pressed the heel of my right boot into his balls, pushing him out the door. He collapsed on the ground, writhing with pain. The two gate guards headed over towards us.

I've never moved as fast as I did then, pulling the door shut and locking it. Then I scrambled back behind the wheel, started the car and took off with the gas pedal pressed full against the floor, spewing sand and grass in every direction.

I was out of that parking lot and down the road like a race car driver. Although I don't think most drive with their pants down around their knees—which was what I was doing. I was hoping to God I didn't meet another car on that narrow, winding path.

I didn't. And I didn't even slow down where the road ended at Highway 17. I just pulled out, fishtailing so hard I almost lost control of the car.

It was late, and the highway was empty. I was going as fast as I dared. Well, actually, faster.

In the rearview mirror was just what I didn't want to see. A car pulled onto the highway after me. It was a big, dark car, and it was going fast.

I pushed harder on the pedal, and managed to maintain the distance between us.

I turned off the highway onto the Main Street of Port Mullet. The town was dead. Nothing was open. No one on the streets.

I slowed some for the red lights at intersections, but I sure as hell didn't stop. I crossed my fingers and counted on all Port Mullet residents being home in bed. The ones that weren't back at the Klan rally, that is.

The dark car was still behind me. My numbness was wearing off to the point I was really scared. I turned off Main Street onto another road that followed the curves of the river. They turned behind me. They were right on my tail now. In my rear view mirror I could see the angry faces in the front seat. I didn't recognize any of them.

They pulled in the other lane, trying to force me off the road.

I gritted my teeth and lay down on the horn. Maybe one of the good citizens would hear it and call the cops. I was still driving for everything I was worth.

Up ahead, I saw the brick building I was aiming for.

I pushed the pedal down further, hitting ninety on a curve with the car still beside me in the other lane of the narrow, two-lane road. They stayed right with me. I never stopped honking the horn.

Then I hit the brakes and swerved right into the parking lot of the police station, nearly slamming into a row of parked cars. I was still leaning on the horn.

My pursuers had not turned off at the cop shop, of course. They had continued on until they were out of sight down River Road.

When two uniformed men ran out of the front door and sprinted over to my car, I frantically pull up my pants. By the time they came to my door I had turned off the car.

"Get them," I yelled. "Those men, the car following me! They were trying to run me off the road! They were trying to kill me!"

The two officers looked at each other. They were barely out of their teens.

"You come on inside the station with us," one of them said. "Everything's going to be all right."

"Stop wasting time and follow them!" I hollered, even louder.

They both stepped back from me and looked at each other. Great, I thought. First time in my life I go to the police for help and I get the Keystone Cops.

An older man was ambling across the lot. "You fellows go on and catch up with the trouble-makers," he said, as soon as he was close enough to talk. "I'll take this young lady inside and we'll get started on her report."

"Yes, Sir," said one of the others.

"Wait a minute, Bill," said the older one. "Don't you want to ask this young lady something?"

"Right. What's your name?"

"There'll be time for *that* later," the older man reproved gently. He turned to me. "Tell me about the car."

"Dark. Blue, I think. Beat-up, old, four doors. I can't be more specific than that. At least five men."

"License number?"

"I was too busy to notice."

"Okay, fellows, you're off."

I got out of the car, moving awkwardly, glad my untucked shirt hid the open zipper. The old guy walked me inside, left me in a plastic chair in front of a desk, and disappeared in an office.

A friendly-looking woman sitting behind the desk asked if I wanted tea or coffee.

"Coffee, please," I said, gratefully, and she disappeared, too, giving me a chance to zip up and tuck my shirt in.

She returned right away with a styrofoam cup of coffee, adulterated with some powdered "creamer" stuff and a lot of sugar.

I smiled and said thanks, and sipped it. Her simple act of kindness had a calming effect on me.

But she was looking at me funny. I put my cup down on the desk in front of me. Then I stood up and did my belt buckle. I buttoned my blouse and straightened it. Nothing I could do about my ripped bra.

I shrugged and sat back down.

"Should I call the rape team?" she asked gently.

I shook my head, "No."

"Can I do anything else for you?" she asked. "Lieutenant D'Amato will be right out. He's arranging for all other units in the area to assist in the search for the car that was bothering you."

I sat there, too tired to be angry and too angry to be tired. My head buzzed with it all. I was angry at Johnny. He hadn't told me that Forrest Miller was the "local guy" who was a big shot in the Klan. I also had my doubts about how seriously the cops were taking my complaint. I could see that, as far as they were concerned, I was crazy. I wanted to call Johnny on what was going down in the little town he policed, and I wanted to see what he was going to do about finding the goons Forrest Miller and George had sent after me. And if it turned out Johnny's loyalties were with the bad guys, I planned to write a hell of a story about it, and to make sure everyone in Port Mullet saw a copy of it. If Johnny thought I'd inflicted my worst on him during our marriage, I planned to show him how wrong he could be.

"Where's Johnny Berry?" I asked.

"Why, home in bed, I suppose," she answered.

"Please call him for me."

"We'll have to let Lieutenant D'Amato make that decision," she said. "Really, he'll be right out." She seemed to regret not being able to do what I asked.

"I'm his ex-wife," I said.

She looked at me, openly surprised. Her sympathy was still visible, but so was her trouble believing me. I guessed I didn't look a hell of a lot like someone the police chief would have married.

I pulled my New York driver's license out of my wallet, and shoved it at her.

"See. That's my name. Laurie Marie Coldwater." It was clear that she didn't see what that proved. I hesitated, and then gave in. "Coach Coldwater, over at Port Mullet High? He's my father." It felt like ashes in my mouth to say that.

She looked at my license, looked at me, and nodded slowly.

"Okay, I'll call Chief Berry."

She didn't use the phone on the desk in the reception area. She went through one of the doors in the back. Almost immediately another officer came out to keep me company. He, too, asked if he should call the rape team. Then he asked if I needed any other medical attention.

Thinking of how many times I had screwed up in so many ways that day, I answered, "Just a brain transplant, thank you."

He looked at me with suspicion. Then he said that Lieutenant D'Amato would be out in a minute.

The nice woman reappeared. "Chief Berry said he's on his way, Mrs. Berry. He said to tell you to just wait in his office until he gets here."

The officer looked very confused.

"Thank you," I answered, "but my name is Laurie Coldwater."

He perked right up. "Really? Are you related to Coach? Coach Coldwater, at Port Mullet High? I played for him. I was a tight end."

I looked at the chubby man. Looked him up and down. "Never would have guessed it," I murmured.

Chapter Nine

I tore into Johnny the moment he walked in. "Why the hell didn't you tell me about Forrest Miller and the Klan? Goddamn it! I had a right to know. I had a right! I almost got raped. I almost got run off the road." I jumped out of my chair, feeling like an avenging angel standing there, hands on hips, glaring at him in front of his yet open office door.

Johnny didn't answer me, but his expression told me he was mad as hell, his face red and his jaw tight with tension. He shut the door, walked behind his desk, and sat down.

I collapsed into a chair across from him. I was feeling the superiority of righteous anger, but, at the same time, I couldn't help admiring the way that Johnny had held his temper. We'd had some first class knock-down-and-drag-outs in our time, but clearly Johnny had learned something in the years we'd been apart.

He said, "I didn't tell you about Forrest Miller because it didn't seem relevant. I know you've always been real fond of Susan's daddy, and you spent a lot of time over there when you were growing up. I didn't see any need to upset you, to tell you something that might make it hard on you to visit your old friends."

I took a deep breath, trying hard to remain calm. "Do you want to hear what happened to me tonight in your law-abiding little town, or not?"

He looked straight at me. "I certainly do."

I told him about the rally, Forrest, George, and the car chase. When I was finished, he was looking down at his desk.

"You just asked me about the sign on Night Lake Road, Laurie. I had no idea you meant to take off on an investigation of the Klan. If I'd even suspected that, you can bet there are a lot of things I would have said to you, and Forrest Miller's position would be the least of it." His voice gained volume and momentum as he went on, "Dammit, Laurie, there's lots of agencies that are dying to infiltrate the Klan, but none of them would send you out there half-cocked to do it! Yes, you could have been killed." His voice cracked there, and he looked down at his desk. "You're lucky you weren't." I could have sworn he was crying.

When he looked back up, his voice was clear again. "When we find this George guy, how are we going to pin attempted rape on him? By your own admission, you tried to turn the guy on. You voluntarily climbed into a car with him and drank bourbon. I want to kill him, but for Christ's sake, Laurie! Use common sense. How would all that look to a jury?"

I got to tell you, it wasn't pleasant listening to what I had thought of as brilliant and daring investigative work referred to in this derogatory manner. And the worst part of it was, of course, that he was right.

Besides chagrin, I was experiencing major exhaustion. I'd nearly been shot in my own home, and then nearly raped in my own hometown. I didn't even want to think about what the guys chasing me had had in mind. Johnny got up and walked around to my chair, then squatted down beside me and picked up my hand. "Laurie, I'll help you, I swear I will. Unless you don't want my help. I'll do what you want. But please be more careful. Don't get yourself hurt." His voice was low and husky.

Someone knocked on the door, and he dropped my hand and stood up, quickly. The door opened, and one of his officers stepped in to talk with him.

From what I heard it was clear that the police weren't going to find the guys who were chasing me. They could have turned down any side street, in any subdivision, and pulled the car into a garage. Hell, they could have left the car on the street. The cops couldn't knock on doors and question everyone who had an old dark-blue car parked outside.

Johnny sent some guys over to the rally to ask about the men who chased me. The party was just about over by then. Of the few people still around, no one had seen me. No one had seen a car take off after me. Nobody had seen Forrest Miller, nor a man with him named George.

Forrest was home in bed when the officers went by to talk with him. He hadn't been at any Klan rally that evening. The very idea was preposterous. His wife confirmed they had gone out to dinner, then spent the evening quietly at home before going to bed. He was sorry to hear that Miss Coldwater had been mixed up in some trouble. He'd heard tell that she did drink quite a bit, and a young lady who does that, why she's bound to get into trouble eventually.

Greg Johnson did admit he'd been to the rally. It wasn't any big deal. Just went there to see some friends, have a drink. Nothing wrong with that, was there? Sure, he'd seen me. Worried about me, too. A woman alone, with all those men. Asking for trouble, if you asked him. Hadn't seen Forrest Miller. Didn't know anyone named George there.

I sat there while Johnny gave me the news. I wasn't surprised, but it made me burn. "So they just get by with it? He gets by with it? Is that what you're telling me?"

"No. I'm not telling you that. Don't think it's over, because it's not. I'm the police chief around here and I plan to make their lives miserable. Every time they turn around, I'm going to be up their asses. I'll ask around, I'll find out who George is, and he and Forrest Miller and Greg Johnson are going to live to regret this."

I was too tired to think any more about it then, and Johnny looked beat, too. It was three-thirty-five by the clock on Johnny's office wall. I wasn't looking forward to walking into my parents' house. I was sure Momma, at least, would be waiting up for me. One look at the state my clothes were in and she'd be hysterical. I was too tired to fabricate a reasonable explanation, and much too tired to deal with her hysterics if I told her the truth. I just wanted to be left alone, and to sleep. I stood up, swung my backpack over my shoulder.

Johnny said, "Come home with me, Laurie. No use upsetting your parents. I swear I won't bother you; you can sleep in my guest room. I'll call your folks and tell them where you are, and they won't worry. You can get cleaned up and face them in the morning when you're rested."

I knew I should say no, but it sounded so reasonable. I had been in a rough spot, and it felt like Johnny was the only person around who was on my side. And I was so drained. I nodded.

Then Johnny said, "You don't look up to driving. Give me your car keys and I'll have someone take your mother's car over to her in the morning. I've already got a unit cruising by your parents' house now and then, just in case your new friends go looking for you there."

I wasn't too tired to feel a shiver of fear crawl up me. That possibility had not occurred to me. That they might come to Momma and Daddy's house. That my parents could be in danger because of me. But no, I thought, nobody would hurt Coach Coldwater, not as long as his football team kept winning.

Johnny drove me to his house. I fell asleep in the car, and he had to wake me up when we got there. I was too tired to notice anything else about it. I went into the guestroom Johnny showed me, took off all my clothes, climbed into bed and went right to sleep.

I woke up to the irritating buzz of a lawn mower outside. At first, I didn't know where I was. A double bed with nice sheets, a beige coverlet, beige blinds, beige carpet. No identifying marks of any sort.

Then I remembered. I knelt on the bed and peeked out through the blinds. Johnny's place was a condominium in a large development, new, and well-maintained. The grass was short and luxurious, the way grass can be if dosed generously with chemicals and water. The edgings were neat, the common lawns were dotted with small bushes and palm trees. There were tennis courts and a pool.

I let go of the blinds and turned to the room where I had spent the night. It looked like all the furnishings had come with the condo. Everything matched. I couldn't hear any other noises in the house, so I assumed Johnny had gone to work. I picked up my clothes from the floor beside the bed. I put on everything except my torn bra which I dropped in the trash can.

I went out in the living room. Same look as the guest room. Everything neutral and bland and matching. I wondered if that's what being made chief of police did to a guy. When I'd lived with Johnny, his taste had run to tons of paperback books on shelves made of old boards and concrete blocks. Weird posters on the wall. Salvation Army furniture.

His new kitchen with almond appliances was spotless. Nothing at all on the refrigerator door. It made me exceedingly anxious. I couldn't find any real coffee, so I made a cup of instant. Taking the foul-tasting substance into Johnny's bedroom which was only slightly more lived-in than the guest room, I checked his night table drawer, and found an open box of condoms. I was happy to see evidence that Johnny was getting some.

The bathroom off Johnny's bedroom was kept neatly, too. Funny, I remembered Johnny as a slob. We'd had some really good arguments over the dishes that had stayed in the sink for weeks. And the dirty laundry that had flowed all over the ugly little duplex we'd lived in.

Experiencing a strong desire to brush my teeth. I searched around, but couldn't find an unopened toothbrush anywhere. At first I hesitated about using Johnny's. But after all, I had once been in the habit of putting various other things of Johnny's in my mouth on a fairly regular basis. And Johnny had put his mouth on some interesting parts of me as well. Should such close old friends stand on ceremony, I asked myself. No, they should not, was my answer.

After I finished freshening up, I was left with another dilemma. I really wanted to do a thorough search through Johnny's drawers and files. After I'd done something as intimate as use his toothbrush how could I refuse myself permission to engage in a much less personal act? Of course, I couldn't. Refuse, that is. If I was going to rely on Johnny, I had to find out what sort of person he'd become.

The dresser drawer in the bedroom contained clothes. What a surprise. But instead of the holey t-shirts Johnny used to wear, this could have been my father's stuff. Almost.

A few suits were hanging in his closet. And, believe it or not, perma-press slacks for casual wear. There was one pair of jeans.

Boxes were stacked on the shelves over the clothes racks. I was a little nervous about getting started on those as I was going to have to pull down the boxes, spread stuff around. If Johnny should come in unexpectedly, I would have a lot of explaining to do.

I stood up, stretched, walked back to the living room and pulled up the blinds that covered the sliding glass door.

I had a good view of the pool from here. A few young people tanned themselves in recliners around the pool. But in the water were a crowd of what Daddy and the boys called "raisins." Old people. Retirees.

The pool was teeming with them. They were more or less lined up. taking some kind of aquatic exercise class. The women all wore bathing caps—most covered with bobbing plastic flowers or ruffles. People from up north move down here, spend too much time in the sun, and it bakes out all their taste. That's the only possible explanation for it.

From this evidence, it certainly looked like Port Mullet was attracting a wealthier class of retirees. Used to be the well-heeled ones bypassed Port Mullet on their way down to Sarasota. The first raisin colonies around Port Mullet had been trailer parks, where the raisins drove gigantic tricycles with flags on the handle bars. The flat, narrow, streets between the neat, precise rows of trailers (not yet called mobile homes) were posted with "No Children Allowed" signs.

The phone rang. In the kitchen earlier I had noticed that the answering machine was switched on.

"Johnny, this is me," said a sweet feminine voice. I wanted to gag. "I know you're not home now, but you will be when you listen to this." He's not dating a brain surgeon, I thought. "Give me a call when you get home and let me know if you can come over for dinner. I'll make it with my own ten little fingers. Bye now!"

Well, I had work to do. First I checked to make sure the front door was locked. It was, but I fastened the chainlock, too. Then I stripped down to my panties. If Johnny came in unexpectedly, I wanted to have some means of distracting him.

Going back in Johnny's room, I pulled over the chair from the desk. I climbed up on it and got down the first box from his closet, set it on the floor and began searching through it. High school yearbooks, athletic awards, report cards. I put it back up and got down another.

The second one was full of photographs. Some loose, some in albums. I picked up a handful of loose photos. They were elementary school pictures of Johnny. I picked the top one up studied it. Second grade, it said on the back. He was cute, dressed neatly in a matching outfit, with a short crew cut, and a cheerful grin.

I scrambled through the rest of them. I knew I shouldn't be wasting the time, but I was hooked. I wanted to see when Johnny had started to become the guy I'd been crazy about.

I started to see signs of it in his junior high pictures. His hair a little shaggy, his clothes not so neat, there was something slightly self-mocking in his smile.

In his high school pictures he had long, flowing hair, ratty clothes, a sweetly ironic, just a bit dangerous, smile. This was the Johnny I had loved. I sat back for a moment, the picture in my hand. What had happened to him? Something must have. In the end, he'd become the man his elementary school pictures had foretold. Just like he'd never met me. Just like we'd never been crazy together.

The next box had old college term-papers and notes, a few snapshots, and the album from our wedding. I didn't even open it. I didn't want to be reminded of that now when I was betraying the last bit of feeling left between us.

There was another box full of receipts, cancelled checks, and stuff like that. Organized by year. It was frightening to think that there were actually people who kept this stuff. And he considered *me* perverse.

Then I pulled down the box labeled "Campaign." There were stacks of campaign literature from the recent Port Mullet mayoral race—letters, notes, financial documents, all that kind of stuff. And a computer print-out of campaign contributions. I sat down and read it all.

Clearly, Forrest Miller and Johnny Berry had both worked on the mayor's campaign. Forrest personally, as well as through his various business entities, had contributed heavily to the campaign. After the election, Johnny had been made Chief of Police. It looked to me like Forrest owned the mayor, and the mayor owned Johnny. So therefore, Johnny was owned by... I felt sick.

One thing I was sure of as I put all the papers back in the box and the box back on its shelf—I wanted to get out of there, away from Johnny and his condo.

I went into the kitchen and ran a glass of water, trying to calm down. Of every bad thing I'd ever thought about Johnny, I'd never once thought he was corrupt. Okay, so I didn't have any evidence that he actually had done anything illegal. But he owed his job to a couple of guys. He was owned. Once in the middle of a heated argument, I'd yelled that Johnny had bourgeois values. That had been the most cutting thing I could think of to say. My saying that had been the notification to both of us that it was over. It had been a much more final act than our acts of adultery, than even Johnny hitting me. It had been the real divorce between us, not the papers I got months later in the mail.

I realized that the only things I knew about how hard the cops had really searched for my pursuers, I knew from Johnny. I was standing at the sink, considering all this, while the glass I was holding filled with water.

About the same time I noticed the water flowing over the top of the glass, I heard footsteps on the front walkway. I turned off the spigot and held my breath. The doorbell rang, just briefly, and then I heard the key in the lock.

"Johnny?" I called.

"Just me," he answered.

"Just a minute. I'll be right there. I put on the chain lock."

I ran and grabbed my clothes, started pulling them on.

I was buttoning my shirt when I heard the front door open. I looked up, surprised. Johnny walked in, smiling.

"You didn't have to break it. I was going to let you in."

"I didn't break it. Those flimsy things are a cinch to open."

"Then why did you bother to install it?" I was sitting on the carpet, pulling on my socks.

He shrugged. "Came with the place."

I put on my boots, picked up my backpack. "I'm ready to go."

He looked surprised. "What's your hurry? I came home to take you to lunch. Thought we'd talk about what happened last night. What we can do about that. And about your girlfriend's father, which folks might remember him. We've got to get organized."

I didn't like his proprietary manner. I'd asked for this, though, by coming to him for help in the first place. I should have known better. At that moment, it seemed to me the major pattern in my life was knowing better and going ahead anyway.

"Never mind me. You're gonna be busy," I said. I walked over to his telephone answering machine and hit one of the buttons.

On came the twittering voice. I held up my hands, waited until she got the part about her "own ten little fingers" and then wiggled mine in front of his face.

He just stood there. Didn't say anything. Then he walked past me to the machine and pushed the reset button.

"Hi, it's me," I said in a Beverly Hillbillies accent, dancing around the kitchen, wiggling my fingers and laughing. I could just picture her, with bleached-blond hair, wrapped nails, fussy clothes. She was probably just dying for Johnny to marry her so she could move into his little condo with their color-coordinated wedding presents, registered at Burdines. I fell onto the couch, laughing, holding my stomach. To think I'd actually been in love with this guy once.

Eventually I got control of myself and lay on my back, trying to catch my breath.

"Are you finished?" Johnny asked, in a cold voice.

I sat up.

"Because if you're finished, put on your boots and I'll take you home. And put one of my shirts over yours. If your Momma sees you in that ripped blouse, she's going to think I'm into rough stuff."

"That's not my home."

"Fine. I'll take you to your parents' house, then." His voice was rough with irritation.

I pulled on my boots, then went into his room and grabbed the first shirt I could find. I walked back into the livingroom buttoning it up. "Thank you for your hospitality, *Chief*."

He was already walking towards the door. He looked over his shoulder at me. "Just so you know… Emma's a fine girl. Real class. She deserves better than me."

"And I didn't?" I snapped.

He was at the door, and opened it without looking at me, speaking so quietly I almost didn't catch his words. I have never been completely sure that I heard him correctly. But I think what he said was, "We deserved each other, Laurie Marie."

Chapter Ten

The mood in the car was frosty, in spite of the sticky, humid air. When Johnny pulled up in the driveway, I grabbed my backpack and opened the door before the car was completely stopped. I slammed the passenger door behind me and was half-way to the kitchen door before I realized that Johnny had shut off the ignition and was getting out, too. Ever the gentleman, I thought. Going to pay his respects to my mother.

I didn't wait for him. I went on in to the kitchen and let that door slam behind me, too. Momma was—no surprise here—standing over the stove.

She looked at me, and I could read her confusion. She couldn't make up her mind how she should react. I'd stayed out all night like the brazen hussy I was. I'd slept at the home of a man to whom I was not married. On the other hand, the man in question was Johnny Berry, whom she would dearly love to see me marry. Again.

Finally she chose. "Oh, Baby. I'm so happy for you. But honey, just remember if you keep giving away the milk, he won't need to buy the cow." She looked like she had a few more pearls of wisdom to toss in my direction when she saw him at the door. She wiped her hands on a dish towel and hurried to let him in.

"Why Johnny! I wondered why Baby Sister didn't bring you in. Have a seat, sit right down here at the table. I was just putting on a pot of coffee, and I have some cinnamon buns here. I'm just gonna warm them up a bit."

"Why, I can't stay, Mrs. Coldwater, but I couldn't drop off Laurie without stopping in to see how you and Mr. Coldwater are doing."

"We're doing just fine, Johnny, and how are your parents? I think of them so often. You know, your daddy was always partial to my fig preserves, why don't you just take a jar of them and slip them to him next time you see him." She was measuring coffee as she spoke, and putting some cinnamon rolls onto a plate and sticking them in the microwave. Momma used to bake them herself, but now she bought these with the texture of cardboard from the big franchise in the mall.

Thing is, I was contemptuous of her for spending most of her life in the kitchen. But I was also resentful when she took shortcuts. But it didn't stop me from grabbing one off the plate that Momma took from the microwave. The cardboard was generously layered with fat and covered with cinnamon sugar. I took a big bite of it, standing there in the kitchen. The crumbs and little avalanches of sugar fell on the floor.

Johnny was sitting at the table. Momma had placed the rolls in front of him. She started setting out the milk, sugar, little pink envelopes of sweetener. I didn't sit down at the place she'd set for me. Without excusing myself I walked over to the little table where the phone book was kept. I picked it up and headed down the hall to my parents' bedroom. I wanted to make a phone call in privacy.

As I entered the room I turned on the light. I felt a shiver up my spine when I remembered how close I'd come to being shot by my own father just the night before. Wasn't I supposed to want to kill him, not the other way around? No, I was getting my complexes mixed up. It was mother I was supposed to want to kill, to have my father to myself. Right, I thought. That'll be the day.

I sat down cross-legged on the bed and opened the phone book. The name I was looking for was there. Or rather, her husband's name. Thomas Dalman. I dialed it, and a child's voice answered.

"Can I speak to your mother, please?"

There was no answer. A clattering noise that sounded like the phone had been dropped. Then a voice called shrilly, "Mom! Mom! Telephone!"

Eventually I heard a soft, feminine, "Hello?" Just that one word, in an accent deep and velvety, much richer than mine. In the difference I could measure the distance between our lives.

"This is Laurie Marie. How the hell are you, girl?"

She gasped and then Susan, my old best friend, and Forrest Miller's daughter, cried out "Laurie Marie! I can't believe it! Where are you?"

We talked for a while, both of us rushing, and laughing, and excited. I heard a child's voice saying, "Who is it, Mommy?" Susan answered, "An old friend of Mommy's. Go outside and play."

Momma opened the door to the room and came in, carrying a stack of clean laundry. She put it away, shooting glares at me every chance she got.

"Listen, Susan, this telephone conversation isn't working. Why don't we meet somewhere? A diner? Better yet, a bar."

There was a long silence on the other end. "I can't leave the kids, Laurie."

"Okay, how about tonight, then?"

There was a longer silence. "I don't think I could go out at night without Tom."

Particularly not to meet the infamous Laurie Marie Coldwater, I added silently.

"Right. Okay"

"Why don't you come over here?" she said brightly.

"Okay. When?"

"Now?"

I agreed. She gave me directions. We hung up. I hopped off the bed to go and change clothes.

"See ya later, Momma," I said, headed for the door.

"Just a minute, young lady." She looked at me for a moment and then walked over to the bed, smoothing out the spread where I'd sat. And brushing off the sand that had come off my boots.

I winced. Another aggravating thing about growing up. I'm starting to recognize it when I engage in boorish adolescent behavior. At this rate, by the time I'm seventy-two, I'll finally stop behaving like a boorish adolescent.

"Sorry."

"Baby, I just want what's best for you. I just want you to be happy. That's all I want."

I sighed, but prepared myself to hear her out. I owed her that, I thought.

"I blame myself for what's happened to you, honey. I shouldn't have let you have your way so much. I should have given you more guidance. Your father should have been more of a help to me. You needed your father to keep you in line."

I was shocked to hear her blame my father for anything. It made me think she really did feel bad about the way I'd turned out. I also had to struggle to keep a straight face. Did she really believe it was more of her advice I'd needed? I'd had so much guidance that I'd had to run a thousand miles just to get a breath of air.

"Momma. Momma. It's all right. Don't worry about me."

She looked at me with fierce determination in her eyes. "You *have* to listen to me. This might be your last chance. I can help you. You'll never forgive yourself if you let Johnny get away again."

"Momma…"

She was having none of my interruption. "No, you listen to me. I don't know why any decent man would have you. But it's plain to see that Johnny Berry still holds a candle for you. If you don't straighten up and fly right, you could lose your last chance. For a husband. For children. For a real home. You'll end up a lonely old woman." Her determination had faded. She was pleading with me now, her stark fears for my future written across her face.

I caught her vision. For a moment, I pictured myself as an old, friendless, homeless woman. Dirty, dressed in rags, freezing to death on a street corner one winter night.

"I can't stay here," was what I said, and I left.

I tore up the roads on the short drive to Susan's house. Or Tom's house. That's how I really thought of it, after all. I was pretty sure that was how Susan and Tom thought of it, too.

Their house was in a new subdivision less than a mile from my parents' house. Smack in the middle of what used to be orange groves. Once Susan and I had "borrowed" my brothers' mini-bikes and chased each other up and down the rows of trees, riding much faster than was safe, wheels sliding in the sand, laughing ourselves sick.

I pulled up in front of the sand-colored house. The yard was small, but meticulously maintained. Tidy azalea bushes, a few orange trees, some palms, a blooming hibiscus bush near the front door.

As I rang the doorbell, I could hear a TV blaring inside. The door was opened by a thin, tan woman with frosted hair, immaculate white shorts, and long, carefully manicured nails. Her face was artfully made-up, the kind of face that gets described as "attractive," but which looked tense and controlled to me. Everything about Susan's appearance seemed to plead, "Can't you see how much I want to please you?" Standing there, the full implication of a "pleasing appearance" struck me.

There was a momentary awkwardness. How were we supposed to greet each other? If shaking hands was appropriate, I was incapable of it. A kiss and a hug—I wondered if that's what old friends our age did in this place? But we had kissed before, Susan and me, and the memory of it was part of the tension between us now.

"Looking good, girl." I meant it to come out loud and hearty, but my throat was tight, and it sounded low and wistful.

Susan smiled. That loosened things up a bit. But the smile fit the rest of her appearance. Neat, sweet, pleasing.

She led me through her living room where two teenagers slouched on the couch, staring at a large TV. Soda cans and candy wrappers littered the coffee table. Their pricey sneakers were parked in the middle of the mess.

Susan introduced the twins to me, but they only barely acknowledged our existence.

Tom must have incredible electric bills, I thought. The house was actually cold, the air-conditioning was turned up so high.

We walked back through the spotless kitchen into the Florida room. It was connected by sliding glass doors to a screened-in pool. The floor was covered with pink and purple plastic toys. A girl around Sarah's age watched another TV in the corner, along with her baby sister, younger than Rachel, perched in a walker.

I wanted this to be real between me and Susan. Best way to achieve that, I thought, was to cut right through the bullshit. None of this pussyfooting around. I was just gonna act like we were the same old girls. The ones who went streaking through the bowling alley, wearing nothing but Walter and Seth's motorcycle helmets.

I sat down, leaned back into the floral print couch and put my feet up on the coffee table. It was one of those glass-topped wicker ones. A flicker of distress crossed Susan's face. I put my feet back on the ground and sat up straight. I was trying to think of Plan B.

Susan asked me if I wanted something to drink. I said, "Yeah, I could sure use a beer." Tension settled in her eyes again. "No," I said, "On second thought, what I'd really like is a nice cold glass of water."

While she disappeared into the kitchen, I stared at the children, at the room, out at the pool. Boy, was I depressed. And the thing was, I wasn't sure why. If this life was what Susan wanted, why couldn't I be happy for her?

She came back with a tray containing two tall glasses of ice, two cans of diet sodas, and two pastel paper napkins, monogrammed. I didn't really believe that this was what she wanted. I couldn't. Let me tell you something. There was a time when, if Susan was chewing gum and I asked for some, she'd give me half the piece she had in her mouth. And vice versa.

Susan flashed me that smile. She poured soda into my glass, handed it to me.

"Nice house," I said. I hate myself when I talk bullshit like that.

"Thank you. We're happy here." Did she think I meant the compliment? Did she really mean that she was happy? Why the hell was I convinced she wasn't? Why was it that deep down, at the bottom of everything, I smugly believed that I was the only one living an authentic life?

"Nice kids," I said.

She smiled again. "Yes, they are. They drive me crazy sometimes, of course, but they are my whole life. And the twins. We're so proud of them. Tom has his heart set on both of them playing football at Alabama."

I couldn't picture the two lumps I'd seen on the couch in the living room engaging in any movement that was not necessary to sustain life.

The excitement and warmth Susan and I had shared on the phone had completely evaporated. I tried to think of a sentence that didn't have "nice" in it.

Susan spoke first. "I've missed you. I've thought about you so much. Tell me everything."

She sounded honest. I tried to tell her about my work and my ambitions, as best I could. She seemed slightly dubious, as if I'd told her I wanted to be a movie star, but also truly interested.

She asked if I had a boyfriend. I said no, I had a woman friend, a beautiful woman named Sammy. I was surprised at how good it felt to say Sammy's name. Blood rose to my cheeks. I smiled like an idiot.

Susan smiled in that pleasant way again as if she hadn't really heard, but her lips were tense, stretched in her all-purpose response. It shouldn't have been news to her, not really. After all, I remembered the time I'd kissed Susan, or she'd kissed me. I guess we'd kissed each other.

Never more than that. And never again. Just that one kiss. It had not been enough; leaving me consumed with longing. Not sure if it was Susan I wanted or just a girl, any girl. Even then, I knew there was a chance that it was just the forbiddenness I wanted to taste. I already knew I'd have a long struggle over my fascination with everything I was told I could not have.

Not long after that, I had met Zack, fell in love with his motorcycles, hard drugs and guitar. We went to concerts all over the state, me on the back of his cycle. So far gone with drugs and alcohol that I never remembered the ride home. Life was everything I had wanted. Dangerous, intense, real. Incredibly sexy. I ran away to live with him right after my high school graduation, just for the hell of it.

One morning, I woke up alone in a scuzzy little trailer, way down a dirt road, within smelling distance of a dairy. The car didn't run. It needed fixing, and it wasn't likely that we'd have the money for the parts any time soon. Zack had taken the cycle to work. My wild man was an assistant butcher at the A&P.

I hadn't learned about his ex-wife and the child support payments until after moving in. And then he told me what he expected from his live-in girlfriend. I thought it was a joke. He really couldn't expect me to keep house and cook and wait for him in that hell-hole while he worked and and then went out with his friends to the places we used to go together. It wasn't until he slapped me across the face a few times that I realized how serious he was.

Up until I'd started spending time with Zack, Susan and I had been inseparable. We'd slept over at each other's house a couple of times a week. Once I met Zack, I saw Susan only at school, where she'd whisper progress reports about her latest project. She was trying desperately to get pregnant. She wanted to get knocked up so she could get married. She said she had to get away from home, didn't I understand, she had to get away.

Sure she had to get away. I understood that. But a baby? I thought that was crazy. She thought I was insane to take up with

Zack. She wanted security. I wanted a wild time.

Susan succeeded. I went with her to the clinic for the test. She had been thrilled. Really thrilled. I felt like someone had knocked the air out of me.

But Tom had balked at marrying her. When she told him she was pregnant, he whined, "I didn't force you to spread your legs." She went in tears to her parents. Mr. Miller had a talk with Mr. Dalman, and two weeks later, I was walking down the aisle of the First Baptist Church in a bubble-gum pink maid-of-honor gown.

Forrest didn't give his new son-in-law access to the Miller money right away. He gave him a job in the groves, and an opportunity to work his way up. Tom was anxious to please his boss. It seemed Tom's parents had thoroughly impressed upon him all the implications of the situation. Forrest was a wealthy man. He had no sons. His only other daughter, Belinda, had been institutionalized for years. Now Mr. Miller owned Tom Dalman and Tom owned Susan. I wondered if Susan still felt that she had gotten away.

"Susan," I said suddenly, too loudly. I startled us both, so I lowered my voice. "Tell me the truth. Why did you have to leave home?"

She looked at me quizzically. The game show played on. The baby was making noises and starting to move the walker around. The other one was picking its nose.

"I was wrong," I said, speaking slowly now, thinking it out as I went along. "I thought you were with me. That you were as crazy as I was about getting away from here. But that wasn't it." I was picking up speed, as it came clear to me. "You just wanted to get way from your parents. Just your parents." I leaned towards her. "Why? Why did you want to get away from them so bad?"

She slumped back in the chair and looked down at her hands. Then she looked up at me. "Not them. Him." Her voice was low. It was hard to hear her over the TV.

"Why?"

She looked up at me, anger clear on her face. It was so rare for her to show raw emotion that I was almost relieved. "You always thought he was so great. I hated that. You saw through everybody *else*! And God, you were so hard on your own family, and I thought they were so neat. Couldn't you see what he was? Is? I was so ashamed of him."

"I'm sorry, Susan. I'm just starting to see how much I missed. I was so wrapped up in my own rebellion that I missed a hell of a lot. Tell me about him now. "

"You mean you still don't know?"

I knew I should tell her then about what had happened last night. But I was afraid. I was afraid it would ruin things between us for good, and I was afraid that she wouldn't tell me all I needed to hear.

She looked over at her kids. "I can't talk here. Let's go out to the pool."

We closed the sliding glass doors behind us and stood on the patio that surrounded the kidney-shaped pool. I stood with my back against the door, facing Susan. Susan looked past me, keeping her eyes on the kids inside. "You only saw his good side. And boy, did he play up to you. I loved you, Laurie, but I hated the way he fawned over you, put his hands all over you. His other side was only for Momma and me. And his workers. You don't know, Laurie. You just don't know."

"What don't I know?"

"He was so mean... Here, listen. One example. One day our senior year, Daddy drove up to the house. He had to pick something up, I don't remember what. He was in his Cadillac, you know?" She paused, and I nodded, encouraging her to continue. "He had his best two hunting dogs in the car. Walker hounds. Senator and Gator, I think. They were in the back seat. And he drove up real slow, you know, because he had the trunk open. And you know why he had the trunk open?"

I shook my head no.

"He had two Mexican grove workers in the trunk. Don't you see? He had his *dogs* in the car and the workers in the trunk." She stopped talking, took a deep breath.

"Oh, Susan." I couldn't think what to say. I wanted to comfort her. I reached out and grabbed her hand.

She didn't pull it away, but she looked at me with an expression I couldn't read.

I squeezed her hand, and then dropped it. "It's not catching. No lezzie cooties," I said.

She laughed. "I wasn't worried."

"Can I ask you something else?"

She nodded.

"Did you know you father was involved in the KKK?"

She let her breath out suddenly, like she had made some sort of decision. "I knew. Eventually. I mean, it was never talked about at the dinner table or anything. But I figured it out eventually."

"Do you know anything about... anything that the KKK did?"

"Like what?"

I took a deep breath. "How should I know? But I want to know what stuff was going on all this time."

She flinched. "Not really. I heard rumors, overheard bits of conversations. Stuff like that. Daddy didn't want me to know much."

"Do you know anything about a black man named Elijah

Wilson? He died when we were kids."

"No. Never heard of him."

I could hear the TV through the glass. I was staring at the clear blue surface of the pool. "Different subject. When we were doing all that crazy stuff, Susan, didn't you mean it? I can't figure it out. How you could do all that with me, and then, you come back to all this."

Finally her eyes left the kids and turned to me.

"What are you talking about?" She was frowning.

I waved my hands about, searching for words.

"All this stuff. You know, houses like this, and the church, and the Rotary Club, and well…" I stopped, afraid that I was not only making an inarticulate fool of myself, but was offending Susan.

She seemed to have caught something of my meaning. "No. I was just having a good time. I don't think I'd have done any of it if it wasn't for you. I mean, it was fun, but this…" She stopped, sighed. "This is what I wanted." Now she waved her hands, indicating the pool, the house, the children, I wasn't sure what. "My father is a cruel, controlling man, and I couldn't wait to get out of his house. But that's all. I always wanted a good life."

She bit her lip. "I'm sorry. I never understood you. You were so brave and strong and smart and full of life. And you went with that creep Zack, who couldn't give you anything you deserved. He wasn't half good enough for you. No one knew what you saw in him. Then you dumped him, and went back with Johnny, and got married the way it was supposed to be. You two seemed perfect together. And then the next thing I knew, you'd dumped him, too. Why do you refuse to be happy? Why do you have to make everything so hard on yourself?"

I shrugged. "Beats me."

She laughed. "But I've missed you all these years. We had so much fun. I always thought we'd live next door to each other, and have our kids at the same time, and take them to the beach together."

I was shocked. I was sure I had never said anything remotely like that. "What gave you that idea?"

She looked hurt. "I thought that was the way it would happen. It's what I always wanted to happen. And I got everything else, but I didn't get you, right here in town, sharing it all with me. I've missed that."

I should have comforted her then, should have told her how often I'd thought of her. But I was still shocked. And offended too, that she could have ever thought I'd end up that way. "But we always talked about backpacking in Europe, or moving to San Francisco, or to a commune in Santa Fe. We never talked about getting married and having kids."

She shrugged. "Teenagers always talk like that. Then they grow up and have real lives. Everybody knows that. Everybody but you."

The kids were hollering. We went back in. Susan yelled at the kids. I said goodbye and started out by myself. The kids quieted down and Susan hurried to walk me out.

We stood on the front porch for a moment. Susan grabbed my arm just as I was getting ready to leave. She spoke so low I had to strain to hear her, and so fast that I knew she'd been storing this up for a long, long time.

"Laurie, I hated you sometimes, too. He never paid me any attention. Not as *me*. Just as his daughter, the one who had to be perfect, like everything else he owned. He was so afraid I was going to shame him, and so he kept me chained up as best he could. I was proud when I told him I was pregnant. I'd done just the thing he'd gone to so much effort to prevent, and I'd done it on purpose. And not only that, it was my ticket to freedom, to get out of his house. When I walked up the aisle on his arm, I should have been thinking about Tom. Instead I was gloating because my father was furious that the whole town would know what a wedding with two weeks' notice meant.

"I hated the way he flirted with you. He went just as far as he possibly could, without giving Momma any real cause for complaint. Momma hated it, too. I saw it on her face. But she still liked to have you around. She said once that something about you reminded her of my sister, Billy.

"And you just ate it up. You'd come over to go swimming, and you'd bring the bikini that your folks wouldn't let you wear to the beach. And then he'd find some reason to come out and prune the roses, and then he'd come right over and give you some tips on your diving form! Did you think Momma and I didn't see what was going on?"

The anger in her voice cut me. I couldn't think of a thing to say. Then her voice changed again, and she said, " I haven't had any real fun since the day you left, Laurie, and that's the god-honest-truth."

The kids were yelling again. I couldn't look her in the face.

"I've got to go see about those kids, Laurie. Don't take these things so hard, please don't."

"I won't. I don't. I'm sorry. I've got to go, too."

I practically ran down the sidewalk and jumped in the car. I took off, but not before giving a real good look at the house next door.

Chapter Eleven

As I drove back to my parents' house, something was crackling, hissing gently inside me. The sight of Susan's bare refrigerator door had started it off. And then it exploded inside me like a firecracker after a long fuse—that intense longing for Sammy.

I pulled up in the driveway and walked to the kitchen door. Momma was stirring something on the stove. She was wearing a hot pink running suit with pink-feathered earrings, and pink rhinestones on her sneakers. Her lipstick matched her suit exactly. I looked at her refrigerator door, decorated with snapshots of my father holding a fish he'd caught, or next to a dead deer. There was a shopping list, and photocopied diet she was following.

I took a glass out of the cabinet and filled it from the iced tea pitcher in the fridge. Without looking at her, I said, "I'm sorry I was rude, Momma. I know you just want me to be happy." Then I looked at her out of the corner of my eye to see how she was taking it.

She kept looking in the pot she was standing over, but the tightness around her mouth relaxed a little. "Well, honey, I'm sorry, too. You know, there's a sale on down at Burdine's. Let me finish up my chicken and dumplings here. Then I was thinking we could go find you some clothes. Something a little more appropriate for this climate. My treat."

I sighed. "I don't think so, Momma. Listen, I have to make a phone call. Can I use the one in your room?"

Her jaw tightened again. "Why do I even keep trying?" she murmured to herself as she turned her back to me to get something out of a drawer.

I could ask myself the same question, I thought, as I left the room.

Sammy answered on the second ring. When I heard her voice, I nearly screamed with joy. I had almost been afraid that I'd made her up. That she was some dream I'd had some lonely night. But there she was, on the other end of that long, long wire, real and calm and warm.

I told her everything that happened. She made me feel like I wanted to feel. Appreciated, understood, special, loved. Then she was quiet.

"What is it, Sammy?"

"I shouldn't have sent you there, Laurie. It was stupid. I did it because I couldn't face it myself. The hole in the center of my life. Not knowing anything about my father. I was afraid I wouldn't like what I found out. Or I was afraid I'd be too afraid of that to look hard enough. And I thought you would tell me the truth, however painful. You're like that. But I shouldn't have asked you. I should have known that once you got started it would be uphill work to get you to quit! You're really something, Laurie. But listen to me, now. Since you've been gone, I've *changed my mind*. I've been thinking that it really doesn't matter what kind of man my father was. The living people in my life are what matters now. *You matter*. Whether Elijah was a drunk, or was messing with someone's wife, what difference can it make to me now? I miss you, Laurie. Just forget about it, and come home."

My heart skipped. When Sammy said "come home," did she mean to her, or to my own apartment? And which was really home to me? But I had no intention of abandoning my quest yet. And I was irritated that one more person in my life was telling me what to do. For my own good. I pointed out to Sammy that my run-in with the Klan had nothing to do with her. It was my own past I had been researching at the rally that night. I wanted to know something more about where I came from, too. And as for Elijah Wilson, I wanted to finish what I'd started. It might well be that there was nothing I could find out this many years later, but I was damn well going to prove that to myself before I quit.

When I told her that while I was down here I wanted to speak with her mother, she protested, "I want to keep her out of this. I don't want to upset her! If it was that easy, you know, I would have done it a long time ago."

"Sammy, she's the one person who might know something. Maybe she'll tell me things she won't tell you. That she's afraid to tell you."

Sammy didn't say anything.

"Come on, be fair," I coaxed.

"All right, go ahead, talk to her. But Laurie, one thing... she doesn't know about us."

I kicked hard with the toe of my boot against the leg of Momma's French provincial night table. "You're ashamed of me!"

"Never." Sammy's voice was so firm and certain that I felt the anger drain away.

"So, why haven't you told her?" To my horror, I could hear myself whine.

"Have you told your mother about us?" There was amusement and warmth in her voice. God, how I loved her right then.

"No," I admitted. "But I told my brother," I added quickly.

Sammy laughed. "What's amatta, you ashamed of me, or something?"

I laughed, too.

"Okay," said Sammy. "I wish that I had told her. But I haven't. It isn't you. I've never told her about any of my lovers. Unless she happened to meet them, which is rare, because I have trouble getting down to visit her, and she hates the city. She was a widow when I was born, Laurie. She gave her life to raising my sister and me. And then after my sister died, she worried herself sick over every little detail of my life. I quit telling her about my lovers, male or female, to give her that much less to worry about."

I wondered if that included the girls' fathers. I wanted to ask if I was just one in a line of Sammy's lovers. Someone making a cameo appearance in her life. Maybe I was just an extra, not even listed in the credits. At any rate, I was someone her mother hadn't needed to know about.

That's the way it was. That's the way I'd wanted it once. But I didn't want it to be that way anymore. And I didn't like to hear Sammy say it.

She gave me her mother's phone number. I felt a little better. She trusted me that much, anyway. I remembered to ask about the girls before we hung up. I was actually interested in what they'd been up to. Then, just before I said good-bye, Sammy said, "I want her to know who you are. When you're there, in front of her, she'll see. She'll understand how good you are for me." Those were awful sweet words to hear. The she added, "And you can tell her as long as you tell your mother first!"

After I hung up the phone, I sat there for a while, staring at the half-dozen framed photographs of my brothers and me Momma had hung on the wall over her chest of drawers. Professional portraits, very formal. Typical sibling poses: five children, in their best starched and ironed clothes, lined up straddling a bench, or arranged in a stiff grouping. Corny to the last degree. My brothers were wearing slacks and blazers, button-down shirts. They all had crew cuts and those friendly, innocent, boyish grins of the fifties and early sixties. I don't think anybody in history grinned like that anytime before or after. You can estimate the date of any male photograph, just by that kind of grin. I guess you can only smile that way if you're the male offspring of the guys who just saved the world for democracy. If you are the ones who are being groomed to tame space, "the last frontier," by wearing coonskin hats, singing "Davy Crockett" and playing Little League while your entire family cheers from the bleachers. Do I sound bitter? Jealous? You better believe it.

I, on the other hand, am visibly sulking in every single shot. I'm wearing fussy dresses with puffed sleeves, lace collars, the whole bit. And my hair was teased, puffed up, and styled. Like cotton candy. Momma had tried so hard to round up the five of us, make sure we were dressed and cleaned, every hair and button in place. Every detail in every portrait fits the scene she was trying to set. Except me. My strong features, brooding eyes, and thick brows were out of place, all wrong.

I appeared about eleven years old in the most recent picture. I didn't know why my mother stopped with the portrait nonsense after that. Did she just admit failure? Give up the idea of trying to make us look like we belonged together?

I had gotten up to leave the room when I was startled by a thought that had never occurred to me before. My mother's first and last vision of me every single day was of that awkward child, frozen in a dress and hairstyle which didn't suit her. No wonder she was desperate for me. She really didn't know that there are places in the world where I fit just fine. And I didn't think she'd believe me if I told her.

In the kitchen, Walter and Josh were sitting at the kitchen table, drinking beer and talking. Momma was serving chicken and dumplings. The boys looked up and said "Hi." I got a beer and sat down at the table with them.

They were talking about the Tashimee Fiesta, something else on the long list of things I hadn't thought about in a long time.

"The Fiesta? They still have it? I can't believe it!"

The boys looked at me, surprised. "Why can't you?" asked Walter.

"Well…" I thought for a minute. "It's so corny. For one thing. And it's so tacky. Fake. I just can't believe it still goes on."

I had offended Walter. "Right. You're calling us tacky. Talk about the kettle. Well, Miss Sophisticated New Yorker, to us poor old country boys, the Fiesta is a hell of a good time."

Momma stopped her cooking and walked over, a potholder in her hand. "The Fiesta is a god-send for the local businesses, Baby. Wait until you see how big it's gotten. You won't recognize it. It's advertised like a big tourist attraction. Why, it brings in people from all over and they come spend money in Port Mullet."

Josh spoke mildly. "Every town has some sort of founder's day celebration. So what if it's corny?"

I knew I should just let things be, but when have I ever done that? "That's just it! I was wrong to say I don't like it cause it's corny. Actually, that's one thing I really do like about it. I'd love an authentic corny founder's day celebration. But this whole thing is so fake!"

Momma turned away and went back to the stove, talking to us over her shoulder. "It's not fake. It's educational. All about the Indians and the Spanish explorers. I would think you'd appreciate notice being taken of the Native Americans, Miss Politically Correct!"

I was stunned. Floored. When had she learned to say "Native Americans" and where had she learned the phrase "politically correct"? Had my mother actually been reading or was this something she had picked up from watching t.v.?

While I stood there in silence, Momma continued. "They were Calusa Indians, anyway. I know that from the pageant. And that's why the club that plans the fiesta is called the Calusa Tribe. They were here, they built their mounds—Mrs. Pierson has one in her backyard, you know—and we have a fiesta to celebrate them."

Walter and Joshua nodded.

I didn't know if she was right or not. That was what I had always heard, but lately everything I had always heard and thought had turned out to be wrong, or twisted, or incomplete. My insecurity made me even more argumentative than usual. "I thought you said the fiesta was about the Spanish explorers."

"That's right," she answered. "It honors the Spanish explorers. They discovered Florida, you know."

"What did they discover? This place was already here. The Indians had been living here for thousands of years. What did the Spanish ever do for Florida? Nothing that I know of. We don't speak Spanish, we don't have Spanish names. Nothing. And, hey, what happened to the Indians that the Spanish found here anyway? Did they just disappear? Are they in a reservation somewhere?"

"The Seminoles are down in the Everglades, Baby," said Walter impatiently.

"I think they weren't originally from here," said Josh. "Didn't we learn in school that they are a mixture of various tribes that were pushed out of other parts of the country?"

Instead of being grateful for Josh's help, I plowed on. "So, why didn't they teach us what happened to the first Indians, the ones that were here when the Spanish arrived," I demanded. "Maybe the Spanish killed them all. Maybe that's what the fiesta celebrates."

"They were missionaries," interrupted Momma. "In the Tashimee pageant, they show the priests converting the Indians to Christianity."

"To Catholicism, Momma. You're the same woman who sent me to Sunday School where I learned the Pope is the anti-Christ."

"I didn't know they would tell you nonsense like that! Now you're blaming me for trying to give you a good Christian upbringing? I never saw or heard tell of ingratitude like this."

Momma turned away from the stove, crying. Walter leapt to her side, putting his arm around her. I felt bad. I hadn't really meant to criticize her for my childhood. I hadn't really meant to make her cry. Not that I have a clue as what it was I did mean to do. I moved awkwardly towards her.

Walter pushed me away. "Grow up, Laurie. You've turned into one of those whiners who blame everything on your parents. Momma did the best she could. As far as I'm concerned she did a damned good job. You just work out your own problems and leave her alone. Don't go blaming your own failures and your own lack of direction in life on her."

I shook my head, unable to respond. I walked past Josh and went to the rear of the house, out the back door into the backyard where I hadn't come since arriving home. There I stood out on the patio, looking at the clear, still water of the pool, then sat at the shallow end, took off my shoes and socks, and dangled my legs in. The water felt cool at first, but almost immediately turned lukewarm, soft and comforting against my legs.

I was in the shade from the live oak tree, protected from the worst of the sun. A pretty tree, the full branches made a canopy over half the back yard. Bird feeders hung all over it. I remembered the day the tree had been planted. I was about nine, I guess, and it had looked like a dry stick, no taller than I was.

Momma had wanted a shade tree for her backyard. Daddy had said he'd get around to it, but he never did. One Saturday, she had pitched such a fit that he'd gone to the plant nursery. But he came back saying oak trees were too expensive. So she'd gone out in the woods, herself, and come back with this stick she planted. She watered it carefully every night, along with all her plants and the orange and tangerine and grapefruit trees.

After dinner, Daddy would come out of the house, sit himself down in a lawn chair, and smoke a cigar. He'd laugh at Momma, watering her tree. He'd say, "I never seen the like of anyone watering a dead stick before." I didn't say anything, but my smirks made it clear whose side I was taking. I had grown tired of my mother's disappointment in me by then, and had begun to return it with my own harsh judgments of her. I was already fading fast from my father's favor, and I hoped the distance I set between my mother and myself would raise my value in his eyes. It didn't work of course. He was fond of her, but his affection was mixed with mild contempt. Meanwhile, I had refused my place in the class of Southern ladies, and there was no other place for me in his scheme. To my father's mind, one test of a strong man is how well he manages his womenfolk.

And that's it, the absolute dirty truth. I had admired my father for his power and freedom, and I had hated my mother for her oppression. Her struggle to create something beautiful, something with her own mark on it within the small sphere allowed her, to fill us with her good food, and the yard with flowers and fruit and birds and butterflies, I had seen as contemptible, pathetic.

Now and then, when the breeze was just right, I could just catch the scent of roses from the trellis against the house. The birds sang. I leaned back on my arms, face to the strong sun, my legs slowly stirring the water.

So why was I so hard on my mother over the Tashimee Fiesta? It wasn't like she'd come up with the crazy idea herself. She didn't write the stupid pageant. The whole idea of it was so absurd, so full of unintentional camp that I ought to love it. If I wrote an article about it, Jerry would eat it up.

As a kid, I had been fascinated by the pageant. Our daily lives were so pale, so lacking in drama. Our churches had no crucifixes, the blood and the wounds deemed unseemly. The history we learned was only dry pages in a book. But once a year, after the orange blossoms bloomed, and then the wild phlox, came the Fiesta and the pageant.

It was a very un-Protestant story. In the days of the early Spanish exploration, a captain, Don Alfonso, along with a priest, Father Hernando and a small contingent of well-armed soldiers, set out from the fort at St. Augustine on the Atlantic coast. They set off into the dangerous wilderness to investigate reports of a cruel tribe of sun-worshipping Indians who sacrificed human victims to their blood-thirsty gods, offering up the still-beating hearts. The arrogant captain brought with him his handsome young son, a youth of fourteen, and his ward, his exceptionally beautiful niece Theresa, a few years younger.

When I thought about it, I could see why they needed to give themselves a history, explain to themselves how they came to be here. Port Mullet was no family's first destination on this continent.

Nobody had ever emigrated directly to Port Mullet. They came from somewhere else first. They came from all over: Ohio, Mississippi, Alabama, Georgia. They were white, almost entirely Protestant, heavily Baptist and Methodist. Their ancestors had arrived in some other city, Boston or New York or someplace in the Carolinas. Some of them stayed, some moved to places where there was more opportunity like factory towns, or ranches in the west. But a lifetime of bad luck, or a sudden bankruptcy or even simple despair had driven these people on. They must have been desperate for a fresh start, those who came to Port Mullet in the twenties and thirties and forties and fifties.

The West already long won, had been turned to dude ranches. But Port Mullet was a wilderness. No good roads in, long, difficult miles to the nearest city, abundant mosquitoes, rough terrain, poisonous snakes of several varieties, alligators, hurricanes.

They were a mixed bunch. They brought little in the way of traditions. They found none here. Or none they knew of, the last natives having left or died more than three hundred years earlier.

The Tashimee pageant gave them something more exotic and exciting than the old First Thanksgiving story. Something more suited to the down-on-their-luck folks who ended their wandering here. Who could picture the pilgrims, in their heavy black garb on the west coast of Florida?

And, of course, the pageant served the greater purpose of encouraging tourism. You've got to admire the sheer audacity of people whose thinking went like this: New Orleans has its Mardi Gras, and Tampa its Gasparilla, why not some grand festival for Port Mullet?

Their ingenuity was almost as breathtaking as their ambition. But the fabulous multi-cultured atmosphere of New Orleans with its scent of coffee and bourbon, the music in the background, and underneath it all the memory of those exotic establishments once filled with half-caste girls devoted to the service of sensuality, that was one thing. And Tampa's Gasparilla had that city's large Cuban and Spanish population with their spicy foods, Catholic mysteries and guilty, exciting abandon before the deprivations of Lent. Port Mullet was Port Mullet. Named for a fish.

My thoughts were rudely interrupted when the back door opened and none other than Josh came out. I didn't say anything, pretended to ignore him. He squatted down beside me on the patio.

"Well now, Laurie Marie, if you won't bite my head off for being such an unsophisticated country boy, I've got an invitation for you."

I kept my face to the sun, my eyes closed. "Yeah?"

"How 'bout you and me going out in the Gulf, catching us some fish? Let's say, Saturday?"

I knew he didn't like me. And while I wasn't sure that he had a clue about what I was up to, I knew he was much too interested. This invitation was certainly not for nothing. Well, now, I was interested in finding out just what it was he was so interested in.

"Okay" I answered shortly.

He chuckled. "Don't get too excited and wet yourself, honey." Then he quickly switched tones. "I'm looking forward to the pleasure of your company, Ma'am," he said with an exaggerated politeness as he stood up.

The back door opened again. This time it was Walter. He told Josh to hurry. Josh did, waving goodbye to me cheerfully. Walter shut the door without saying anything to me.

Chapter Twelve

Sometimes, now and then, I get it. I understand why some people want to live here. Sitting with my legs in the warm water, the sun on my face, the smell of Momma's flowers, and the singing of the birds, I thought I might not want to leave.

In just a split-second I came to my senses. How does anyone write, take photographs or even think in the midst of all this? Maybe it's just that I'm a masochist. Maybe I like to torture myself with the city's gray and grime and filth. I don't know. But I'd be somebody else if I had stayed here, I'm sure of that.

I jumped up and went inside the cool, dark house. Momma was in the kitchen.

"Sorry I flew off the handle about the Tashimee Fiesta."

She looked at me suspiciously. Then she asked if I wanted some coffee. She poured us both a cup, and we sat down at the kitchen table. I felt that I'd spent more time at her kitchen table in the last few days than I had spent at my own in the last year.

"Momma," I started. "What about the black people in town?"

She looked puzzled. "What about them?"

"Well, where are they? I don't see them anywhere."

"Where are they," she repeated to herself. "Well, around. There weren't many here to start with. This part of the state wasn't big slave-holding country, not like where I grew up. There are black communities in the cities, of course, but I guess there isn't much to cause a black person to move here.

"I'll tell you what, though. That black girl who was in your class—Terri, her last name is Hawkins, now—she's a teller at the bank. I make it a point to get in her line, no matter what folks have to say about it."

She said the last bit with such pride in her voice. I had trouble not laughing at what my mother thought was a daring stand for civil rights. She was trying to be honest with me, and that felt good, and I didn't want to ruin it.

We were quiet for awhile. I was noticing how tired she looked, when she started talking again. "Laurie, I don't know what it is. I try. I believe you're trying. Why doesn't it work?" She sounded tired, too. Defeated. I didn't like to see Momma, who had always given extra meaning to the word "perky," like that. But I couldn't think of anything to say. I just shook my head.

"You're my only daughter. My baby girl. I'm surrounded by these men who don't really care about me. Your father, your brothers, their friends."

I couldn't bear it. I interrupted her. "Don't say that, Momma. It isn't true. Everybody loves you. Everybody."

"They love my hot meals. They love the way I do their laundry. I buy every piece of your daddy's clothing. He hasn't bought himself so much as a pair of shoelaces since the day we got married.

"Any of them can walk through my kitchen door anytime, and there's something good for them to eat there. How much time do you think your brothers and their friends would spend around here, if it weren't for that? And that's about all your daddy and I have in common. That we sit across from one another at the table.

"When you were born, that was the happiest day of my life. Finally, I had a baby girl. I wouldn't spend the rest of my life alone in the kitchen.

"I'd raise you up, and you'd be right there beside me. We'd go to the beauty parlor and shopping together. Even after you grew up and got married, we'd be in the kitchen together for Sunday dinners and the holidays. We'd cook beforehand, and, afterwards, we'd be there alone together, doing the dishes. We'd talk, share things that we couldn't tell anyone else. And you'd have children, and they'd be all over the house. I could spoil them. Don't you see?"

I nodded, clutching my coffee cup so hard my fingers hurt. She didn't seem to expect me to say anything.

After a moment, she continued talking in that far-away voice. "My happiest memories are from when my Momma came to visit me when I was first married. Most of the time, I was lonely. You don't know. I was all by myself all day in the house with the babies. Momma would help with the ironing, and she'd watch the babies so I could run out and get my hair done." She was staring into space as she spoke.

"She'd make the biscuits for breakfast, while I fried the bacon and eggs. Then, when your daddy had gone to work, she'd pour us both a cup of coffee and sit down.

"I never knew her to waste time, other than that. But we'd sit there, fifteen minutes, maybe half an hour. Drinking coffee, watching the birds at the feeder. And she never said it, but I knew she was proud of me.

"She had high standards, you know. For housekeeping, for child raising. And she was proud of the way I was doing."

Momma quit staring and took a sip of her coffee. "Good Lord, how I miss her. It's been fifteen years, and I still miss her everyday."

She looked at me. "I always thought it would be like that between you and me, Baby."

We sat there for a while in silence. Then I said, "You want another cup of coffee, Momma?" and before she could say or do anything, I went in the kitchen and got the coffee pot. I poured us both some, and then took the pot back in the kitchen. Then I sat back down, and pointed out to her that the cardinal was at the feeder nearest to the window.

I called Sammy's mother, Mrs. Williams, at her house in Alabama. She was polite, sweet, sounded a lot like Sammy. She said Sammy had called and told her to expect to hear from me. I asked if I could come talk to her in person. She hesitated, and then graciously made it sound as if the invitation was her own idea. I said I'd be there the next night.

I went looking for Momma and found her folding clothes. Mine were mixed in with hers and Daddy's. I never asked her to do my laundry when I was there. She always just got it and did it, and I had never thought much about it.

"Momma," I said, "now, please, don't get your feelings hurt."

"Why are you saying that?" she asked.

"Because I don't want you to get your feelings hurt. I told you I have some work to do while I'm here. Well, I've got to go on a visit up north of here for a day or two. I'm leaving tomorrow morning."

"Your daddy will miss you," she said.

I restrained myself from snickering, or saying something like "Fat chance."

"I'm going to rent a car," I said.

She got that hurt look on her face. "I can't believe that you think no more of us than to think we'd let you make a trip like that in some rented car. Take mine, it's got a car phone. Your daddy won't want you on the highway alone without a phone."

"All right, Momma," I said. She looked surprised. I knew that after a victory like this, she would figure she ought to try for more. She'd take this to mean I was ready to listen to reason about becoming a police chief's wife.

I decided I had to get out of the house quick, before she started after me. I put on my bathing suit, pulled a pair of jeans over, grabbed a towel, and told Momma I was going to the beach.

"Wait a minute," she called after me. "This trip you're going to take doesn't mean you'll miss the Tashimee pageant, or the parade, does it?"

"I wouldn't dream of it," I called back over my shoulder on the way out the door.

I was driving through town when I passed the bank where Momma and Daddy had done business ever since I could remember. I turned around at the next intersection and went back.

When I walked in, I saw Terri right away. The last time I'd seen her, at our high school graduation, she'd been thin and rangy with a huge afro. Now she was magnificently rounded and her hair was a gorgeous, waist-length mass of braids. She was wearing a drop-dead royal blue dress with huge gold buttons that matched her earrings.

I stood in her line and when I got to the front I said, "Terri, do you remember me?"

She smiled sweetly. "Of course I do, Laurie Marie Coldwater. Your mother and I talk about you every time she's in here. But I wouldn't have forgotten you, anyway. How can I help you?"

"I'd like to talk with you," I said. "Can I take you to lunch?"

She looked up at the clock on the wall. "Sure. I get my break in twenty minutes. How about the coffee shop across the street?"

While I was killing time, waiting for Terri, I went into the drugstore down the street. The owner's wife was still at the cash register, and she was still a huge, talkative woman, but her hair was now completely white. I took a bottle of sunblock to the counter.

She grinned in excitement and started in on "Why, my goodness gracious, if it isn't…" I tuned it out until she got to the part where she started asking me the questions and I had to reply. You know, "How long are you down for?" and "How do you stand it up there in that big city?"

I replied, "A few more days," and "Oh, I like it fine."

"You know," she said, "I used to feel so sorry for you, poor little thing way up there in that nasty city, but you know, things aren't like they used to be around here anymore, either."

"No?" I said, politely.

"Absolutely not. Why my Greta, she's taught at the elementary school for years and years, you know. And the things she tells me about those Yankee children, you wouldn't believe. They don't know enough to say "Yes, Ma'am" and "No, Ma'am" when they answer a question. And some of those little…" She dropped her voice, "Jew children," and then she raised it again. "You wouldn't believe how arrogant they are. You just wouldn't believe it." With that she handed me the white paper bag with the receipt stapled to the front.

"Sometimes I don't know what to believe," I said. "I never would have believed that there was anti-Semitism in this town."

"Why, honey, what are you saying? I don't have anything against the Jews, it's just the ones that don't teach their children how to behave. You're calling me names. Your momma and daddy are going to be real disappointed to hear about this." She was agitated, pulling at the glasses that hung from a chain between her gigantic breasts.

"I'm thirty-five years old," I answered wearily. "You can't keep threatening a woman my age with her parents' disapproval." I walked out with my head held high. As I stepped out on the pavement, I thought about Sammy's sweet voice asking, "Did you tell your Momma about me?"

Terri settled in across from me gracefully, handling her pocketbook with an elegance I don't ever hope to match. That's why I always carry a backpack—a real backpack, worn around the edges, not a dinky little designer one. It may not be graceful, but there's something solid about the way it bangs against my back when I throw it over one shoulder. It lets me know that that's the sort of girl I am, not the sort who can tuck her tiny gold-colored purse on her lap like Terri did. Me, I'd spill food on it, or forget it, get carried away laughing and it would fall on the floor.

Terri was friendly and talkative, just like we were two old friends. We talked about our school days and her work at the bank. When I asked her what had happened to the black kids from our school, she laughed as if I had said something funny. "All twelve of us? Am I our keeper?"

I blushed, and felt silly. I was the big city girl, and yet I had the distinct feeling she knew a thing or two I didn't.

"Well, let's see. Just like you white folk—" and here she laughed again "—we went all sorts of ways." She was able to eat and talk and smile at the same time, and to look classy doing it. I was impressed. "You want me to say that some of *us* ," and I was definitely the butt of her humor, "moved to the city and became drug dealers and pimps?"

"Of course not," I gasped.

"Too bad," she answered, "because that's what my brother did."

She laughed, but there was something kind in it, and I began to realize that she wasn't laughing at me, but genuinely found the ironies humorous. She was also compassionate enough to go on talking when it was clear that I was frantically searching for the proper reply.

She did give me the run-down on what had happened to the black kids who went to high school with us, as varied in direction as the rest of my classmates. David, the center on the basketball team, had moved to Washington D.C. and was an accountant. Sheryl was a real estate agent. Which reminded me of some more questions I had to ask, even though I risked looking like a fool once again.

"Where did your family live when you were in school?" I asked.

"Take a guess," she answered, and again, she chuckled as if this were really funny.

"Okay, where do you live now?"

"Not on Piney Woods Road, that's for sure. I've got a condo by the beach, over near Miller's Inlet."

"Do you mind me asking you these questions?"

"Good heavens, no. You want to find out how the rest of us live, I'm happy to oblige."

She told me, too. She said that during high school her parents had lived out on Piney Woods because her mother was a nurse in a hospital up north a bit, while her father taught school in Tampa. Port Mullet was about midway between, but no houses in Port Mullet seemed to be available at the time when her folks were looking. Again Terri laughed. Her expression changed, though, when she told me how much she had hated living on Piney Woods. Her parents had a nice house in Port Mullet, now, and Terri had no trouble buying her condo.

"So, you're saying there's not a race problem around here nowadays?"

"Well, no, I can't say that. Haven't you heard the Klan even adopted a highway around here? There are folks filled with hate everywhere. But God's love is winning them over, bit by bit. That's what I believe. I tell you, hate ends you up like my brother, or like Willy, remember Willy? One good-looking boy, he was. Mmmmm. Well, he's a member of this group and they all believe that blacks and whites got to be totally separate, because any time they get together, the blacks will get the short end of the stick. Me, I just do what my mother and father always told me. I just love everybody, and keep faith in my soul that love will win out. I got a good job, and good friends, and a good apartment, and I love everybody. That's the ticket."

I asked her if she'd heard of Elijah Wilson, and she said no, that didn't ring a bell. I was feeling that she thought I was sort of backward, not knowing any more than I did about the black community in my own hometown. I wanted her to know that I wasn't like that, that in the city, my friends came in all colors. So I told her about Sammy.

Her face lost its good-natured glow. "Oh, my. Oh no. I tell you, that just breaks my heart to hear it. But I don't believe that God has abandoned you, Laurie Marie. I tell you what, I'm going to bring up your situation in prayer meeting tomorrow night. The Lord hates the sin, but he loves the sinner, that's what the preacher always says, and I'm going to pray for your soul, you better believe it. I surely am."

As politely as I could, I looked at my watch and made motions to leave. "Nice talking to you, Terri. Why don't I take the check?" And I was out of there as fast as I could.

I dragged myself in Momma's kitchen door hours later, sandy, sun-burnt, beach-logged. I could easily go another decade without a day at the beach. For a few minutes it felt great. Then I became restless and ached to do something. But it was too hot and bright to read, and too hot and sandy to do anything else. I decided I'd lie down in the dirt when I was dead, and that would be soon enough.

The kitchen was empty. I heard the TV in the front room. I figured that meant Daddy was home.

When I walked into the room he said, "Hi, Baby," without looking away from the set.

"Hello, my patriarch."

He glanced at me for just a moment. "Don't sit on anything with those wet, sandy clothes. Momma won't like it."

"I was just going to change," I said. "Have you spoken to Momma today?"

"What, Baby?" he said, concentrating on the screen.

"Did she tell you that I'm going on a trip tomorrow? She's loaning me her car."

"You've only been here a few days."

"I know. And I'll be back in just a day or so. I have work to do." I said it as provocatively as I could, hoping he'd ask me what kind of work, hoping I was on his mind enough he'd wonder what I was doing.

"You know your Momma will miss you."

I didn't even bother to answer. Just headed for the shower.

Later, as I was leaving the bathroom, he yelled to me, "You got some phone calls."

I dressed quickly and walked into the living room toweling my hair.

"Who?"

"The police chief." My father finally looked at me, the muscles around his face twitching like he was holding back a smile. "Guess he's still kinda sweet on you, Sister. You got another call too. From Susan used-to-be-Miller. You know, she always was a right pretty girl. Nice, too. Easy to get along with."

At least he didn't say, "Unlike some people I know."

I called Susan first.

She said, "I have to talk to you." A pause. "I'm sorry. I didn't tell you everything."

"Okay. Now?"

"No, I can't get away now."

"Tonight?"

"No, Tom won't let me tonight."

"Okay." I was getting annoyed, but tried not to sound it. "What about tomorrow morning? I'm leaving on a trip, but I could meet you in the morning."

"Trip? My God, Laurie, whatever you do, you've got to be careful!" There was nothing artificial in her voice now, I was sure of it. That was real fear I heard.

"Careful of what?"

"I can't tell you now." Her voice had dropped so low that I strained to hear her.

"Well, when can you tell me?"

"What about Saturday, after the parade?" Her voice rose then and became sweetly cheerful. "I have so much to do for the fiesta, I won't have a chance to see you before then." I was sure someone had walked in on her.

I sighed. "Okay, I'll see you then."

"Sure, I'll hold," she said brightly.

"Susan, what's going on? Do you want me to come over?" There was no answer. I was really getting worried.

Then she whispered again, hurriedly. "There. He's gone. Just be careful. Very, very careful." There was a click, and she was gone.

I was trying to decide whether or not to return Johnny's call when the phone rang.

"Hello."

"Hi, Laurie. Did you father tell you I called?"

"Yes, but he didn't say why." I meant to sound cold, but it came out petulant and whiny.

"I wanted to see how you're doing," he answered evenly.

"Fine, thank you. And you?" I countered.

"Would you like to meet with me and we can talk about how

your project is coming along?"

"Maybe later this week."

"Oh, are you busy the next few days?"

I snapped. "Cut it out, Johnny! I know damn well that Momma called you and told you I'm going out of town! So now you're checking up on me. The two of you think I can't take care of myself! I'm tired of this shit!"

"So how long have you believed in this conspiracy theory? Are you feeling more paranoid than usual, and does the doctor know you're off your medication?" His voice was still mild.

I almost said something nasty and hung up, but something stopped me. I wasn't sure what.

I was still a little shaky from my escapade the other night. But I really didn't believe danger lurked in my trip to visit Sammy's mother. Still, "if something happened to me" I wanted someone to know where to start looking. Johnny was the only someone I knew who had the resources and knowledge. Damn it, if I was wrong about this and got hurt, I would want to be avenged. And as much as I hated to admit to myself, I thought Johnny would do that. I was disgusted about Johnny's relationship with Forrest Miller, but some part of me still believed that Johnny would hunt down anyone who hurt me. Part of my heart—a childish, sappy, part for sure—was as romantic as it was in the long ago days when I thought all the love songs on AM radio were written for Johnny and me. In spite of everything, I believed there was still a place in his heart that corresponded to that mushy place in mine. I know, it's shocking news, but there it is. There's this tiny, but stubbornly incurable streak in me. It's another one of my short-comings.

I agreed to meet Johnny at Bobby D's in half an hour.

I walked back into the living room where Daddy was still staring at the TV. "Hey, where did you say Momma is?"

"She's out buying herself more clothes. I told her that she has closets full of clothes. She took my car and went, anyway. She did say she'll be back in time to put supper on the table."

"Good thing, you might starve, otherwise," I mumbled under my breath.

"Did you say something, Baby Sister?" he asked.

"Tell Momma I'm meeting Johnny for coffee, but I'll be back in time for dinner," I said.

"Your Momma will be hurt if you're late for dinner."

I left.

Johnny was right there, waiting for me in the same booth as

before. I slid in. Immediately the waitress appeared with a piece of hot pecan pie with a nice scoop of vanilla ice cream melting all over it.

"Peace offering," said Johnny. "Your mother told me about your road trip plans, but don't hold it against her. She's an awful sweet woman. And neither of us mean you any harm."

"I know," I said, through a mouth full of achingly sweet goo, "you both just want what's best for me."

"Right," he said, looking at me funny.

I ate slowly, carefully arranging each spoonful to contain the perfect proportion of sweet, syrupy pie to ice cream. I studied Johnny, while trying not to let him see.

Who was this guy? I'd divorced him and Florida and the entire South at the same time. But in the end, I couldn't get rid of any of it.

I couldn't even forget how happy I'd been when Johnny and I first started screwing. He was worlds away from the other boys I'd had. They were frantic and impersonal, as if fucking was a form of slightly embarrassing physical therapy. But Johnny and I hit it right off, with tender explorations of every body part, every taste, every sensation. Sometimes, hours later, I would find that my hair smelled like sex, or my knees, or maybe even the inside of my elbows. The thrill of those moments was so exquisite, the thought that we had such an intimate connection between us, that I would actually tremble. Well, I was beginning to think that I still carried with me, would always carry with me, Johnny's scent.

I thought, "Isn't marriage a pisser." Then I thought about Zack, and realized that it wasn't the fact of marriage. I hadn't seen old Zack since the day I left his trailer on foot, walking in the hot sun down that sandy road, dragging my clothes behind me in a plastic trash bag. I hadn't missed him one bit. His mangy person hadn't crossed my mind a half-dozen times in a dozen years. I didn't have a clue where he was or what he was doing, and I didn't care. Not that I hoped anything bad had happened to him. I just didn't care.

I hated Johnny for selling out, but I still cared about him. I wanted only good for him. I swallowed the last piece of pie and came to a decision. I knew Johnny. Forrest Miller might own a part of him, but Johnny would never actually betray me, not if it counted.

So I told him everything. He listened.

Then he looked me in the eyes and said that he wouldn't try to stop me. I bit back the "Just try it and see what I do, buddy!" that buzzed on my tongue like an itch that wanted to be scratched.

He went on, sounding like Susan for a moment, when he told

me to be careful. He spoke slowly, saying he was of two minds about my safety. His first mind was that I was fine. Yes, I had played the cock tease and pissed off George and his friends the other night, and they had chased me to teach me a lesson.

But, he told me, he could count on the fact that after they got over their hangovers the next day, they would surely realize they could only make things worse by continuing to harass me. He smiled for a moment, and then said that George probably cleaned their plows when they had to tell him I led them right to the police station. He said that their superiors in the Klan, including Forrest, would be stern with them for carrying on like that. The new Klan was working hard to become a political force in the county and the state. Their whole agenda was to look like a legitimate organization for white men who were tired of feeling the system was against them. Their treatment of me was just the kind of thing they wouldn't want public. No, he knew these guys' thinking pretty well, and he thought they were going to leave me alone.

On the other hand, he went on, I'd been going around mentioning Elijah Wilson's name everywhere I went. Now, we didn't know for a fact that there was anything out of the way in his death, but we both knew that bridge and Deadman's Creek was an awful funny place to drown, all by one's self. Even if someone else had been instrumental in Elijah's death, it was a hell of a long time ago. Chances were real good that nothing could be discovered, and certainly nothing proved at this late date. Still, he said—and here his drawl slowed down to such a leisurely pace that I almost couldn't stand waiting for him to get his words out—something about the whole mess made him nervous. He wanted me to be extra careful, stay out of stupid situations, and call him if I had any doubts.

He was looking off over my shoulder as he said the last words. His expression changed from concern to surprise. Then he actually blushed, the red streaking up to his cheeks from where it started on his solid neck. I turned around to see what the problem was, but could see nothing out of the ordinary. Didn't see anyone I recognized.

An attractive woman in a suit approached our table. She wasn't classically beautiful, but she walked with energy and self-confidence and had an open, intelligent look about her face. And she was a snazzy dresser. Her suit was yellow silk and she carried it off with a red t-shirt and red high-heeled pumps.

She reached our table, leaned over to kiss Johnny on the cheek, and said, "Come on, scoot over, give a lady's legs a break."

He did, and she sat down beside him and extended her hand

towards me in a graceful gesture.

"Emma Lewis, friend of Johnny's. You must be the famous Laurie Marie Coldwater." Her voice and her smile were warm and didn't seem the least bit forced.

"Nice to meet you," I mumbled, hurrying to adjust my earlier notions about Johnny's girlfriend.

Johnny had been momentarily stunned himself, but he was coming back to life. "I thought you said you'd be in court for weeks."

"That's what I thought. But when the defendant's attorney got a taste of my case, he decided that the best defense would be a quick plea bargain." She giggled. The sound was pure Southern womanhood. I looked at her hands. The nails were long, lacquered a shiny red.

"Emma's the best ADA in the whole damned county," offered Johnny.

"And she's got the best damned legs," added Bobby, as he walked by our table.

"Well, boys, I just don't think little ol' me can take all this flattery," she drawled with just enough irony to keep me from hating her.

"Emma," I asked suddenly, "are your parents living?"

She looked at me, surprised. "Sure. They live down in Naples, where I grew up. Why?"

Damn. My theory had been that only Southern girls with dead parents could stay near home and still make their living with their brains. I tried again, "Do you get along with them?"

"Sure I do. My Daddy and I are the best of friends. And why, there's nothing like the relationship between a girl and her momma, is there?"

Johnny nearly choked on this, but he didn't say anything.

"Well," I said carefully, "there's certainly nothing like the relationship between me and my mother."

I was actually sorry when Emma said she had to get back to work. I liked her. I couldn't help turning to watch her walk away on those spectacular legs rising out of those high-heeled shoes. When I turned back to Johnny I was embarrassed to see that he had been watching me watch her. I couldn't really classify the look on his face, except to say it was strange.

He drained his coffee cup and looked around. "I've got something to say that can't be said in here. Let me walk you to your car."

Out in the parking lot, both of us leaned against Momma's car. Johnny spoke quickly, looking straight ahead, not at me. He told me Walter was hanging around with a rough crowd. There was a big drug bust coming down soon. He didn't want Walter getting pulled in. He said that he trusted me not to tell Walter all this, but if there was anything I could do to get Walter set on a better course, I ought to try it. Real soon. He looked embarrassed. He said he didn't like himself for what he was doing, but he'd like himself less if he didn't.

The last moments felt awkward. I couldn't decide between a friendly hug or a handshake. I was intensely aware of Bobby's customers watching us through the big plate glass windows of the diner.

Finally I just punched him on the shoulder and walked away. I was almost across the parking lot when an irresistible impulse hit. I decided to liven things up around town, give Johnny a little explaining to do to keep him busy while I was gone. I turned, ran back across the lot, threw myself against him, and planted a big kiss on his lips. Then I turned toward the diner, and waved my hand like a beauty queen acknowledging her audience. I trotted back across the lot, hopped in the car, and peeled rubber speeding away. Gave the folks a little something to think and talk about. I bet Emma heard about it before I was ten blocks away.

Chapter Thirteen

I was up early the next morning, shoving some clothes in a backpack. Even so, by the time I walked in the kitchen, Momma had already finished the breakfast dishes and was washing windows. I dropped my backpack beside the door and poured myself a cup of coffee. Then I poured one for Momma and asked her to come join me. To my surprise, she put down her cloth and her spray bottle of window cleaner and did.

As she was sitting down, she said, "Daddy said for me to tell you he's gonna miss you. He would have seen you off himself, but he had to get to the golf course before it gets too hot."

"Right," I said. I thought I had kept the tone unprovocative, but I guess it wasn't enough.

Momma looked at me. Her eyes were pleading, but I didn't know what for. "He *did*, Baby. Now don't be that way. You know your daddy loves you."

I knew I should let it drop, but I just couldn't do it. "I do? How?"

"Well, of course, he loves you."

"I'm supposed to know that on the basis of the fact that he never calls me, or writes me, or sends me a present? Or makes any effort to spend time with me even when I'm staying here in the house?"

"Don't be ridiculous. Daddy and I call you once a week. We send you cards and birthday presents. Of course Daddy wants to see you, but he's a busy man. Don't expect the whole world to revolve around you. I didn't raise you like that."

I looked around the kitchen at white eyelet curtains with blue ruffled tie-backs. Yellow and blue geese marched around the wallpaper. The floors and windows were spotless. If the family that ate in this determinedly cheerful kitchen wasn't happy, could anyone be?

"You. *You* call me. *You* write the letters. *You* buy the presents. *You* spend time with me when I'm here."

She looked puzzled. "Sure, honey, that's the way the world works. But Daddy wants me to. It's all from both of us."

"I know that's the way it works, but I'm tired of it. You're assigned to do the stuff Daddy wants done, but doesn't want to do himself. Cooking, cleaning, buying clothes. You're assigned to love his problem child for him, too."

"Why do you have look at everything like that, Baby? Why do you try to make yourself unhappy? I don't want to hurt your feelings, but I really think you need professional help. I've spoken to Dr. Franklin, and I think he'd be willing to work you into his schedule. As a favor for me."

I started to say something, but she shook her head. "I swear I won't say a word to your father or your brothers. Now don't worry. Dr. Franklin says there's no stigma to receiving professional help these days."

"Momma, don't. Please don't."

The rims of Momma's eyes got red and she started sniffling. I went to the bathroom, got a box of tissues, and brought them to her. She took one and blew her nose. I patted her on the top of her hairdo. I wasn't sure if she could feel it through the structure. "It's all right, Momma. I'm sorry I made you cry. It's okay. I'm *not* unhappy."

"You might try thinking about someone else's feelings now and then," she sobbed.

That's how I left her. I picked up my bag, and walked out, shutting the door carefully behind me.

It felt good to turn onto the highway and drive, just drive—radio up loud—sing and drive. I was headed north, into the deep Deep South.

It was a tacky hour's drive past all the new shopping centers. The highway was four-lane, the traffic heavy.

But after a while, the highway was two-lane and the scenery was palmetto scrub. For long stretches, there were no cars behind me. Now and then I passed small towns, after awhile not even that—just places where three or four buildings were clustered out by the highway. I couldn't find a radio station that appealed to me anymore, so I turned it off and sang to myself. Pulled a soda out of the cooler Momma had packed for me, and had left on the front passenger seat.

I was having a good time, relieved to be out of that house where all my ambivalence and anxieties and failures lay around like ashtrays.

After all those years in Manhattan, I missed driving. This kind of driving, not the slam-dance driving in the city. Just a long road, and me. Kind of like meditation. As close as I get to it, anyway.

I had plenty of time to organize my thoughts, figure out what was going on. I'd pretty well decided that I would do an article for *The*

Rag on the Klan rally. Maybe I'd describe it in the breathless tone of one of those articles telling about black-tie charity balls in the style section of the *Times*. I thought Jerry would probably go for that.

My first priority, of course, was my upcoming talk with Sammy's mother. I'd chat with her, try to get her to open up about Elijah, to tell me what kind of man he really was. And, of course, I'd find out what she knew about the circumstances of his death. I'd ask her for the names of some of his friends who might still be around, then see if I could look them up when I got back to town. I thought maybe I'd write up all the interviews I did, put them together so Sammy would have a sort of family history to give the girls. Just thinking about it make me feel warm and generous.

I'd called Walter's place the night before to try to set him straight, like Johnny suggested. But he'd been out, and I'd left a message for him that he should really behave himself until I got back and had a chance to talk with him. I hoped it was clear enough for him to catch the meaning, and cryptic enough to keep Johnny out of trouble.

It wasn't until I'd been on the road for several hours, and almost two-hundred miles, that I realized that the same brown, nondescript car was in my rear view window every time I looked. Way back, but there all right.

First, I felt a little nervous. Then I was irritated at myself. I was being paranoid. After all, anyone wanting to head due north would take this highway. Once they got on, they'd naturally be behind me for quite a while.

So I slowed down to about forty-five. Which was real hard for me. Made me antsy. The brown car slowed down, too.

I went back up to seventy. It sped up, too. I stepped on it, went just about as fast as I dared. So did the car behind me. But it continued to stay far enough behind that I couldn't get a real look at who was in it. I thought there were at least two of them. My stomach was tying itself up in Boy Scout knots, but I forced myself to remain calm and functional.

I pulled off into a gas station. The car drove on past. I looked hard. There appeared to be the driver and just one passenger beside him, both men. Not the least bit familiar.

I filled up with gas, used the predictably filthy bathroom, bought some of those peanut-butter-filled cheese crackers Momma used to buy for me and my brothers on long car rides when we were kids.

Then I hit the road again. Checked my rear view mirror a couple of times. The brown car was nowhere in sight.

After a few more hours, I was getting bored with my own

singing. When I passed through a town with a K-Mart on the highway, I pulled off into the parking lot and went in.

I hadn't been in one of those in a long time. After you've spent years shopping in those cramped places in the city, you start to appreciate the wide aisles. And there were whole families wandering around, pushing carts, leisurely picking out things to buy. Mothers and fathers who didn't look like they'd wasted any time worrying about what to wear; kids with stained t-shirts, messy hair, dirty knees.

Wasn't long until I found what I'd come in for. The bargain bin of cassette tapes. All of them a dollar ninety-nine. I took the best of the lot, which wasn't saying much—Tony Bennett, the Monkees, Pavarotti, the Best of Disco—an eclectic mix. I paid for it all, along with a giant-sized box of Milk Duds that I couldn't resist. Those stores are dangerous for me, and as I paid, I made a decision to abstain from them for at least another decade. I walked back across the parking lot, fully equipped for the last leg of my journey.

Except Milk Duds don't really constitute a meal. Instead of pulling back out on the highway, I did a quick turn through the streets of the town, looking for nourishment. I saw a small bakery, bought a dozen doughnuts and a large cup of coffee. There now. A few more turns and I was back on the highway.

I stuck Pavarotti in the tape player. Seemed appropriate to eat doughnuts by. The land was hillier now, the vegetation greener, and the earth looked darker. I was in northwestern Florida, a completely different place than the one I'd left that morning.

There I was, driving, munching, sipping and singing my way north. I glanced into my rear view window, and my heart dropped into my doughnut-stuffed stomach. It was there again. I felt nausea churning as I realized that I should have gotten the license number when it passed me at the gas station back there. I thought about calling Johnny on the car phone to discuss this turn of events with him, but I didn't want to have to tell him how stupid I'd been.

I was almost to the next turnoff on my journey, onto a smaller, less-traveled highway. It was getting late, and I could feel the dark getting ready to settle. The recent car chase fresh in my mind, I definitely didn't want the brown car behind me as I drove down lonely, unfamiliar roads through the night.

I burrowed my coffee cup down among the doughnuts for safe keeping, and picked up the phone. I put it back down. I couldn't very well call Sammy's mother and ask her to come get me, could I? I mean, that'd be rude, and, besides, I didn't want to put her in danger. And right there, it hit me. I was putting people in danger. I'd left my parents without telling them that the Klan was angry at me. I'd felt sure my daddy's reputation would protect them, but then I'd been sure I could handle George that night in the car. I'd been worse than stupid. I'd been so prejudiced it had turned me stone blind. I'd been sure that no redneck southern Klansman could outsmart me that I'd ignored all the evidence of being in the wrong place at the wrong time, with all the wrong moves.

Sure, Johnny said he'd look after my folks, but didn't they have a right to know that I may have endangered them? Shouldn't I have owned up to my stupidity? And why was I so trusting of Johnny all of a sudden, when I knew about him and Forrest Miller? Maybe he just told me all that stuff about the drug bust and Walter to get me to let down my guard. I desperately wanted to believe that Johnny was a decent guy. I wanted to believe it in spite of the fact that he'd stayed in that crummy little town when he could have done better. In spite of the fact he'd once made two years of my life a living hell. In spite of the fact that I knew he owed his new position to Forrest Miller. And what kind of guy wants to be a police chief anyway? The only way I could get a handle on that was to picture him kind of like Furillo used to be on "Hill Street Blues." But Furillo wouldn't have told me about the drug bust, would he?

And Sammy's mother. If it was the Klan tailing me, and they were still mad at me, I might be putting her in danger, too. I only had Johnny's opinion that they wouldn't keep pursuing me for my stupid behavior at the rally that night. Unless, of course, the guys in the brown car had nothing to do with the rally and instead were interested in my interest in Elijah Wilson. I'd been dancing around this in my head, but it was time to stop and face it. Johnny was right, I'd mentioned Elijah Wilson to almost everyone I'd spoken to since I got to Port Mullet. Just thinking about the possibility of his murder, even a thirty-five-year-old murder, chilled my guts. Up until that moment, I'd been thinking how brave I was. Strong, invincible. But I wasn't brave, I was just stupidly impulsive, and careless with other people's safety.

Sammy had faced this already, when we were talking on the phone. The minute she had realized that this wasn't just a little human interest research problem she'd given me, but a mystery with unsavory possibilities, she had tried to get me to drop it. She hadn't wanted to put me in danger. And I'd been too wrapped up in my pride, and this macho idea that I was gonna drag her daddy's life story home to her, like some caveman with a dead mastodon. More like a kindergartner with a finger painting.

I saw what looked like a diner up ahead and pulled off into the small parking lot. I backed into a spot, parked right by the front door, under a pool of light.

I watched the highway for a few minutes. The brown car didn't appear. I had made up my mind. I was going to call Mrs. Wilson and cancel my visit. Then I was going to drive back to Port Mullet, tell my parents about all the stupid shit I'd done in my short visit, and get the hell on the first plane to LaGuardia. I was determined to quit screwing around with things that were none of my business or over my head.

After two rings, someone answered the phone.

"Mrs. Wilson? I asked.

"Who's calling, please?" asked a female voice.

"This is Laurie Coldwater," I stuttered. "Is this Mrs. Wilson?"

Instantly the voice changed, became that sweet-sounding voice of the South that I have—okay, I'll admit it—a certain incurable fondness for.

"No, honey. You're Samantha's friend Etta Mae is waiting for, aren't you? I'm Sapphire, her sister, Samantha's aunt. We are looking forward to your visit, child. Etta Mae is out in the kitchen right now, making her lemon pound cake, the one with the pudding mix in it and that sweet glaze, don't you know.

"You just hang on, now, while I go get Etta. And drive careful, honey. Don't hurry, but Lord, are we looking forward to seeing you."

I held the phone, nearly busting my eyeballs trying to look through the dark south down the highway. Searching for the brown car that I was half afraid was a figment of my imagination, and half afraid wasn't.

"Where are you calling from, Laurie?" came Mrs. Wilson's voice, as sweet as, and very much like, Sapphire's.

I told her where I was.

"Oh, you're less than an hour away. Don't eat anything, dear, if you can help it. I'll have supper ready when you get here."

"Thank you, but...Mrs. Wilson?"

"Etta Mae. Yes, honey?"

"I appreciate all the trouble you've gone to, but I really don't think I should come."

She didn't say anything for a while. The cars that passed by in front of me appeared first in the distance as headlights. The light rushed closer and closer, bigger and brighter, but I couldn't see the bodies of the cars until they were right in front of me.

I spoke in a rush, feeling like a small child, trying to explain some mess I had made. "I should've told you this when I first spoke with you. I'm not sure it's safe to visit you, Ma'am. Not safe for you, I mean, not me. I'm not sure I'm safe anywhere right now, so it isn't me I'm worried about—"

My predicament became more real for me as I spoke, trying to tell it all to a stranger. I shivered, and then realized the doors to my car were unlocked. I locked the one on the driver's side, and I reached the one on the front passenger side. But I'd have to put the phone down and lean way over the seat back to reach the ones in the rear.

"Just a minute," I said. "I've got to lock the car doors."

I did it quickly, but as I was sliding back down into the seat, I caught sight of tail lights on the back of a car headed north on the highway. No way of telling if it was the brown car.

"Shit," I murmured as I picked up the phone again.

"What's that?" asked Sammy's mother.

"Nothing," I said. "Just, I'm sorry to put you to all the trouble for nothing—"

She cut me off. "Now, I want you to listen to me, Laurie."

"Yes," I answered, miserable at my complete incompetence.

"This is about Samantha's father, isn't it? That's why you wanted to see me. That's what you want to talk to me about."

"I don't know," I said, realizing how little I did know. Bumbling around in the dark, screwing things up, unable to keep my priorities straight. "I made some people mad at me. Not anything to do with you, or Mr. Wilson. Some dangerous people."

I started to say something, but stopped, exquisitely aware of the dangers of car phones. This wasn't some innate detective sense; I'd read all about the marital problems of Prince Charles and Princess Di.

She didn't wait for my answer. "I'm telling you that if you're in trouble, it most likely has to do with Samantha's father. Just come here, now. Just start up that car and drive. You get into any problems, you call me. When you pull into my driveway, you honk. I'll hit the automatic garage opener and let you in. You got that?"

"I don't think—"

"Don't talk back to me," she said sternly. "Just do what I say. We can talk when you get here."

I wasn't sure it was the right thing to do, but it felt good to turn the ignition and pull out on the highway headed toward that voice. Headed towards someone who sounded a lot like Sammy. It felt like heading home.

Chapter Fourteen

Following the directions Sammy's mother had given me, I found myself deep in the countryside, not far over the border into Alabama. The roads were dark, houses few and far between. I kept looking in my rear view window. I didn't see the brown car.

I wished that I'd indulged in something even more calming than chocolate doughnuts. Maybe something alcoholic. A tranquilizer, that sounded right. I was in a bad way. Never before in my life had I wished, even fleetingly, to be dull to sensation. I wanted it all, the sharp and the sweet. That's what I had always loved about life, what I had craved. The ups and downs. The ride.

Turning into a long clay road with just a few houses, all of them set far apart, I finally pulled up in the driveway of a trim little house with its porch light burning. I tapped the horn lightly, then looked back over my shoulder, up and down the street a couple of times until the garage door lifted. A modest blue car was parked in front of the house. I guessed that the women had moved their own car to the street so I could park in the garage.

The interior garage light wasn't on, and for a moment I was surprised. Sapphire and Etta May had seemed so concerned with the details of my comfort and safety. As I slowly eased my car into the dark, windowed garage, I realized that it was safer that way. Quickly I shut off my lights which illuminated the concrete wall before me so it would be harder for anyone outside to see in.

I turned off the ignition. In the dark, strange shapes loomed around my car, all your usual garage-type stuff, I was sure. But I nearly jumped out of my skin at a sudden, loud, grating noise behind me.

The garage door was closing. Then the overhead light flicked on, and the door into the house opened. Two women in flowered dresses stood at the door, smiling at me. Smiling like Christmas, like a good back rub, like cotton pajamas after a cool bath on a hot summer night. I smiled myself, and opened the car door carefully. I eased out of the door and around the front of the car in the cramped little garage.

The women stepped back to let me in, crying, "Are we glad to see you!" and "Let me hug your neck, child." They both embraced me warmly, but my height, and their lack thereof, resulted in their faces pressed against my boobs, or, rather, my lack of those.

The sisters looked a lot alike, and they both looked a lot like Sammy. Sweet, full, intelligent faces. Etta Mae and Sapphire did not have that flash of sassy self-awareness, that spark of exuberant sexuality that Sammy carried with her. I wondered if Sammy's would fade by the time she reached her mother's age. I wondered if I'd be around to watch it go, and if I could bear to see her with it gone.

They hustled me to a small table set for dinner. They sat me down, and started carrying serving dishes out to the table. Dish after dish of Southern delicacies—so much like my mother's way of greeting me, but it felt different. Was it because they were still strangers to me? I hadn't had a chance yet to disappoint their expectations, to hurt them just by being who I was. Or was it something else, something condescending? You, know, a white, middle-class woman demonstrating love with food is pathetic, but a black woman doing the same is a warm earth mother? I don't know the answer to that, but I know I dove into that food like I'd never had a decent meal in my life.

They chatted and entertained me while I ate. They talked about Etta Mae's beautiful grandchildren. They got out their album, filled with pictures of Sarah and Annie and Rachel in all stages of development. Framed crayon drawings by Sarah and Annie covered the dining room walls.

I asked if Sapphire had any grandchildren, but was told no, Sapphire had never married. She had taken care of their daddy until the day he died.

They talked about the grandbabies' talents, and skills, and beauty, all in great detail. They bragged about the achievements of their Sammy. They were thrilled at the coincidence that in a big city like New York, Sammy and I had run into each other. They asked me for details about the girls. How many teeth had Rachel lost? Had Sarah's front two grown in yet? Wasn't Annie a terrific violinist? Did she need a music stand—they'd seen a fine one, with hand-carving around the top—and did I think that would make a good birthday present for her?

When I worked my way through the food, they cleared the table, forbidding me to help. Then they brought out the lemon pound cake and coffee. Sapphire took the plates and coffee cups into the living room which was comfortable and tidy. The furniture all matched, early American style. The colors were a brown tweed with gold and brick red with a matching rag rug on the floor, and an eagle insignia on each side of the brass-colored magazine rack.

Sitting on the couch, I started to compliment them on the room, then stopped. I was afraid they might think I was being ironic, referring to the position of Afro-Americans in colonial society. Which was convoluted thinking and far from the point. I took a bite of the cake, complimenting Etta Mae on it instead. Without a trace of irony or fear of misinterpretation.

Sapphire was sitting across from me, perched in an early American armchair. She leaned towards me, holding her plate with both hands, and asked with an intense excitement that made her sweet voice husky, "Tell us more about how our Samantha is doing."

It was funny, I thought of her as my Sammy, and they thought of her as theirs, but surely we all knew that she came closer to belonging to the girls, to Annie and Sarah and Rachel, and maybe even to her patients. Surely we knew that, in truth, Sammy belonged to herself.

I saw myself in comparison, then, so afraid of being engulfed by others' expectations that I strenuously avoided all strings and complications. But there was Sammy, with ropes and knots and harnesses of relationships all over her, and still she was free, herself. She was a goddamned Houdini, that Sammy. "Well," I said, "she's doing great. I don't know how she does all she does, but…"

"Does she have a boyfriend? Is there someone special? Oh, how I'd like for her to find some nice man who'd take care of her. Really appreciate her and be a father to her babies."

I took a hard, quick breath that burned my throat. I put my plate and fork down carefully on the coffee table and sat back into the couch.

Etta Mae looked at me, distress in her face. She was trying to communicate something to me, but I couldn't tell what. She put down her plate, too, and turned to her sister.

"Now Sapphire," she began, her voice gentle, "you know that Samantha doesn't need a man. She's doing fine by herself."

Sapphire looked at her blankly, then an expression of comprehension rose in her face. Startled, she looked me full in the face, then, embarrassed, she looked away.

"Laurie is our guest," Etta Mae continued, evenly. "Now, Laurie, I know that you've come for some information, and here we've been talking your ear off."

"I don't believe it," announced Sapphire in a loud voice.

Etta Mae, in a voice that combined fire and honey, said to me then, "I do believe that Sapphire and I need to step into the kitchen and take care of a few things. Please excuse us just a moment, Laurie, dear."

"No," said Sapphire. "You're not going to take me off into the kitchen and dress me down like you were Daddy. Uh-uh. No way. It's not happening."

In spite of myself, I was rooting for Sapphire. I like that kind of spirit, you know. "Okay," I said. "You wanna talk turkey, Sapphire, I'll talk. You know who I am, don't you, Sapphire? I'm Sammy's lover." For a moment, I was startled by how good that felt, how freeing, after the days I'd spent with my parents, hiding the truth. The next moment I was suffused with shame. Sure I could be brave with Sammy's parents, but I was a low-down, yellow-bellied coward with my own.

Sapphire laughed, a hearty, happy laugh. "Don't tell me a story like that, Laurie. You think I can't see that you're a girl?"

That stopped me for a moment, but I took a breath and went on. "I'm her lover."

She laughed again, bending over, holding her round stomach. "Samantha is not a lesbian, honey. For one thing, she has three children by three different men. She's the kind of woman that likes a good-looking man to park his car in her garage, if you see what I mean."

I was speechless yet again. I looked over at Etta Mae and saw that her complexion was gray and she appeared to be in shock, so I couldn't expect any help from that direction.

Eventually, I gathered my wits and plunged in again. "Well, both of us are really bisexual." I didn't like the way that sounded. Instead of bold and free, it sounded sheepish.

"Why, honey, all that means is that you two are making do until a real man comes along. I understand that, I do. Two fine, smart girls like you two, and good men being few and far between." Then she lowered her voice, her tone became more confidential. "But Laurie, honey, now you listen to me. When Mr. Right comes along, I know you won't stand in Samantha's way for happiness." Her voice shook a little, then, and I could see tears glinting in the corners of her eyes. "She's up there in that big city, with three babies to raise, and her own way to make. Etta and me, we worry about her."

There was a lump in my throat. I could feel her concern for Sammy all the way down to my toes. I wanted all kinds of good stuff for Sammy, too. I wanted to promise Sapphire and Etta Mae that I'd take care of Sammy and the girls. Instead, I waited while Sapphire dabbed at her eyes with a handkerchief. "I care about Sammy," I said stiffly. "And the girls, too."

"You don't have to say that, honey," said Sapphire, with a pained smile. "We know that. We can see that."

There was a strained silence. I looked around the room. These two women had spent most of their adult years in this house. It had looked so warm, so cozy, when I walked in. Now I didn't know. Maybe it was a prison to them. Was Sapphire bitter and unhappy that she had never found a man to take care of her? And Etta Mae had found a man, but it certainly hadn't done her much good, I thought. Then I thought, yes, he did her good. He gave her Sammy, after all.

Etta Mae cleared her throat. "Laurie came here for some information about Samantha's father. About Elijah." The way she said his name made me suspect that she hadn't said it to Sapphire for a good long time. "This must be very important to Samantha, for her to send Laurie down to see about this. I plan to tell everything that she thinks might help her."

She picked up the coffee pot and poured some more into my cup. The air conditioner hummed. I realized that part of my brain had been straining all along to hear over it, listening for something outside.

We all sighed. Etta Mae looked at me. "So, what do you want to know?"

"Anything. Everything, I guess. What was he like?"

Sapphire snorted. "Worthless," she said.

Etta Mae gave her a stern look, but Sapphire didn't seem fazed. "He was a handsome man," Etta Mae said. "Looking at Samantha, you can tell that, can't you? Yes, her daddy was a fine figure of a man."

Sapphire didn't say anything.

"Smart, too," Etta Mae continued, speaking slowly. "Sharp as a whip."

"Too dang smart for his own good, that one was," said Sapphire, under her breath, but loud enough for us to hear.

Etta Mae ignored her. "Well-spoken. Charming."

"A paragon of virtues," mocked Sapphire.

Etta Mae glared at her. "You liked him, too. You thought he was terrific. You told me so every time he came courting. You encouraged me."

"I didn't tell you to run off and marry him. Daddy said for you to wait, and I told you to listen."

They continued to stare at each other across the coffee table.

"So you married Elijah Wilson, then what?" I asked.

Etta Mae began to speak, but she didn't answer my question.

She spoke in a dead voice, as if she was in a trance.

"Daddy wanted me to stay here with him. He said he just wanted me to wait, to make sure." She opened one arm in Sapphire's direction, then let it drop. "What he really wanted was for me to wait forever. Like her. Like Sapphire. Forever, in this house, with the two of them. To wait on him, until the day he died, like she did."

"Well, you showed him, didn't you?" snapped Sapphire.

"So I ran away with Elijah, and he took me down south to a... a... I can't even call it a house! It was out in the woods, on Piney Woods Road. Nearest town was Port Mullet, and that was a good drive over bad roads away.

"Good Lord in heaven, I still remember the day when we drove up. That row of shacks, trash everywhere, boards over windows. No yards to speak of, just sand and sandspurs. Rusting little house trailers, dirty babies all over the place."

She stopped for a moment, then continued. "I knew Daddy had been right, then. We'd been married less than twenty-four hours, and already I could see I'd made a big mistake. But I had to see it through. There was no going back until I'd seen it through to the bitter end. Oh, I knew right then that it was gonna end bad. I couldn't see exactly what it was that was going to happen, but I knew what it was going to feel like. That's right. I knew it when they came to me to tell me Elijah was drowned, and I was a widow. There was nothing for it then. Nothing to do but turn around and come back home to Daddy with my tail between my legs. Beg his forgiveness and beg him to take me in so I'd have a home for my girls.

"And he never let me forget it, either, all the years he lived. He'd been right, and I'd been wrong, and the good Lord had punished me for my stubborn headedness, he'd say. Punished me, but not cured me, he'd say, anytime I dared to disagree with him. About anything. Anytime my opinion wasn't the same as his. Anytime at all."

Etta Mae was staring off into space. Sapphire looked angry. I was angry, too. Angry at Etta Mae. Sure, things had been hard on her. Real hard. Harder to a factor of ten than anything I'd ever been through, for sure. But still I thought, she should have kept fighting. She shouldn't have come back here to live under her father's thumb. She should have gone somewhere, anywhere, raised her girls on her own. She should have done something. Yeah, I was real good at judging what someone else should have done in circumstances I'd never faced. A white girl with all the advantages, who couldn't even tell her folks the truth about her own life.

The phone rang. Sapphire got out of her chair reluctantly and went into the kitchen to answer it.

I hated Etta Mae right then. I hated her for giving in, for knuckling under to her father. I hated to think what it had been like for Sammy, growing up in that atmosphere.

In a few moments, Sapphire came back. She didn't sit down. She just stood in the little archway between the dining room and the living room.

"Who was it?" asked Etta Mae, finally.

Sapphire smiled then, a bitter smile. "I was just going to ask you that. Or maybe I should ask Laurie."

The import of her words hit me, and time congealed around me. The moments felt like molasses in the air. Time felt like something I couldn't move through. Then all of a sudden, everything sped up. I had been hating Etta Mae for bringing up Sammy in an atmosphere of oppression and shame. This poor woman, who had done her best, and raised the fine, free woman that Sammy had grown into.

And against Sammy's wishes, I'd brought the threat of physical danger right here, into the home of these two nice old ladies.

"Who was it?" Etta Mae repeated.

"The lousy coward didn't leave his name," said Sapphire, with a calm dignity.

I couldn't wait any more. "What did he say?" I demanded.

"He said..." she began, then walked over to her chair and sat down before she went on. "He said— Now let me try to get this right. I believe he said this, the very best I remember—'Nigger bitch, you listen up. This is your last chance. One more mistake and you won't be around to make any more. Same thing with that filthy white whore you got in your house. You send her packing back to that shithole of a city where she comes from. You understand me, bitch? Last chance, nigger bitch.' Then he hung up. That was the gist of it, although I may have gotten a word or two wrong. And, of course, I am incapable of imitating effectively the ignorant, low-down, white trash accent in which he spoke."

Etta Mae and I started to speak at the same time, then we both stopped. We both motioned for the other to go ahead.

Sapphire ignored us. "This is about Elijah," she announced. "He's still doing it. He caused trouble from the first moment he walked into this house. Now he's been dead all these years and he's still messing things up." She looked at me. "Samantha wants to know the truth about her father, but she doesn't dare ask us herself.

She knew we never wanted to talk about it."

Her voice rose. "Hell, yes, we avoided that subject. The man who ruined our lives." She stopped, and started again, her voice quieter, under control. "But it wasn't right of us. If we'd told the child everything she needed to know, she wouldn't have needed to send Laurie down here, poking around in a mess she's got no way of understanding. She wouldn't have stirred up trouble that's been sleeping for along time. We wouldn't be getting nasty phone calls. So I'm gonna tell the truth, soon as I get us some glasses of iced tea."

Sapphire got up and went back in the kitchen, taking the coffee cups with her.

Etta Mae turned to me and spoke in a considered tone. "I do believe I need a cigarette. I'm sure you don't smoke, Laurie, but would you mind if Sapphire and I indulge ourselves? I do feel the need just now, what with this particular conversation ahead of us."

I had no objection, of course. Live and let, that's my motto. But I knew it would have given Sammy fits to see anyone, let alone her loved ones, recklessly risk their health like that. Etta Mae got ashtrays from behind a platter on the highest shelf of the hutch. She went back to her bedroom and came back with a pack of Marlboros.

Sapphire put down glasses of iced tea on coasters in front of us, along with a plate of cookies. Etta Mae passed her the pack of cigarettes, still speaking to me in that polite, but distant way. "We never smoke in company, Laurie. This is an exception."

Sapphire laughed. "Until Daddy died, we had to sneak out back in the woods to smoke."

Etta Mae loosened up a bit then. "Lord, yes. Daddy agreed with Preacher Thompson. 'A woman who'd smoke would do anything,' that's what the two of them used to say."

I laughed too. "Our preacher said the same thing. So Momma would smoke only when Daddy wasn't home. We'd have to hurry around, opening windows and turning on fans, right before Daddy was due back."

Etta Mae nodded, smiling. A real connection between us had been established: we knew how it was to be the daughters of a certain kind of man.

Sapphire broke into our sisterhood suddenly. "Did Samantha ever tell you about her sister? About Clara?"

Etta Mae looked stricken.

I answered, "Yes, she did. A little. The fact of her. That she died a few years ago."

"She didn't tell you that Clara bled to death on a city street? She was stabbed. By a john, most likely. She was a crack whore. Her own babies both died of AIDS. She would have died that way herself, soon, anyway."

Again time thickened on me. "Sammy didn't tell me that. She just told me she'd had a sister, Clara, who died young. I never asked for details." As I spoke, I was wondering at my own willful blindness. I hadn't thought to ask why, or when, or how, or to consider what effect her sister's death might have had on Sammy. I had been a lily of the field, neither spinning nor toiling, just planted there in Sammy's graces, enjoying myself. And once again I said to myself, "A hell of a detective you are."

"Clara wasn't really Samantha's sister," said Sapphire.

I just looked at her. Waiting for her to go on. Waiting to hear what else I'd overlooked, refused to see.

"Clara was her cousin. Clara was, is, my child."

"Oh," I said, brilliantly.

Etta Mae put her hand on her sister's arm. "You don't have to go into all this. We can just tell her about Elijah, and leave it at that."

"I am telling her about Elijah," Sapphire snapped.

Etta Mae jerked her hand back as if she had been stung. She began to cry, quietly.

"We have never once spoken about this," Sapphire continued, in a calmer voice. "Not once. We didn't need to. Etta Mae ran off with her shining knight in August and seven months later, I gave birth to Clara. Wasn't anything to say. Nothing to ask. Daddy and Etta Mae knew who it had to be. Elijah, you can bet he knew."

I looked from one sister to the other, unsure what to say.

"By then, Etta Mae knew exactly what she'd married into, anyway. I'm sure she had figured out why her lover-boy had been in such a hurry to get her away and marry her. Why he couldn't wait a little while, and have Daddy find out that he'd gotten me in the family way. Daddy would have made him marry me, and Etta Mae was the pretty one."

I looked at her, wondering if it was possible that one had been considered prettier than the other. To me, they looked alike, two bookends.

Sapphire sighed. "I went away to relatives in Mississippi to have my Clara. Left her there. Came back to take care of Daddy. Folks said, 'Your poor daddy. What you girls have put him through. You should go do for that man.' As if I hadn't been through something myself. I left Clara with my aunt, Daddy's sister, and I came back home. To do for him. To make it up to him. It wasn't that long until

Etta Mae was back here with little Samantha. We sent for Clara, and called her Etta Mae's oldest. We made their birthdays almost a year apart when it was more like six months. We never discussed it, mind you, we just started doing it. Of course, there were those who knew the truth. People aren't blind, you better believe that. But the years go by, and you say a thing enough, and people lose interest in what the truth really was. It made Daddy feel better to talk about his widowed daughter and her two girls, and his other daughter, the maiden aunt.

"We never really meant to lie to Samantha and Clara. It was kind of like Santa Claus, you know. A nice story for when they were little, but when they got old enough, why we thought they'd notice the holes in the story and start asking questions. But, you know, Samantha never did. Finally, we figured she didn't want to know. Smart as a whip, that girl, but if she still wants to believe in Santa Claus, what could we do? That's what I thought. But now I know what we should have done."

Etta Mae had been sitting so quiet through all this that I was startled when she broke in. "What we should have done! I did the best I could! I don't need you telling me now that I should have done this, or I should have done that! There were a lot of true stories that I never told Samantha. Why should she have been burdened with all this? I wanted her to be strong enough and brave enough to make herself a life. And I was right. Look how far she's gone, look at what she's done! If I'd told her the truth about her chances in life, she might have given up before she ever started."

Sapphire turned and stared at her. "And if we'd told the truth about a black girl's chances in life, maybe Clara would have been more careful. Maybe she wouldn't have ended up in the street with her blood running out of her. My God, with strangers just walking around her! And her dying, alone there, with no one who loved her to hold her hand."

We sat there in that little room. Etta Mae was crying quietly. Sapphire seemed filled with rage and could barely sit still. She kept shifting in her chair, crossing and uncrossing her legs, glaring first at me, then Etta Mae.

There was a buzzing, or maybe a rumbling kind of noise, distracting me. I thought it was the air conditioning again. I almost said something to Sapphire, but I stopped. Then I almost said something to Etta Mae, but I couldn't. This was for the two sisters, and for Sammy, to work out. I had no part in it.

I was tired and the sound of the air conditioner was really getting on my nerves. I wondered if Etta Mae and Sapphire would take me to a room where I could shut the door, open the window, climb into bed and then lie there, with no noises, no voices, just the sounds of the peaceful country night.

I looked over at Etta Mae. She had a strange expression on her face. Sapphire got up out of her chair. First she flicked off the overhead light. Then she snapped off the lamp on the side table. She walked over and stood beside the window, careful not to stand in front of it. She picked up the edge of the curtain and looked out.

The sounds grew louder, then louder still, and then began to fade. There was a loud squeal of tires, and then the sound of an engine gunning. The buzzing grew louder again.

Someone was driving a loud, noisy vehicle up and down the lonely street outside the house. Sapphire dropped the edge of the curtain. "It's a pick-up truck. Etta Mae, where's Daddy's gun?"

Chapter Fifteen

Now, you got to believe me when I tell you that guns make me very nervous. There was this sweet little dyke I met once, cocky and arrogant and boyish, with the most charming little tattoos on her wrists, her ankles, and one on that sweet place in the back of her neck, just visible under the wispy ends of her short silky hair. But the charm evaporated for me when she stood beside my bed, pulled off her black leather vest, and I saw the gun inked into her flesh, just over her heart.

Apparently, though, Sapphire and Etta Mae felt differently about the subject. When came back down the hall, Sapphire was carrying a rifle.

The truck was still tearing up the road, back and forth in front of the house.

"I should just leave," I offered.

"No, you're not," said Sapphire. "Not now. Not with them out there. Don't worry, I have a plan. Just stay away from that window in the mean time."

"Let's move back to the kitchen table," said Etta Mae. The tone was more of an order than a request. She softened it by saying, "I thought we could pass the time by playing Monopoly."

I didn't move. "Don't you think we should call the police?" I asked, while Sapphire set up a Monopoly board. The two sisters were seated at the table, smoking fiercely.

Sapphire chuckled. "I already did. I called the sheriff's wife. Says he's out fox hunting. Says she'll try to find him. I don't want to talk to his deputies." She took a long, graceful drag on her cigarette, then continued. "They're all idiots and what I have to say, I have to say to the sheriff. Believe me, when he hears it, he'll take care of those creeps out there." She waved her cigarette towards the window. "Don't get me wrong. We've got friends we can call—black and white —and if we called them, they'd be here before you could blink twice and spit. But I think we can settle this by ourselves." She put down her cigarette and started counting out the money.

"I don't mind trouble in the end, if that's what it comes to. But I'm not dying to start any, if it doesn't have to be that way."

She gently dabbed out her cigarette out in the ashtray and stood up. "I do believe we could use a drink, what do you say, ladies?" Without waiting for an answer, she headed back into the kitchen.

She came back with three cans of beer and three glasses. "Now, look here what I found. I keep these around for the man who does our lawn work. You know how a man who's been working out in the heat appreciates a cold beer."

Etta Mae said, "No need for tall tales, Sapphire. I have an intu-ition that Laurie won't think any less of us if we own up to taking an occasional sip of beer now and then."

I agreed that I would not think less of the sisters, and started right in on my can. They chose me banker, and the game com-menced.

While we played, I talked. I told them everything. Why I had come, everything that had happened so far, every little detail I'd learned. I even told them about Forrest Miller, and how I'd run into him at the Klan rally, and then gotten some Klansmen pissed off, so that now I couldn't tell who was chasing me why. We kept playing, moving around our silly little silver-colored pieces, getting in and out of jail. Collecting two hundred dollars every time we passed Go. We were all listening to the truck outside, but we didn't mention it. I did flinch once. The roaring sound got so loud that I thought the truck was going to bust right through the front wall. Etta Mae saw me, and reached over and patted my hand. "They're just trying to scare us. That's all."

Sapphire looked up from where she was rearranging all the hotels she had on Boardwalk. "Well, they are succeeding in that," she said drily.

"So what is it?" I finally demanded, unable to wonder any longer. "What is it that you know that they don't want told? What is the deep dark secret? Do you know what really happened to your husband, Etta Mae?"

I thought I might have gone too far. She was clearly nervous, her eyes darted like hunted birds. She shook her head no, but didn't say anything.

Instead, Sapphire answered. "I'll tell you how much I've guessed. He got into trouble. He did something foolish and he got himself killed. If it were anyone but Elijah, I'd say it could be anything. Maybe some white man didn't like the way he tipped his hat. But knowing what I do about Elijah, I always figured it was a woman."

Etta Mae nodded, her eyes down. She was fiddling with her lit-tle metal top hat, turning it over and over in her hands.

Sapphire went on. "One thing worried me all these years,

though. If he got involved with a white woman, or even if he just said something to a white woman, or even if somebody thought he might have said something, they would have lynched him in a big to-do. The whole purpose would be to make sure all the uppity niggers knew about it. A warning." She spat out the words like they stung her mouth, then paused, lit another cigarette. "They murdered him all right, but quiet like. Just left his body in a river. Not hanging in a tree, no burning cross. So this is what I always figured. He did something that was so stupid they killed him for it, but whatever it was also reflected so shamefully on the white folks that they kept it quiet."

In the silence after Sapphire's question, I strained to hear sounds of a motor outside. Nothing. Maybe whoever it was had gone. Or maybe they had parked the truck and were sneaking around the house right now. Maybe they were going to murder us all.

Etta Mae spoke into the silence. She put down the top hat, and her voice was clear and firm. "It was a woman. A girl, really. A high school child. Not any older than you were, Sapphire, when he started messing with you. White girl. Her family had packed her off to a mental hospital once before, for whoring with the Mexican workers in her father's orange groves. Just lay right down in the sand between a row of trees and took them all on, one after the other.

"So when her daddy caught wind of her and Elijah, he wanted the situation taken care of. But not advertised, with a burning cross, or Elijah's body found hanging from a tree. In the end, they dumped his body in the river so the papers would say he drowned. The girl was so easy, you see." Here she laughed, a hard, sharp humorless bark. "Any other girl or woman in town, they would of called it rape. But even Forrest Miller couldn't have claimed that anyone, even a nigger boy, raped Billie Miller. Her name was Belinda, but everyone called her Billie. Not a soul would have believed she'd been raped."

We sat in silence. When she'd said Forrest's name, I had felt a shock go through me. Forrest had been involved in Elijah's death. And so had Susan's sister, Billie. The silver-framed picture of her at the Miller's flashed into my head. I could hear Susan's voice, across the years, saying, "That's my sister. She's away, where she can get special care. Momma goes to visit her." And I had thought that it was one of those family embarrassments, that she was retarded or maybe just feeble-minded. So I hadn't asked anymore. I hadn't even wondered how Susan felt having a sister put away in a home somewhere. Finally I managed to ask, "What happened to her? What happened to Billie Miller?"

Etta Mae looked me straight in the eye. "Packed her right back to the looney bin. Tassahatchee Mental Institute. She's probably there still."

"The slut," hissed Sapphire.

"Don't blame her," snapped Etta. "That poor child must have been out of her mind. I was surprised her father didn't kill her, too. Old Elijah, though, he was strutting around his last few weeks. He must have thought he was something, slipping it to her like that. I bet he didn't even see what was coming. More dick than brains. That child surely knew what was going to happen to her in the end. I think that must have been what she wanted. I think she wanted to get away from her father's house that bad."

"How did you come to know so much about this girl?" asked Sapphire.

Etta face tightened, and she looked away. "I worked in the Miller house."

Sapphire was shocked. 'You cleaned house? Sweet Lord of Mercy, it's a good thing Daddy died never knowing that. 'I didn't raise my girls to scrub white folks' toilets,' how many times did he say that?"

Quiet tears ran down Etta Mae's face.

"I'm sorry," said Sapphire, helpless sadness in her voice. "I'm sorry. I don't mean to make you feel any worse."

"I did what I had to," said Etta Mae, ignoring the tears. "Men came calling for me before Elijah. Daddy didn't think they were good enough for me. Men who worked with their hands. He'd raised his daughters for something better, that's what he said. But for what? I had a college degree, but there weren't any teaching jobs around here. He wouldn't let me go North. What was I to do?

"And even Daddy was fooled by Elijah's smooth ways and nice clothes at first. About the time Daddy was starting to see through him, Elijah talked me into running away to marry him. Problem was, Elijah underestimated Daddy. Didn't dream he'd abandon me completely, refuse to send us a cent. Not even a wedding gift. So when Elijah couldn't find any work 'befitting his situation in the community,' what was I to do? I took what work I could find to feed us both."

We sat in the silence, thinking about that for awhile. Then Sapphire, said, gently, "Well, it's good we are finally talking. Things are in the open now. In all these long years, I've never once been able to poke you in the side with my elbow and say, 'My, wasn't that Elijah a fine companion in the sack.' For all his faults, he had that one fine quality. That was the best thing that ever happened to me, and, until now, we've never been able to share it." She sat back in her chair, a smile on her face. Boy, did I like her just then.

"The best thing that ever happened to you! Why, Sapphire! He left you in trouble. He ruined your life."

"It was worth it," Sapphire insisted.

"A roll in the hay with Elijah was worth it! Come on, Sapphire, he just wasn't that good. What he had in confidence, he lacked in technique. He may have been cocky, but that isn't the same thing as being good with his cock!"

Sapphire's smile faded. She sat up, grasped the edge of the table with both hands. "How would you know?"

"You don't think Elijah is the only man I've ever had, do you, Sapphire?"

"What do you mean?" Sapphire asked sharply.

"You want me to say it right out loud, Sapphire? Okay, here goes. I've had others, and I've had better." She spoke defiantly, proudly. This was something that she'd needed to say for a long time. But the moment she finished speaking, her resolve crumbled some and she collapsed a bit.

Sapphire was obviously flabbergasted. "What? You've kept this from me all these years, Etta Mae, acted and pretended and flat out lied that you were a respectable lady?"

I'd been just sitting there, enjoying the show for quite a while by then. I had the feeling that without an audience, without me there, they never would have been telling each other these things.

"Well, I don't have to tell you, you know. Some things a lady keeps to herself," said Etta with dignity.

"At least tell me this. Tell me you're referring to things that happened a long time ago. That I can understand. When I succumbed, I was young and foolish, and I thought I was in love with Elijah. And then you were an awful young widow. I can understand you might have felt the need for a man's company. Just tell me that you're not running around with men behind my back at your age!"

Etta Mae's smile then was a bit self-satisfied. "Let me just tell you that there's something Wallace Henry appreciates more than a cold beer on a hot day. You don't really think he does such a careful job pruning the shrubs because of the measly little amount you pay him every week, do you?"

Sapphire was speechless at first, then recovered just long enough to gasp, "You slut," and collapsed back in her chair.

I felt that it was time for intervention. "Please, I think we have to get back to the subject here. It's getting late and out there," I pointed to the window, "are some people who don't mean us well. We're in this together and we've got to get organized here."

I turned to Etta Mae. "It's time to stop fooling around and tell me everything you know about Elijah's death. Why you think it has something to do with those thugs driving up and down the street out there."

To my surprise, she told me. "I could tell what was going on, even though Elijah probably thought he was doing a fine job of hiding it. Meanwhile, Billie was doing everything she could to make sure her folks knew. They were meeting in orange groves, down by the beach, out at Deadman's Creek.

"If I knew what was going on, you can be sure that Forrest knew. He'd been watching Billie like a hawk ever since she got back from Tassahatchee the first time. Billie disappeared one afternoon. Elijah didn't show up to pick me up from work that evening. Mrs. Miller, she gave me a ride home. Not all the way, mind you. A white lady didn't drive her car alone down Piney Woods Road. After she dropped me off, I walked the mile or so home. I had gotten accustomed to Elijah's unexplained absences, so I didn't really miss him until I woke up the next morning and he was still not there. Well, that had happened before, too. I got a ride into town in the back of a truck full of grove workers. When I got to the Miller house, I knew right away. Knew that this was the day I'd been waiting for, been dreading, but had known was coming. I'd known that being Mrs. Miller's colored help wasn't the only misery I was destined for. That was only a kind of a hallway to hell, and I was fixing to be ushered into the main room.

"The exact truth of what had happened dawned on me in little bits, all day long. Mr. Miller was in Billie's room. She was screaming and crying and carrying on. I was doing the breakfast dishes when Dr. Foster arrived. He went back to her bedroom, and pretty soon she got quiet. I guess he gave her some kind of shot. I remember wishing someone would give me a shot like that. Something to dull the pain. Felt I deserved that, at the very least.

"Groups of men came in and out of the house, off and on, all day. Mostly they just ignored me, of course. Like I was a piece of furniture. Sometimes, though, I caught someone looking at me, and the way they were looking told me I was right to be afraid. A lot of men. All day long. Some would go, some would come, some of them were just there. They spent a lot of time in Mr. Miller's study. With the door shut."

Here she stopped for a minute. When she continued, her voice was dreamy, like she had forgotten Sapphire and I were there and she was just talking to herself. "I hated that room most of all. Of all the rooms in that house, I hated it the most.

"It stunk of that nasty cigar Mr. Miller was always smoking, for one thing. And it looked ridiculous! The rest of the house was all light and Florida-looking, but he did up his 'study' like he was some lord in some English manor house. Dark paneled walls, mahogany desk, heavy leather couch and chairs. And bookshelves full of books. I hated him for those books more than anything else. No, that's not true. I hated what he did to Billie, to his own daughter, more than anything. But anyway, he had rows and rows and rows of books. All with the same leather cover. He got them all from one of those companies. They sent him 'guaranteed classics,' one a month. He never read them. I'd bet good money on that. Never." She snorted with derision. "I so missed having something, anything, to read. There wasn't a single book in that shack Elijah took me to. I would have liked an indoor toilet. I would have liked hot running water. But I think I could have taken it better if we'd had some books.

"I knew better than to try to use the Port Mullet Public Library. Besides, it was a pitiful little thing." She looked at Sapphire again. "I only saw it from the outside, but from the looks of it, there weren't as many books in that library as you and I kept in our bedrooms here at home. I couldn't keep from hoping that you and Daddy would send me something to read."

"I didn't know," said Sapphire softly. "I didn't think."

Etta Mae went on as if Sapphire hadn't spoken. "I coveted those books. I did. And it wasn't fair that he had them and never even looked at them, while I was aching for a chance to read them."

"Couldn't you have asked to borrow?" I broke in.

She shook her head slowly. "Of course not." She thought it over, and then shook her head more vigorously. "No, I could not."

"But you being trained as a teacher and all…"

She stopped shaking her head and looked at me, puzzled. "What makes you think they knew that?"

"Well, didn't they?"

"Oh, Laurie." She sighed, and waited, as if trying to decide if she had the energy to deal with my ignorance. "I was a good worker, and a good cook. That's all they wanted to know about me. If they knew anymore, they probably wouldn't have kept me."

Sapphire was growing restless. "I'm gonna call the sheriff's wife again," she said. "Tell him to get the word to those guys out there that they can end their little visit. I'll let him know, in an oblique sort of way, that we haven't told you a thing. That we don't need some outside agitator looking into the water under the bridge, as it were. Then I'll get him to promise safe passage for you."

"How are you going to do that?" I asked, surprised.

"Won't be hard," she said. "I got a little something I've been saving for just the right occasion. Alice Parson, our cousin's wife, she does the washing and the ironing for the sheriff's wife. She told me about some bright-pink lipstick she keeps encountering on the sheriff's uniform shirts. Well, I put two and two together, how the sheriff's young secretary overdoes it with her make-up, and how the sheriff's cruiser is parked by the woods near that secretary's house on a good number of the nights when her husband is out of town, and well…let's just say I've got a feeling he will cooperate."

I chuckled. Sapphire grinned and went into the kitchen. Etta Mae sat there, staring at the table.

"So, how did it end?" I asked.

Etta Mae spoke without looking up. "Billie was committed to Tassahatchee again before nightfall. Elijah's body was found two days later. The day after the funeral, I borrowed the money from Mr. Miller for bus fare home to Daddy. I could see he was relieved I was going when he handed me the money. I never paid it back, but I'm telling you now that I don't have any outstanding debts.

"I raised Sammy, the sweetest, smartest little girl I could wish for. Better, even. And Clara, I loved her just like she was mine, too. She was as sweet as Sammy, but she wasn't as smart. But the main thing was, she wasn't as strong.

"She was troubled, that one, from the time she was tiny. Things went wrong for her, no matter how hard she tried. And she always thought it was her own fault. That partly comes from having Sammy to compare herself to, I think. She saw how well things went for Sammy. She got so she blamed everything on herself. I got the feeling that she sensed there were bad things in the past, the things we didn't talk about, and the very fact she didn't know what they were, made her feel guilty.

"I tried so hard so make a clean, new future for the girls. But looking at what happened to Clara, I swear, I could no more change what she was headed for than I could change what had already happened. Just like I knew Elijah would end up bad, I knew Clara was going to have a hard time. She sensed all our faults, all our failings, and she made up her mind to pay for them. That's what I believe."

In the silence that followed, we could hear the murmur of Sapphire's voice in the kitchen but not the words.

"Have you seen Forrest Miller's study?" Etta Mae asked suddenly.

I was surprised, but I nodded yes.

"There were these big leather bound photo albums. Made in Italy. Oh, so finely made. Pages of black paper, filled with pictures, and little descriptions written under them in white ink. Not snapshots of the family. Mrs. Miller kept those on her desk in the bedroom, in scrapbooks from the five-and-dime."

I was a little irritated at Etta Mae for going on about trivia then. My head was filled with the sad, terrible things she'd told me, and I didn't have the patience for chitchat. And I was trying to listen to Sapphire's side of the telephone conversation, since my immediate personal safety seemed to be the main topic.

But Etta Mae kept on. "He kept pictures of all the important things he did. The stuff he thought made him a big shot. I only took quick peeks at them now and then, when I was in there cleaning. I was afraid someone would catch me. But there were lots of pictures of him. Of Forrest. The vanity of that man. Every event that he thought reflected well on him, he had a picture of it. Every time he gave a speech, got an award, organized an event, anything. Did that man think highly of himself!"

After a long day, I was tired. I had gotten what I had come for, and yet I couldn't help remembering something Momma used to say: "Be careful what you wish for." I was too tired to listen anymore. But now that Etta Mae had finally started talking about the past, it didn't look like she could quit. I was grateful when I heard Sapphire hang up the phone.

"I think you ought to see if you can get a look at those albums," said Etta Mae, droning on in my ear. "You know what I mean?"

"Uh-huh. Sure do," I said, not paying attention.

Sapphire walked back in the room, smiling. "Okey-dokey. It's all clear. Sheriff is going to have a talk with those boys. Let them know we're just two old country girls that want to be left alone. We're not interested in telling ancient tales to our young guest here. Sheriff's going to escort the young lady to the state line. And he's promised me those guys are not going to bother her."

I was grateful, but I couldn't help asking, "Do you believe him? What makes you think that he's not going to double-cross you?"

"He won't," Sapphire said sharply. I think she was miffed that I hadn't praised her accomplishment.

Etta Mae spoke quickly, "Don't you see, Laurie, the sheriff doesn't want any race trouble here. That'd be the last thing he wants. This is a rural county, lots of land, few people. Local economy needs the cheap black labor, and Lord knows the sheriff's worthless wife needs help to do the washing and ironing.

"And this can of worms belongs to another state. Nothing to do with these country boys."

Sapphire broke in then. "No, he wants an easy out, and this is it. Truth be known, I don't believe that Forrest Miller wants to mess with you unless he has to. He knows the rules have changed in the last twenty years. Something happens to you, no telling what kind of investigation might get started into a lot of old stuff that he just wants to keep buried. But look at it from his point of view. You told him you write for a magazine, right? He hasn't seen you in years, and then you show up to ask him about Elijah's death. And that very night you go showing up at his Klan rally. Your behavior has been more than enough to spook him, if you'll pardon the expression. When I told the sheriff it was Forrest Miller behind those boys out there in that truck, you should have heard him gasp. Your old Forrest is one big man in the Klan this part of the South. Hear tell that they have all sorts of political ambitions for him. I don't think the sheriff minds this chance for Forrest to hear his name. He's passing on the word that your investigation dead-ended right here, and Etta Mae and I are sending you home empty-handed. That's what Forrest wants to hear. That you're not a threat and you'll be getting yourself back north where you belong, and out of things that aren't any of your business."

Etta Mae interrupted. "Nothing anyone can do now, after all these years anyway. We can't prove that they did what we know they did." Her voice trailed off at the end there, tired, and bitter.

Sapphire said, "The sheriff said to sit tight, he will be here for you in just a little while, Laurie, dear."

Chapter Sixteen

When Sheriff Pierre showed up at Etta Mae and Sapphire's door, he had his ridiculous, cowboy-esque, standard-issue sheriff's headgear in hand. He spoke politely to Etta Mae and Sapphire. They responded graciously. I was seething. For hours we had been scared silly by the stupid behavior of a bunch of jerks in a truck. And here was another good old boy condescending to extend his power on my behalf. I hated him. I was filled with raw, powerless, hatred.

He said that I should follow him to the intersection of Highway 21, then turn into the parking lot of the motel at that corner. I followed the red taillights of his cop car with the radio turned up loud to drown out the pulse of anger beating in my ears. When he turned into the lot, I followed him, and when he stopped, I did, too, and shifted into park, but I didn't turn the car off. Sheriff Pierre got out of his car and walked over to me. I rolled down the window with my left hand, kept drumming the flat of my hand hard against the steering wheel in time to the music.

He motioned that I should turn the music down. I did, but not until the song, "The South's Gonna Do It Again," was over. He waited, but his expression wasn't quite as good-natured as it had been earlier.

"It's late at night for a lady to be driving alone," he said blandly. "This here motel is owned by my uncle, and his boy runs it. I'll tell Cousin Howard to look out for you. You can get a good night's sleep and then get an early start tomorrow."

I thought about this for a moment. "How do I know that those guys won't bother me here?"

"I set those boys straight. I talked to their boss, Mr. Miller, and he called them off. They won't be bothering you again. Not in my part of the country."

His self-confidence irked me. He was proud of his power, that much was clear, and yet it was guys like him who protected guys like Forrest, someone who had done the terrible things I had just heard about from two sweet old sisters leading a quiet life on a dirt road in rural Alabama. Still, I wanted to gloat over the way they'd been able to make Sheriff Pierre dance to their tune.

I was dead tired. If I was going to have to drive the highway home with my brain on high alert, I was going to need at least a couple hours of sleep, and then a couple of gallons of caffeine. So I turned off the car and stumbled out of it onto the gravel driveway. Sheriff Pierre accompanied me to the front desk, where his cousin Howard conducted his business. Howard was almost a Sheriff Pierre look-alike, but he wasn't wearing a uniform.

I was thinking about a hot shower and a good night's sleep, and a temporary reprieve from all remedy-less old sorrows. It sort of reminded me of standing in the murky, salty water at Deer Key, and feeling that gentle biting around my toes and thinking it was probably minnows, but worrying a little, too, that it might be a crab getting ready to get a good hold of me. I didn't want to worry about crabs for awhile.

Anyway, so I was out of it, but not so out of it that I didn't notice a little drama at the front desk, a little momentary embarrassment, when Cousin Howard obviously figured the Sheriff and I were going to check into the room together. It was clear that the sheriff's usual course of behavior made that a natural assumption. But they both jumped on it quick, smoothing over that little misunderstanding, hoping I didn't catch all the implications.

I should have left it at that, I know. But I was angry and tired beyond reason. Sheriff Pierre started to take his leave, and I just couldn't help myself. "Oh, no, Cousin Howard. You don't think that the Sheriff and I... No, you couldn't think that. Oh my. I don't want people thinking that about me. Not when I'm hoping to be his new secretary."

Cousin Howard blushed. Sheriff Pierre blushed. I went on, in my best imitation of a sweet Southern girl voice. "I'm not that kind of girl. And the sheriff is not the sort of man. Right, Sheriff Pierre?"

Howard started assuring me that I didn't look like that kind of girl at all. And, of course, his cousin's reputation was beyond reproach.

The sheriff's face may have been red but as he turned to me, the look on his face made me decide that my future travel plans would not include Sheriff Pierre's part of the country. He left.

I picked up my room key. "No thanks," I said sweetly to Howard. "I don't need any help with my luggage."

Sheriff Pierre waited until I stepped outside the office before burning rubber on his way out of the parking lot.

I had room number three. I walked along the shadowy concrete sidewalk in front of the units which had few outside lights. Both of the doors I passed had torn screens. An ancient air conditioner chugged in each window, leaking a dark stream of water onto the sidewalk. It was just water, but I was careful to step around it. I sensed unclean, invisible vapors rising from it, thick and nasty and contaminated.

From the looks of the parking lot, only those two rooms I had just passed were rented out. I wondered if business was always so slow at the Warm Breezes Motel and Motor Court. Then I thought what I knew about the sheriff and figured the place probably did better with its by-the-hour rates for lusty locals than with the overnight tourist trade.

I unlocked the door to my room and pushed it wide open. Finding the room even darker than outside, I was reluctant to step in, so I stood there in the doorway, giving my eyes time to adjust to the lack of light. Finally reaching along the wall by the door, I found the light switch, but still resisted flicking it. I was afraid somehow that there was something in the room I didn't want to see.

And of course there was. I turned on the light and found the room depressing instead of scary. Very shabby, from the worn brown shag carpet and brown curtains that didn't quite cover the windows, to the worn, dirty cover on the sagging bed.

I started to drop my backpack on the floor, but the carpet, with dark spots and places where the nap was matted together, was so unappealing that I put it on the small chest next to the bed instead. There was no chair.

Now, this is the thing. I've stayed in worse places, places that were far more unsanitary. I've slept in a bed in a youth hostel in Paris that was definitely dirtier. One night in Italy I slept on the filthy floor of a train. And I can't even begin to describe some of the dilapidated rooms in the East Village, where I've lain in a lover's arms. Those were adventures; that was romantic. So a rustic inn run by Italian peasants thrills me, but Alabama dirt, the tackiness of a run-down highway motel disgusts me.

I wanted a hot shower. I wanted to feel clean. I felt tired and confused, an overdose of other people's sorrow clinging to me like a layer of oil all over my skin.

The light in the bathroom was poor, but it wasn't so dim that I missed noticing how dingy the tiny room was. A tiny lizard perched on the shower floor. I stripped off my clothes, stuffing them in the sink, as it was the only surface that looked partly clean. Then I stepped in the shower, scaring the lizard away, and turned on the water. I was expecting a cleansing, healing blast of hot water. Instead I got a drizzle of brownish, rotten-egg smelling liquid.

The one tiny bar of soap, supplied by the management of this establishment, had a strong, artificial violet scent that was worse than the sulfur water. I rubbed it vigorously against me, then stopped, proceeding more gently when I found the texture similar to that of steel wool. After I had soaped up, I stood under the shower head for a long time, hoping that eventually I would feel, if not clean, perhaps a little cleaner. The water began to run cold, but I still didn't feel clean. I got out.

I dried off on the miniature towel, so threadbare in places that I could see right through it. I was hesitant to put my dirty clothes back on, but then sleeping naked between those questionable sheets seemed even less appealing. I pulled on my t-shirt, then rinsed out my underwear in the brown water from the faucet. I turned on the air conditioner and hung my wet underwear in front of it, hoping that would encourage it to dry.

Then I lay down on the bed. I pulled up the top sheet over my shoulders, to protect myself from the air conditioner. The air wasn't cold, but it emanated from the machine with the force of gale winds, even on the lowest setting.

At first my body rejoiced at the relief of stretching out. "Yes!" cried my calves, my thighs, my back, my neck. "This is what we were waiting for!" I sighed, sank deeper into the bed. My tired red eyes closed automatically, and it felt so good. I thought I was maybe thirty seconds away from a good night's sleep.

But it didn't happen. Even my nose was too tired to keep registering the mildewy smell of the room and the sulfuric, violet vapors from my hair. All conscious thinking ceased. But damn it, some hidden part of my mind refused to take my orders.

And so there it was, trying to listen for car engines, for footsteps, for voices, straining to hear over the hum and spin and clunking and blowing and dripping noises of the prehistoric air conditioner. I was never going to get any sleep that way.

I got up and turned the air conditioner off. The air hadn't been very cool, but it certainly had been moving. I crawled back in bed, and, within minutes, the heavy, hot, full air hung over me, making sweat drop down the back of my neck, under my arms, down my thighs. I was suffocating.

I got out of bed again. I couldn't open the front window, the one with the air conditioner in it, without the air conditioner falling out the window. I walked to the back wall, to the other window. It was behind dusty curtains and venetian blinds with a heavy layer of dirt.

The crank to open the jalousie panes had cobwebs hanging from it, with some dried, withered, dead insects. A big palmetto bug skittered away as I fought with the crank. It was hard to turn, didn't feel like it had been used for years, and probably hadn't been oiled since it was installed.

When it was fully opened, I pressed my face against the screen, embroidered with dust, cobwebs, and filth. No hint of breeze, no relief from this direction. I tried to see what was out there in the dark, behind the motel. At first there was nothing but blackness, but I peered hard, so hard my eyes hurt. After a while, I could see shapes. Trees and bushes, I thought. I saw no lights, it didn't look like any houses or buildings of any sort anywhere near by. I really was in the boonies.

The full import of that began to dawn on me, even through the layers of fatigue. I was really in the boonies. Those who were following me, chasing me, threatening me, could do what they wanted with me, and no one would know. I had the word Sheriff Pierre had given the old ladies, and I knew they had believed him. They were sharp all right, but they led such isolated lives. Could they really judge how well he could be trusted?

They put great credence in what they had to hold over him. But for all I knew, his wife wouldn't particularly care that he was sleeping with his secretary. She might already know. She might even be grateful that she was relieved of the nasty chore of being the object of Sheriff Pierre's desires.

Maybe Sheriff Pierre planned on getting rid of Etta Mae and Sapphire himself, and turning me over to whoever it was that wanted me. I was, for all intents and purposes, one of those nosy Yankees, and I had stupidly annoyed the hell out of the sheriff by revealing I knew his secrets.

And here I was, putting myself at his mercy. I was still playing this like it was a game, a good story I could pursue when I felt like it, and then take a little time off, rest up. But this was real life, this was twenty-four hours a day. And since I had made a mess of things, it was my job to clean it up. I had obligations to people, to Sammy, and to Etta Mae and to Sapphire, and even to my parents. And to myself.

Now was the time to think everything through, to consider everybody who had a stake in this, to decide what the game was worth, what risks I should take. I was going to make plans, get as prepared as possible.

I sat cross-legged on the bed, doing just that. I was also listening to the occasional car or truck passing on the highway, waiting for the crunch of gravel that would tell me someone had pulled into the parking lot.

Then I heard it. I held my breath, hoping I was imagining it. I wasn't. I walked to the window, pulled aside the curtain and peeked out. An old clunker of a car was pulling up in front of the office. It was hard to tell the color. I thought it might be gray, and then thought no, it's brown.

A guy climbed out of the driver's side. He was tall, jeans and cowboy boots. Another one stayed put on the passenger side. I didn't recognize either of them from that distance, in that light, but that didn't mean anything.

I looked out at my car, across the lot from me. Cursed myself for not thinking to move my car directly in front of my room. I grabbed my jeans, wiggled into them, slipped my bare feet into my boots, and peeked back out the window. The brown car was still there, and the two men were in Howard's office.

I grabbed my backpack and slid out the door, running across the gravel, slipping, struggling to keep from sliding on my ass. The keys were in my hand.

Then I had the door unlocked and I was behind the wheel, turning the ignition. Pressing that gas pedal, and slamming the door at the same time, I swung out on the highway. Headed south. Fast. I kept looking in the rearview mirror, and no one was behind me.

Exhilarated, I turned up the tape player, sang along for all I was worth. The dark trees raced along beside me. I rolled down the window and the wind dried the sweat on the back of my neck, and under my arms.

I'd been on the highway for a good half-hour, no other car in sight, before I relaxed my foot a little on the gas pedal, down to where the car wasn't shaking. I was still way over the speed limit.

A half hour later and still no other cars in sight, I couldn't fight the fatigue any longer. I pulled into another motel, checked in, parked my car around back, but took a room next to the office, facing the highway.

I fell into the bed in my clothes, and slept deeply, dreamlessly, until the sun was high and the day had heated up.

Chapter Seventeen

I lay awake in bed for a while, my eyes shut tight. I had so much to do. But all I wanted to do was go back to sleep. The first thing I should do was get up and drive over to the Tassahatchee Mental Institute. See if I could speak to Billie Miller. See if she would—or if she could—tell me anything. I was starting to feel that Billie and I had a lot in common. We were both refugees from the claims of Southern ladyhood. Maybe she would sense that, and maybe she would trust me, and tell me what I needed to know. Once I just wanted to know about Elijah's life. Now that I knew why he had died, I wanted to know how it was done, and who did it, and how I could prove it. It was pretty wild to hope that Billie would help me, I realized that. And there were a lot of hurdles I had to jump first. Like getting permission to speak to her at all.

I sat up in bed. There was a mirror over the desk across the room from me. As soon as I saw my reflection, I realized I had a problem. If I showed up at the mental hospital looking like that, I would definitely be taken for a patient rather than a visitor.

After a shower with ordinary clear, unscented water flowing from the pipes, and normal motel soap, I felt I'd made some improvement. My clothes were not looking the better for the wear, though. I was going to have to do something about that.

As I paid my check at the diner where I had eaten breakfast, I asked the cashier for directions to the nearest store where I could buy some clothes. She was good-natured and helpful. She'd been patient about giving me change during the meal so I could keep feeding quarters to the little jukebox at the table. My parents would never let me play them when I was a kid, and I still can't get over the thrill of being able to do it.

After searching through racks of polyester housedresses and muu-muus with those ugly ruffles at the bottom (and trying to restrain myself from asking out loud, "People still buy this stuff?") I found a flowered rayon dress in the junior department. I pulled it over my head and studied myself in the dressing-room mirror. I was trying for the sweet Southern girl look, but was achieving something closer to Courtney Love. I would have said to hell with it and bought some jeans and a t-shirt, but all the jeans were all stone-washed, decorated with cute buttons, or studs or fringe, or lace, or all of the above. All the t-shirts had lace, or maybe a depiction of long-eared white bunnies with pink bows around their necks.

So I paid for the dress and some cheap white pumps, and then changed in the dressing room. In a few more minutes, I was on my way to Tassahatchee. I started out full of bravery, but faltered when I pulled up to the large, imposing building, set far back from the road. From the feeling it inspired in me, it might as well have been a nicely-landscaped prison. So this was where bad girls got sent. This was one of the futures my mother had spent her life trying to protect me from, one of the reasons she had tried so hard to make me toe society's line.

Once inside the front doors and at the information desk, I asked to see Belinda Miller. I'd grown up with her sister, I said. I was an old friend of the family, home for just a short visit, thought I'd do my Christian duty and visit the sick. I tried batting my eyes at the young man I was speaking to, but from his slightly alarmed expression, I gathered the effect was more demented than femininely appealing.

In spite of that, he seemed helpful enough. He disappeared in a back room, and came back shaking his head. "I'm sorry, Ma'am, Miss Miller died a couple of years back."

I stood there, shocked. The young man offered me a chair, a glass of water. I wondered dully why I couldn't have married a nice man like that, someone to take care of me, polite, gentle, solicitous. I could have kept him in thrall to me with my sexual expertise, and lived a quiet life of constant adoration. Then I recovered just a bit, and saw there were thousands of reasons why I couldn't have married a nice man like that, including the fact that I tried it once and it was a disaster.

I shook my head at him, mumbled my thanks, and turned around to leave. Susan hadn't even mentioned to me that her sister had died. Susan knew enough about what had happened to avoid talking to me about Billie. Or maybe I was reading too much into this, looking for connections where there were just coincidences. Billie had never been the subject of confidences between Susan and me. So why would I expect her to inform me of her death?

When I reached my car after a long journey across a sun-baked parking lot, and then put out my hand to turn the ignition, I realized that I was crying. I sat there a while, in the stifling hot car by the manicured lawns of the expensive looney bin. I cried for Billie, for all the things I'd never know about her, for her adult life lived almost entirely within those walls.

I knew so little about her. But I had already started to believe she was like me. Wild and passionate and truth-seeking. She had not been as lucky as I had been, for I'd escaped to the wicked city and she had ended up in Tassahatchee. But I think that I'd been hoping that I could save her, somehow, even at this late date. Now it was too late for that unlikely redemption.

I hoped that she'd found passion and sweetness and life in the arms of Elijah Wilson, my lover's father. I hoped she'd loved the sand underneath her back. I hoped she had thrown her head back laughing, her legs wide apart. I hoped she came and she came and she came. I hoped when she bathed that night, when she stood in her immaculate pink-tiled bathroom in her father's house, she smiled again at the hot, fishy smell when she pulled off her panties, and then cupped her hand between her thighs, catching the sticky abundance flowing out of her. She'd paid for the freedom of those moments with her life's imprisonment, and I fervently hoped it had been worth it to her.

I thought about Billie for a while, and then I said to myself, "A good female gumshoe can't spend her whole day sitting in the parking lot of the crazy house, making myths about a dead woman's life. No, a girl detective's work is never done."

So once more I headed out onto the highway. And this time I knew where I was going and what I was doing. I had some things to settle in Port Mullet. I had been away long enough.

I started seeing the signs for Weeki Wachee, and knew I was a little more than half an hour from Port Mullet. Another thing that hadn't changed. Live Mermaid Shows, Spring of Live Mermaids. The girls on the billboards were sexy in that homogenized, too-clean, too-healthy way of the '50s. Weeki Wachee still has the bird shows—a bird sets off a tiny toy cannon, rides a little bicycle, stuff like that. But the main event was still the girls. All those people from all over the country, working hard all year to save their money so they could go to Florida and spend a chunk of cash in Weeki Wachee. Old sunburned guys from Ohio still wanted to have their pictures taken next to a pretty girl in a bathing suit, wearing a fake fish tail.

I just saluted the flags out front as I passed by.

I'd kept a pretty good look in the rear view mirror, and I still hadn't seen the brown car. No one else seemed to be following me, either. More and more stores and strip malls appeared on both sides of the highway, and more and more busy roads intersected it. Traffic had picked up considerably, and I was forced to restrain my rather wanton ways with the gas pedal. I couldn't decide whether I was reentering civilization, or not.

I finally pulled up in my parents' driveway, and it looked strange to me. Weird. Like the lighting had changed or something. When I walked in the back door, my mother was on her way out. "Sunday School teacher's meeting," she said cheerfully. "I'll be back in an hour or so." She stopped and put her hand on my shoulder. "Why, Baby. You look so sweet. What a nice dress, and the shoes, too! It's a pleasure to see what an improvement you can make in your appearance when you just put a little effort into it." Then she was out the door.

My father was sitting at the kitchen table, baseball cap on, eating a tomato sandwich. He had a plate of green onions next to it. "About time you got back, Sister," he said, without looking up from his plate. "You know, you're breaking your mother's heart. She looks forward so to you coming to visit. Then you're no sooner here than you're back out on that highway, headed somewhere else."

I dropped my bag on the kitchen floor and took a seat across the table from my father. "Dad, I need to talk to you about the Klan again. I know it was pretty active around here, and I can't believe that you didn't know anything about it."

Now he did look up. "Just who are you to come in here talking to me like that? What is it you are accusing me of? And why do you come home at all if you're only going to aggravate us like this?"

I felt that old feeling rising, the one where I realize the part of me still wants desperately to please my daddy, but knows that it's impossible. But I decided to ignore it. "Daddy, listen to me. There's something I have to know. It's at least as important to me as winning the next football game is to you, or shooting the biggest buck next season, or catching the most fish. I'm your daughter, Daddy. Don't you see that's where I got it? The drive to do something right if I'm gonna do it at all. I got it from you. And there's something I'm trying to do. I've got to do it right. And I need your help."

He looked at me, as surprised as if the deer he was aimed at, or the fish he just pulled out of the water, had opened its mouth and spoken to him.

"Why didn't you say so, Baby Sister? You need my help, well then, I'll do my best to help you. Why don't you just tell your old man what all this secrecy, and running around, and foolishness, is all about?"

So I did. I told what I felt I could, as best I could, as quickly as I could. Leaving out the rape attempt and the guys chasing me around in cars. I figured if he knew about that he would feel compelled to get one of his guns out of the cabinet in the living room and go shoot somebody. I didn't think that would solve anything for me, and I didn't want my father spending time in jail defending my honor.

"Dad," I said, looking right at him, "I do need your help. I don't ask much…" I realized that I'd made a mistake even before he started to interrupt me. I knew what he was going to say. If asking my father to put up with having a daughter like me wasn't asking a lot, then he didn't know what the hell was. He'd gladly loan me money, wrestle alligators for me, or shoot any man who dishonored me. But asking him to accept me for what I was, that was just too much.

"Forget that, " I said quickly. "Let's start over. I'm a human being and I'm trying to find out the truth about something here. Tell me what you know."

He sighed, took off his cap and set it on the table beside his plate. "Okay, Baby Sister. I never wanted you to have to listen to things like this. I always tried to protect you from this kind of thing. But here goes. The way I always figured it was, the Klan was for white trash. You know, the lowest guy on the totem pole's gotta make sure there's somebody beneath him. I wasn't ever interested in their dressing up and foolishness. But I heard things, sure. Wasn't my business to interfere, though. Hell, sometimes it was the guys running the town that ran the Klan.

"When I was growing up, Sister, we had it hard. I know, I can see that look in your eyes, you've heard it too many times. I told you the stories when you were a kid, but it didn't mean any more to you than a fairy story.

"Well, here's something I never told you before. When I was maybe ten, and I had five younger brothers and sisters, and one of them a tiny baby, too, my daddy up and left. Said he was going to Mississippi to look for work. Hell, even I didn't believe it. He didn't work when he had local jobs, that's why he was always getting fired. That's why we went hungry most of the time.

"But anyway, he left. Was gone a couple of weeks. Then he showed back up, walking funny, bruises on his face, acting like he felt shamed or something, and that was one feeling I didn't think he was capable of. Got to talking with my cousins a few weeks later and that's when I found out what happened. The Klan, they hunted him down and beat the hell out of him. Let him know they wouldn't put up with him leaving his wife and children for the community to support. Or watch starve, one or the other.

"Folks used to say my family was lower than niggers. One year we moved into a house that coloreds had just moved out of, and I knew then that my daddy didn't have a scrap of self-respect.

"But I was good at sports, that's what got me out of there. Got me to college, only one in my family. Got me to marry a fine woman like your mother. And then it turned out that I'm even better at coaching than I was at playing. I look at those boys and I see myself. I think that maybe one of them needs a ticket out of a miserable life, and an athletic scholarship might do it for him. Sometimes I get so frustrated that you and your brothers don't know how lucky you've had it.

"But to get back to the point, I moved here and settled in, and the town folks here were tickled pink about what I did for their athletic program. I tell you, in the beginning the salary wasn't much. To them, I mean, not to me. To me it was more money than I thought I'd ever see. So, when they saw I was making their boys into something to be proud of, something to make them hold their heads up high when they said they were from Port Mullet, well, they did take care of me.

"I wasn't any more interested in their Klan than to be polite, you know, when they'd talk about it. I was so grateful for what I'd got, that I didn't care about pushing down someone lower than me. If you can remember back that far, I didn't fight integration like a lot of them. In fact, I was for it. There was some talk about putting all the white kids in private Christian schools, like so many towns did. But I pointed out how much better our chances were for a state championship in football if I could get a few of those big black boys on my team. And I was right, wasn't I?" Here, he stopped and chuckled. "You should of seen some of those crackers! Same ones as hadn't wanted any colored kids in their schools. We went into the state finals, they were saying, 'Coach, those niggers on the other side are roughing up our colored boys.'" He laughed again. "Hell, Baby Sister, I saw that colored girl reciting her poetry at the Presidential Inauguration. You see it?"

I shook my head no.

"You ought to watch historical events like that, Sister, it's educational. Anyway, I saw that colored girl, and I went out and bought one of her books, and damned if I didn't like it. She was a country girl, grew up poor, like me. A lot like me. I didn't know anybody had written any books on that. She understood, and *conveyed*, don't you know, what it was really like. You think you could pour me a little more coffee, Baby Sister?"

I got up and poured him some coffee. I hadn't ever heard so many words from him directed at me in my entire life. It was tempting to leave it at that, to not push him. After all, this might be the beginning of some kind of understanding between us. But I had to know.

"But Dad," I said, "what about Forrest Miller, and the Klan here in Port Mullet? And do you know anything about Elijah Wilson's death?"

"You really are a Yankee, aren't you?" he said. "You can't let a conversation make its way where it's going by itself. You have to force things, don't you?"

"Yeah, I guess I do," I said, but not defiantly. Just telling him, yeah, that's who I am, not because it's what you don't want me to be, but just because it's who I happen to be.

"Well, then, now that we got that settled," he said. "Forrest Miller had an upbringing about like mine. Maybe some better, but not a hell of a lot. But he moved to Port Mullet at the right time, took some pretty good business risks, and that's all there is to it. He's been pretending to be a gentleman farmer with a pedigree so long that he probably believes that's what he was born. But hell, there's a few old-timers who remember when he didn't have a pot to piss in, nor a window to throw it out of.

"Now, I'm getting there," he said. I thought I had been hiding my impatience better than that. "Don't hurry me. He's been involved with the Klan around here just about since he came to town. Like I said, I didn't have much to do with those boys, but I never saw any reason to interfere, either. Wouldn't do me or anybody else any good. I'd just disappear one night, and there'd be no one to take care of your momma, or you children.

"They've been involved in their escapades over the years, but I did my best not to hear the details. It's not like they made a practice of killing people. Most of what it amounted to was parties where they congratulated themselves for being white. Like their skin color was a reward from God for being so good, or something.

"I know Forrest was concerned about the way his older girl was tramping around. It didn't look right in the community. If a man can't control his womenfolk, he loses all respect. Nothing nastier than a girl from a good family turned bad. And that colored boy should've known better than to mess with Forrest Miller's girl. But that doesn't mean they should've done what they did to him. A good many of the men of Port Mullet were in on it. They got together, and tied him to a tree. Then they shot him all at one time, so they could all share in the responsibility. I always figured that was Forrest's doings. It was his daughter. If he wanted it done, he should have done it himself, was my way of thinking. But some men, to hear them talk, you would think it was a great honor bestowed on them, to get to take a shot."

"How many is 'a good many of the men in town'?" I asked.

"Well," he said, "maybe that's an exaggeration. But it was a group of them who were important, who ran the place. They didn't talk to just everyone about it, but me, being the coach, they thought I was a proper one to be bragging to. And I'm not proud to say that I didn't set them straight about that."

"Why didn't the coroner notice the bullet holes at the autopsy?"

"He was most likely with them when they shot."

"Oh." I should have figured that out already.

"I'd rather not think much more about it," he said. "Every which way I turned for a week or so, there was someone wanting to show me the goddamned pictures."

Chapter Eighteen

I tried to pin Daddy down, to get him to be more specific. Find out exactly who said what to him, and exactly what the photographs looked like. He was evasive. It was a long time ago, he kept saying. Maybe he was telling the truth the best he knew how. It *was* a long time ago, and for him to keep on living with these people, maybe he had had to forget. He had to go, he said. He stood up, leaving his dirty dishes at the table, on his way to get things ready for the Big Game Cookout that always kicked off the Tashimee Fiesta.

I had just finished changing back into my more customary attire when Johnny dropped by. I opened the kitchen door, and he was standing there with a big newspaper-wrapped package tucked under his arm. There was a pungent, smokey smell I recognized but could not place.

"Hi there, Laurie Marie. My father sent me by with a mess of smoked mullet to show his appreciation for your mother's fig preserves." He looked for all the world like a good old boy dropping by on one of those friendly errands that make up the texture of life in a town like this. A town where a large group of men may get together one night and murder a man, then brag about it and show the pictures around town.

"Cut the crap, Johnny, and put that down on the counter. You're going to draw flies carrying whatever that is around. I know you really came here to talk to me. What the fuck about?"

"It's nice to see you, too, Laurie," he said evenly. "I was worried about you, you know. Why don't you invite me in and we can sit down and chat about current events?"

I didn't want to stay in the house. All those little connecting rooms, and twisting hallways. Someone could approach and you wouldn't know it until the last minute, and then you were left wondering what it was they had heard. Besides, I didn't even trust the house itself anymore. Nothing was the way I remembered it. Everything had been much worse than I had suspected. I'd been so concerned with my own freedom, my own obsession with breaking away, that I'd been willfully ignorant of what was going on around me. I'd never wanted to find out that there might be responsibilities here for me, things I should do.

I led Johnny out back, and we sat down in the old white garden swing under the oak tree. It creaked as we swung. This had to be an afternoon in somebody else's life. Like, next maybe some lady in a flowered dress and a picture hat was going to step through the back door and offer us lemonade.

I'd forgotten to take Johnny's package, and he had carried it out with him. He finally put it down next to him on the swing. We just sat there and swung for awhile. Johnny absentmindedly opened the package next to him. He started breaking off little pieces of mullet and eating them.

At first I thought the oily smell was going to make me sick. After a while, though, it smelled appealing, comfortably familiar. Something I'd liked once, and forgotten completely. Next time Johnny picked up a piece, I leaned over and took it right out of his fingers.

It was rich and earthy and smokey. Various people in the city had insisted that I try smoked whitefish. I did, a few times, and each time I hated it. But this reminded me of something. I knew that I'd had it before. Then I remembered. As a kid, one afternoon, Daddy had taken me—just me, and not my brothers—on a trip out into the country. We went down a shaded country road, to an old unpainted wood house with a big front porch. Skinny dogs came out from under the steps and barked at our approach. An old lady came out of the house and greeted Daddy. She gave me a glass of iced tea, and my daddy a glass of buttermilk. I sat on the porch, drinking my tea. Daddy and the old lady went out back to the smoke shed. They came back with big pieces of smoked mullet. She wrapped them up in newspaper for us, except for one piece Daddy and I ate in the car on the way home, licking our fingers clean. "Now let this be a lesson to you, Sister," Daddy had said. "Good eating like this is worth the trouble."

Johnny said, "I expected to hear from you, Laurie. When you didn't call, I was worried about you."

"You know what, Johnny? I like Emma. She seems like a hell of a woman."

Johnny smiled. "Yeah, Emma's good. Too good for me. She knows she's not you, and that I'm such a damned stupid fool that I'm never going to forgive her for that."

"Johnny, did you sell out to get your job?"

"Hell, yes. What do you think? They go around giving away Chief of Police to just anybody? Happy now that's clear?" His voice was cold and clipped.

"Did you know that Forrest Miller and his Klan friends killed

Elijah Wilson? Are you protecting them?"

He sat there a moment, chewing on the inside of his cheek.

"Shit, Laurie, are you sure? Can you prove it?"

"Yes to the first. Not yet to the second."

He chewed a little more. "Hell no. I didn't know that. I would have told you already if I did. Now listen. George White ran for mayor. He's an old buddy of my daddy's. It was pretty clear that if he got elected, I was going to be Chief. Well, what's wrong with that? I'm a damned good chief. Then Forrest Miller, for reasons of his own, got behind George. So what? Two guys running for mayor, the other one was a real jerk. Should I have supported the guy who wouldn't give me the job? I tell you now and I mean it, if I had any evidence of Forrest Miller committing a serious crime, I'd arrest him. I might have let his parking violations go in the past, but since the night you got in trouble, that's all changed. Everyone knows there are skeletons in his closet, but he's been awful good at hiding his tracks."

"Yeah, well, if I can get proof, what would you say to that?"

"I'd say, let's lock him up and throw away the key."

"Even though he's in tight with the mayor, your boss?"

"I'm not going to try to make you believe in me, Laurie. Either you do or you don't."

I didn't answer.

"What do you know, Laurie? If I'm going to help you here, you have to tell me what you know."

I started talking. Not because I thought he could help anymore. I could see for myself that we had no evidence. But because I need-ed to say it—Forrest Miller had incited a brutal murder. And the men involved hadn't even seen it as that, and had bragged about it around town. But as the years went by and the town grew from an isolated little village to the commercial sprawl it was now, they had learned to keep their mouths shut. By now, some of them were sure-ly dead, some had moved away, and none of the rest of them had any motive to tell the truth. Sitting there in that swing, I felt that trusting Johnny was the right thing to do. I'd have preferred to guess wrong about him than to go on doubting him.

Johnny's tanned, lined face grew paler as I talked. I believed that he was truly shocked. After awhile he said that what really got him was there was practically no chance of finding any admissible evi-dence after so many years. "It's a tragedy and a crying shame, Laurie, but it's also what's going to keep you safe. Forrest and them know you can't prove anything, they're not going to bother you. For extra insurance, I'll go pay another little call on Forrest. Make it perfectly clear that I'm going to be keeping an eye on you from here on out, and, if anything should happen to you, I'll be mighty interested in it. He'll get the picture."

No, I thought, I will. The one thing I didn't tell Johnny was that Daddy's mention of the photographs had reminded me of something Etta Mae had said to me. I had a secret plan. There was one more place I planned to look before I gave up on getting solid evidence.

After a while, Johnny said, "Laurie, there's something important you should know. I never told you, and I should have. You and I know each other like no one else will ever know us. I shouldn't go messing with that by keeping things from you."

I said, "I don't know what in the hell you're trying to say."

He ignored me and went on. "You know that something can happen when you are a child, something important, and you just completely forget about it, until all of a sudden it just comes flooding back to you?"

"Johnny, please. I'm just not ready for your repressed memories right now. I'll give you the phone number of the therapist of one of my ex-lovers. She's been on Oprah, so she must be good. But I don't want to hear that your mother and the other ladies of the Eastern Star forced you to commit unnatural acts in the Masonic Lodge."

Johnny didn't laugh.

I sighed. "Okay, Johnny, go ahead."

"When I was a little boy…"

"I knew you were going to start like that."

"Don't interrupt. When I was a little boy, I came home early from Vacation Bible School one day. I got sick, and Pastor Green brought me home. He dropped me off by the front gate, told me to give my mother his regards. I went in the kitchen, and your father and my mother were drinking coffee."

"And…" I prompted.

"And nothing. Your father finished his coffee and left. His car had been parked around back. That's why I didn't see it."

"What were they wearing?"

"I don't know. I don't remember. Probably my mother was wearing a housedress and your father was wearing grey trousers and a starched white shirt and a tie. That's what people generally wore back then, far as I can recollect."

"So? What's your point?"

"Come on, Laurie Marie. Why on earth would your father talk to my mother—to any woman—if they weren't having an affair?"

I ran my tongue over my teeth, started to argue with him. But he was right, I knew it.

"My daddy and your momma? Good Lord, Johnny!" Even as I said it, I wondered what had got into me. I couldn't remember ever using that expression before in my life. Horrified, I wondered if this was the corollary to another discovery I had made. I saw my mother everyday in the bathroom mirror. In the softening under my chin. In the lines around my eyes. Shit. And now I had started talking like her. I added, "And hell, they might as well fuck as drink coffee alone together in the house, because no one would ever believe that was what they were doing,"

"That's right," Johnny agreed.

We were silent for a moment. To break free from my father, it had been absolutely imperative that I sleep around like crazy, every time I got a chance. But when I did that, who was I imitating? Shit. I hate all this self-knowledge stuff. Being a self-absorbed teenage ninny had been much less painful.

Then something occurred to me, and I jumped right out of the swing, startling Johnny. My leap set the swing in furious motion, and it banged into my leg. "Ouch! Oh no! Maybe you and me... Maybe we're..."

Johnny grabbed my arm, pulled me back down on the seat. "No, no, don't worry about that. I thought about that, too. Back when we were married, and we were having one of our major battle scenes, and all of a sudden, I remembered. I remembered them sitting there at the kitchen table, how shocked they looked when I walked in the door. I worried about it for a long time. I still wanted you, damn it, even though I was afraid you might be my half-sister. And I hated you for turning me into that. A depraved person, a pervert. I hated you then for everything you did to me, all the crazy things we did together. All the guys, my friends, they were still going to watch high school football games every Friday night, just like they hadn't ever graduated. And spending their weekends fishing, and talking about girls. Jesus Christ! You had me doing mushrooms and hallucinating, and sleeping with you and another girl at the same time!"

"That's not fair," I interrupted. "We didn't do mushrooms and sleep with Marla the same night!"

"That's not what I meant!" he spat at me. Then he calmed down, and took my hand. "I didn't mean to get into all this. What I meant to say is, your brother Seth, when he started dating Jody Howard, your daddy took him aside and told him she was his half-sister, and that was that. Seth lost interest in Jody right then and there. Your father wouldn't have let us get married if there was any chance that we're, you know, related."

"I can't picture my daddy telling me that," I said, doubtful.

"No. But he would have taken me on a fishing trip or something, and he would have told me."

"How do you know about Seth and Jody?"

"Seth told me."

Seth didn't tell me, I added to myself silently. I sat back down in the swing. The breeze moved the small oval leaves of the live oak tree, shifting the lacy patterns of light and shadow on the grass. We pushed our feet against the ground in unison every time the swing went forward. I knew that he was right. That was the worst of it. If Johnny had been my half-brother, my father would have told Johnny, but not me. The next worst thing was that Jody Howard was my half-sister. That simpering, empty-headed, homecoming queen. Bitter jealousy rose up in me. Did my—our—father prefer her? Did he wish I was more like Jody?

"Let's go swimming," I said. I pulled off my shirt and jeans. I had on a red satiny bra and panties that were less revealing than my actual bathing suit, so I didn't see why not.

"I've got to get back to work right now, Laurie Marie. Ever since you've been in town, it's been hell on my reputation as a steady worker."

"Okay, then. See you later. I'm going for a swim," I said. I turned my back on him, walked the few steps to the pool, and stood near the deep end, dipping the toes of one foot in the water. I knew he couldn't resist.

I was looking down, watching his shadow approach me on the white concrete. He thought he was sneaking up on me. I edged right up, balancing on the edge, the lip of the pool cutting into the soft skin in my arches. One push from Johnny and I'd be in deep water.

I waited until I could hear his breathing, and right as his arms reached out to push me, I turned from the waist, wrapped my arms around him, locked them together tightly. We fell with a satisfying splash into the clear blue water. Johnny's nice starched uniform and all.

He was startled, and he let loose of me right away. I pushed with my feet against his chest, and shot away from him across the length of the pool. I'm not in great shape anymore, and my lungs were aching for air when I reached the shallow end and broke the surface. My wet hair dripped on my shoulders, and my skin felt cool in the air.

I climbed up the steps and out of the pool, not looking back at him. Walked a careful distance away, in case he should seek revenge.

He was over at the ladder, hanging on tight and coughing. And laughing. And cursing. "You could have at least let me take off my watch!"

I smiled sweetly, waved good-bye and went in the back door to the house. The air conditioning brought immediate goose pimples to my flesh.

Momma was back home, unpacking groceries in the kitchen. She looked up at me, surprised. "What are you up to?" she asked.

"Oh, Johnny and I just had a nice swim. I think I'll go take a shower now, Momma."

I walked on down the hall, Momma watched in disapproval at the wet footprints following me down the hall.

Chapter Nineteen

Over the sound of my hair dryer, I heard someone knocking on the door. I opened it and Momma said I had a phone call. "Lovely girl," she said. "Her name is Sammy? We had a nice talk."

I dashed down the hall to the phone. "I want to talk to you later about what you did to Johnny Berry, Baby Sister," she called after me.

Sammy was there, on the other end of the line, in the city, in the universe, in my life. Sammy, the center, the heart of my quest. The moment I heard her voice, I felt it in my heart. She was her patients' Sammy, and her own Sammy, and the girls' Sammy, but she was my Sammy, too. And there was something different about the way I was thinking about Annie and Rachel and Sarah. The girls, I thought. Sammy's girls, and their own girls... and my girls, too.

We talked for a long time. She had spoken to her mother, she knew some of what had happened. She was afraid for me, and didn't try to hide it. I told her that the Chief of Police had given the matter some serious thought, and he didn't believe I was in danger, but he was taking steps on my behalf anyway. That seemed to make her feel better. I didn't tell her about the idea Etta Mae had given me, about what I planned to do. I knew she would only try to stop me, because she believed it was still her errand I was on. But it wasn't anymore. It had gone on far beyond that now, and this was something I had to do for me.

I asked about Annie, and I listened to what Sammy said, then asked for Sarah and Rachel the same way. I even asked about Elena. I cared, she could tell that, and, as a result, I think, there was something lighter and more serious in her voice, in the way she talked to me. When she talked about her children before there was this little note of apology, of saying she knew that I was humoring her by listening, that this wasn't really my thing. Sammy seemed sense the difference in me. We had a talk as warm and intimate as any we had ever had in bed. But just as Sammy said something about coming to get me if I didn't come back soon, I knew I must be hearing wrong. I knew she couldn't leave her patients or her daughters, and I was going to be back soon anyway. Then I saw the trap. If Sammy and the girls were a part of me, that meant I was going to get torn apart when the relationship ended, right? I couldn't quite listen anymore, and Sammy had to go anyway, so I managed to hang up pretty fast. Shit, I thought, there's always a catch.

I walked into the kitchen, stood leaning against the sink, and stared out the kitchen window. A nice enough little street. Small, neat houses, and little concrete driveways with cars parked out front. Just like a small-town anywhere. Except, because this was Florida something was contradicted by the lush vegetation, by the fierce heat, and even the tiny lizards darting everywhere. Go ahead and pretend, it all seemed to say, go ahead. But right here is the evidence that things are stranger and more fertile than you can imagine. There is more going on here than you know.

The phone rang, startling me. It was Susan. She sounded too cheery. She spoke quickly, said she couldn't talk then, but there was something important she had to tell me. She said she'd see me tomorrow at the parade.

"Parade?" I asked, stupidly, still thinking about traps, and me always wary about the wrong things.

"The Fiesta Parade," she said, explaining how she and her family would watch from the mayor's front yard. I should meet her there. Afterwards, she said, the pageant would be in the park, down by the river. The first day of the fiesta, how could I forget?

Suddenly my mind shifted into gear. I asked about her father's plans. I could tell from her voice that she was surprised, and suspicious. But she told me. He was going to the Big Game Cookout. Tomorrow he'd be a judge for the parade. And then he had a part in the pageant. And, of course, there was a party after the pageant.

She said she really had to go. There was noise in the background. Tom was asking her impatiently when she'd be off the phone, and the kids were making kid racket. She'd see me tomorrow, she said. She was ready to hang up, so I had to talk quick. I told her what I needed. Just a key. Just for a little while. I had to take it on faith she'd do this for me, without an explanation, and without betraying me. It wasn't like with Johnny. I hadn't made a decision to trust her. But I asked her this anyway, and she could be the one to decide whether she would be trustworthy. She waited a while before answering, and when she did, her voice was so still, so composed, that I knew she had made her decision. "Okay. At the parade then."

I folded some laundry, and then kept pouring wine while Momma kept cooking. After the dishes, I spent the evening with Momma watching all her shows. Momma was careful not to say anything, not to act too pleased. But I could tell she was. This was the best thing we could do together, better even than getting our hair done or going shopping. The nice, normal kind of stuff. The stuff families do together. She didn't criticize me or make a suggestion once during the evening, unless you count the time she said, "Don't you love the way Loni wears her hair? And it's just about your color."

TV was worse than I remembered. Not that I had ever watched much of it. Anyway, somehow, we got through that evening, even though it seemed to me to take longer than the last twenty years of my life. I asked her once if she was hurt that her husband and sons were off on the Big Game Cookout where no women where allowed. She looked at me like I was crazy. "I don't have to cook dinner tonight or breakfast tomorrow. And why on earth would I want to be out there in the woods with a bunch of men drinking too much and eating that foul stuff they call cooking? No thank you very much just the same!"

Organized by the most respected businessmen in town, the Big Game Cookout was the first event of the Tashimee Fiesta, always on the Friday night before the opening parade. The men went out in the woods somewhere, and cooked copious amounts of venison, gator, wild boar, and rattlesnake—any creature that had lived free and they had managed to assassinate. Not my idea of a good time. As a kid, I wouldn't even eat ice cream if it was in the freezer next to what I thought of as Bambi's mother. Johnny had confessed to me once, back when we were married, that when the exotic stuff ran out, plates of barbecued pork were handed out, called boar, and no one was the wiser. The women in town disapproved of the extremely liberal use of alcohol at the event, but, I tell you, that's the one part of it I understood. If I was going to eat that disgusting mess, you better believe I'd want to wash it down with something alcoholic.

The men stayed out all night, then stumbled back into town just in time to get the parade going the next morning. Sitting there with Momma, a thought occurred to me. No women at all? Why did we believe that? How did we know that they didn't bring in strippers, dancers, whores? I could ask Johnny, but I wasn't sure he'd tell me the truth. For a moment I thought about sneaking out after Momma went to bed, to check it out for myself. But I rejected that pretty quickly. There are some things I really don't want to know.

A little later Daniel and Paul dropped by, on their way to the cookout. After they left, I asked Momma something I'd been wondering about. I couldn't believe the boys came by the house so often just to see me. Did she see them this often when I wasn't in town? She said she was sure they were coming by to see me, but then she did see a good bit of them. Most weekdays, she said, at least one of them showed up for lunch. That's why she always kept something ready. Most week nights they showed up for dinner too. And on the weekends, of course, all of them were there for big dinners, and to watch the games.

I was amazed—not that Momma spent all that time cooking for five grown men nor that they enjoyed being catered to. But that those grown men could visit their parents that often and still lead their own lives. This was my first extended visit in more than a dozen years, and it was taking everything I had to keep from losing myself.

When Momma went to bed, I was too keyed up to sleep. I drank some bourbon, but I still wasn't sleepy. I prowled the house, edgy to get ahold of that key and wishing I had it tonight while Forrest Miller was off with the men, and no one around his place but timid Mrs. Miller. This was the night for action and all I could do was wait.

Finally the bourbon hit its mark and I fell into bed.

In the morning, I wandered into the kitchen thinking that, for once, Momma and I could just sit and eat Cheerios. She wouldn't be jumping up to make eggs and grits and buttering the toast. But Momma was already waiting for me. Sitting at the table, dressed in her parade outfit, a magenta nylon running outfit, with matching shoes and earrings. Her gigantic gold handbag was on her lap.

I stared at her magenta rhinestone earrings for a moment, and then turned around, considering going back to bed until I was strong enough to face this day.

"Hurry up and get dressed, honey. I'll take you out for breakfast."

Quickly I did, dressed in jeans, tank top and sneakers, ready for action, and went back into the kitchen.

Momma took one look at me and said, "Oh, Baby..." The disappointment in her voice cut me deep. She had worked hard all her life, so hard, for no appreciation, and why would her only daughter, out of pure spite, dress that way, with a deliberate lack of attractiveness? That's what I knew she was thinking. But for once she didn't say, "Why don't you put on something nice?" Neither did she ask me if it would kill me to dress in a way to please her, just this once. I appreciated her silence; she really was trying.

She took out me out to breakfast, to one of those franchise Southern, country-cooking places, with the plastic-coated menu and colored photographs of the various breakfasts. I ate the Farmer's Breakfast, country-fresh scrambled eggs with home style buttermilk biscuits smothered with old-fashioned sausage gravy, designed to evoke some kind of security, something implicit in a traditional family. But the food tasted only of fat and sugar and salt. Afterwards, I felt heavy and slow, all my perceptions, responses and functions dulled but satisfied—not quite the same thing as unconditional family love, but hey, it was pretty close.

Then we went to the parade. Momma parked the car on a side street a few blocks from Main. She didn't lock it. We walked the few blocks to the mayor's house.

The front yard was filled with people in lawn chairs, drinking iced drinks. Momma knew everyone of course, and everyone knew Momma, and they thought they knew me. I recognized a few people here and there, but, for the most part, I was lost.

A chair was pulled up for Momma right up front, where she would have a good view. I opted to sit on the curb. It dawned on me slowly, that I did know a lot of the women, the young matrons in pressed white shorts, with tidy belts and sherbet-colored blouses. They had trim figures, and their legs and arms and faces were deeply tanned. They all smiled that bright, cheerful, optimistic smile they had practiced since the days when they were cheerleaders, majorettes, or pretty girls in pastel dresses being escorted to a dance. These were the girls I'd gone to school with, my old classmates.

A group of them started to move in my direction. I felt a moment of panic, then out of the corner of my eye, I saw someone coming towards me from the other direction. It was Susan. She sat right down on the curb next to me, heedless of her nice white shorts. She gave me a big hug, and started in with "How good to see you!" and "Don't you look nice!" The others, seeing me occupied, regrouped.

She put her hand on my thigh, just briefly, when she leaned over to kiss my cheek. When she lifted her hand, I pocketed the key she'd placed there. She turned and said something nice to my mother, then, "Oh look, here comes the parade!"

I hate parades. The Port Mullet High marching band was headed towards us, with the majorettes out front. My Momma had been a majorette in her day, and she had hoped I'd be one too. Just one more way I'd disappointed her. I remember her telling me once, when I was, I don't know, ten or so, that the majorette with the biggest smile was the one that would go farthest in life.

There they were, in front of us, in the feathered, sequined costumes that remind me of Las Vegas show girls costumed by a Baptist preacher. The way they kept twisting and twirling their shiny metal batons depressed me. Behind them came the band members, marching in wool uniforms with plastic overlays, designed for a cooler climate. They had red faces, and sweat poured down their cheeks. The band was playing "When You Wish Upon A Star," in honor of King Philip and Queen Tashimee in the float behind. A pretty blond high school senior, in an equally fluffy hair-do and dress, waved and smiled.

Momma and Susan admired her dress. While I had been on my road trip, both of them had attended the beauty pageant, sponsored by the Rotary Club and the Port Mullet Council of Churches, where the current Queen Tashimee had been selected.

"Oh, you should have seen her in the talent competition," said Momma. "She just stole the show. It was so sophisticated. She wore a long black dress and gave a dramatic presentation of *The Raven*. You really should have seen it."

The captain of the football team was her King Philip, Susan said. The king and queen were surrounded by other girls dressed as Indian maidens. Their hair was in braids, and their faces reddened with make-up provided and applied free of charge by the local Merle Norman shop. They wore fringed dresses of brown cotton, meant to look like deer skin, with red rickrack around the neck and hem. The football team was standing around topless, wearing pants of the same brown cotton with the same red rickrack and fringe.

There were plenty of floats still to come. Momma and Susan were discussing each one and who was on them. When I thought they were absorbed enough to miss my exit, I bolted.

I slipped between two houses, ran two blocks to Main Street, and ducked into the Golden Nugget for a quick beer to facilitate my thinking. While I waited at the counter, I felt a big, hot hand on my shoulder and turned. It was Josh.

"Hey. You scared me. Buy you a beer?" I asked.

"So where the hell were you?" he snarled.

"The fishing trip! I really am sorry. Something came up," I said. "Come on, let me buy you a beer or two, make it up to you."

"I never let a girl pay," he said.

"Suit yourself." I shrugged, paid for my beer, took the bottle back to my corner.

Josh bought his and then, to my surprise, joined me. When I saw him coming, I put my feet up on the chair next to me so he had to take the seat across from me. As he took a long drag on his bottle, his face looked different, none of that arrogance, none of the stuff that gives a good old boy his good old boy look. He looked defeated and stupid.

"What's the matter? It's not a big deal that I didn't go fishing with you because I know you don't give a damn, really." I remembered my warning to Walter on his machine, and the connection to

Josh and his invitation clicked. "So how about you tell me what this is all about? "

"Doesn't matter. Turn us in, do whatever the hell you want. I'm out of it now. I don't think you can prove anything on me. If you can, then, I'll bite the bullet and be a man about it."

I urged him on, "What's the deal with the fishing trip that you wanted me to go so badly?"

"I couldn't have done it." Josh flushed and shook his head. "I wasn't going to take you out there in the Gulf and dump you. Not Walter's sister. Not after eating Momma's food and being welcome at your home. When you didn't show up, I was glad. You know, when I first got into it, it was fun. You go out in your boat after dark, you wait to get met by the big boat carrying the shit. It was like the games we used to play when we were kids. And hell, it was fun to be selling the stuff everybody wanted. Kind of like a public service. But it hasn't been so much fun lately. I thought I knew what I was doing, but, since the heat has been on us, I really found out who I was dealing with."

"Big time smugglers, right?"

He just looked at me, anxious and morose at the same time. "I'm not naming any names. And you don't have anything on me. Nothing. It's over."

"Just tell me this. It was Forrest Miller, right? He wanted you to take me out on your boat and not bring me back?"

"Forrest Miller? That jerk? Hell, no. It was the guys I work for. We've had rumors that the feds were looking into us. You're a lousy cop, you know that? You show up here, like a fish out of water, poking into everybody's business, you think we're that stupid?" He looked embarrassed. Ran his finger through the condensation on the table. He looked up suddenly panic on his face. "You're not wired, are you?"

I laughed. "I may be a lousy cop, but you're a worse criminal. Listen, someday soon you're going to be real glad you got out when you did."

"You *do* know something! I was right, you are a cop!"

"I am not. Don't you have someplace you can visit for awhile? Get away from here? I think a change of scenery would do you good. And why don't you make sure you take Walter with you."

He looked more cheerful. "You think you could help us find something in New York?"

I laughed again. "I'll try, Josh. Any friend of my brother Walter is a friend of mine. At least as long as he doesn't dump my body over the side of his boat into the Gulf of Mexico."

Chapter Twenty

After Josh and I had parted ways, I walked down to the Main Street Bridge, needing to wait until I knew Forrest Miller was distracted or involved in the festivities. The parade had passed by a while ago; the crowd had dispersed to the park to wait for the next stage of the festivities. I climbed down under the bridge, took off my shoes, and sat with my legs over the sea wall, dangling in the tea-brown, brackish water. I could still hear, faintly, the music of the parade while it made its way to the end of the route.

I stirred the water with my legs and remembered the last parade I'd seen. I'd taken Annie and Sarah to the Gay Pride parade in the city. I'd planned on going with Sammy, but at the last minute she couldn't make it. As always, the brash spectacle and the exuberant variety of human desire exhilarated me. Sarah had loved it, too: "Look at the tall lady wearing nothing but feathers! Oh, Look! It's really a man dressed as a lady wearing nothing but feathers!" But Annie had been miserable. The raucous music blaring from the floats gave her a headache. She was embarrassed by the muscular guys posing in bikini briefs. She was frightened by the big men in drag. And she turned her head away from the women with their arms around each other.

I hadn't been very understanding. Sarah and I had teased her, called her a stick-in-the-mud. But now I was thinking about how overwhelming it could have been to a young girl on the cusp of puberty. Where I saw freedom, perhaps Annie, daughter of a mother with an irresponsible, sex-obsessed lover like me, saw chaos.

I hoped I'd have a chance to show Annie that freedom can be tender, too. And maybe tenderness in love could be demonstrated by caring concern for the loved one's child, just as much as by the sweet soft licking of the loved one's salty, silken flesh. Or maybe not. I didn't know. But I aimed to find out.

Later, I left my hiding place under the bridge, and wandered over to the carnival grounds. I watched some of the baby beauty contests, bought some blue cotton candy. Didn't need to stop at the guess your age and weight booth; construction workers in the city are always giving me personal evaluations, free of charge. I felt no need to try the rides. The roller coaster, the octopus, the scrambler. I guess my adrenaline glands had had enough workouts lately.

I was turning away from a booth when I saw Terri. She noticed me in the same moment. Our eyes met, and she smiled in greeting, just as if she didn't believe with all her heart that I was a sinner. That's what I told her after we sat down at a picnic table with paper plates of fried catfish and grits and hushpuppies.

"But I love you, Laurie Marie! God loves the sinners, each and every one of us, and it's His love pouring through that you see in me."

"Right. Listen, Terri, are you going to the pageant?"

"Sure I am. I never miss it."

"Doesn't it bother you?"

"Bother me?" She was genuinely puzzled. I had confused so many people since I'd arrived in town that I was beginning to feel that I spoke a foreign language.

"You know, the whole racist nine yards."

She laughed and picked up a hushpuppy. "Honey, you think too much. My brother, now, he'd agree with you. He wouldn't come within a mile of it unless he was carrying a sign and leading a demonstration. I just don't think it's worth worrying over. The audience doesn't think about things like that; it's just a story to them. My parents always said, don't worry about seeing racism everywhere, you just worry about behaving your own little self, and letting the love of God shine through you. Everyone's equal in God's eyes. But I have to run now."

Now I was puzzled. "But, Terri, how are we gonna move towards that future you were talking about, you know, the kingdom of God on earth, unless we face the racism in our past, in this town, and in that stupid pageant?"

But Terri had already gotten up and was throwing away her paper plate. She turned, and called, "Don't forget. Jesus loves you and I love you," and then she was gone, back into the crowd.

A little later I saw Susan. She was taking a picture of Tom. He was going around on one of the little kiddie rides with the two youngest children. I watched them for a few moments. I'll tell you this, for what it's worth. They looked, at that moment, like a happy family. And she was right, you know. It was me that talked her into every one of those pranks in high school. All the while I was having myself a great time and it never occurred to me to that she wasn't. I had pressured her. I wanted her to be one way, and her father wanted her to be another, and, between the two of us, we'd nearly pulled her apart. Maybe life with dull Tommy was a big relief after that.

I felt so distant from her then, as if they were a Martian family I was observing. All the people all around me felt alien. The whole town I'd spent so much time not thinking about for the past dozen years. I'd spent a lot of energy trying hard not to be a person from Port Mullet. Did I really, secretly, believe that people in the city were morally superior? Didn't the sheer numbers of investment bankers, lawyers, and muggers in the city illustrate the insanity of that idea? And every day, the inhabitants of the city, sophisticated city dwellers, stepped around people living on the street. Maybe the real reason we chose a city so big, so immense, so crammed with humanity, is that we thought it excused each of us from personal responsibility. Maybe that's really what I like about the city. Maybe I left Port Mullet so I wouldn't have to see what I didn't want to deal with, those very things that I had been confronting the last few days. Why had I ever thought that leaving made me superior to those who stayed and did nothing? Had I thought that absolved me from responsibility?

There was a general movement in the crowd towards the little outdoor theatre at the edge of the park, over by the river. It was nearly time. I followed, pulled along by the energy of the crowd. Once there, I stepped aside, let the ones behind me climb up the bleachers. Instead, I stood over to one side, near a tree, waiting.

It was the tail end of dusk. Night was just about to fall. The sun was down beyond the line of trees, live oaks between the theatre and the river. The sky was rose and crimson over the trees, and dark above and behind us. The colors were fading fast. I could hear the humming and buzzing of the insects around us. People were slapping at their arms and legs, leaving little smears and blotches of blood. The brush under the trees was alive with rustling noises. I thought of darting lizards, and snakes, both rattle and coral. I had learned to identify them as a kid, like everybody else. The sound of the rattle is frightening, I was taught, but the silent coral snake is more deadly. Behind the trees, in the dirty river water, swam cottonmouths while alligators floated, disguised as partially submerged logs, or lay buried in the thick mud, just waiting.

Then it was completely dark. I was tired of self-examination, of soul-searching. I turned my irritation out to the crowd on the bleachers. The inhabitants of my home town seemed to me then to possess the heartless, mindless festivity of the audience at a lynching: their small talk as they waited for the performance, the way they slurped at the soft drinks and dug their hands into the greasy bags of popcorn, seemed to me ugly, crudely carnal.

The taped music came over the sound system, the lights

dimmed, then a small oval of light centered on the semicircular stage area. From the deep shadows at stage right came a tall, slightly-stooped man dressed as a Spanish priest. The audience was silent, waiting.

In a moment the priest would enter, holding a scroll of parchment. He'd stand with his head bowed. This was the way the pageant always began. Then he would slowly unwind the scroll, and read the prologue.

I knew what would happen next. I had seen it so many times. The priest, Father Hernandez, would tell how he had set out with the Spanish captain, Don Fernando, his son Philip, and niece, Theresa, along with a handful of soldiers. Then Father Hernandez would roll up the paper, the lights would dim, he would leave the stage. When the lights came back on, the priest and the children would be captives of the Indians. The captain and his soldiers would have all been massacred. The chief, bedazzled by Theresa's European beauty, would adopt her as his daughter. Another noble family would take Philip as their son. Father Hernandez, by the grace of God, would convert the entire tribe to Christianity. They would become good Catholics and abandon human sacrifice.

Theresa, renamed Tashima, would grow ever more beautiful and, of course, the braves would prefer her to the Indian maidens. As the chief's daughter, she would be permitted to choose her own husband. The single young men would compete for her favors, but she would choose Philip, her kinsman. Together they would rule the tribe, after her adopted father's death.

A jealous, rejected brave, would enlist the medicine man in his cause. The medicine man, bitter that the priest had turned the people against his superstition and magic, would gossip among the population, spreading rumors. He would say that it was wrong for the people to turn against the old ways, and point out signs of the gods' disapproval: illness, poor weather, bad fishing, and hunting. The ignorant Indians would believe the medicine man and turn against Tashima and Philip, imprisoning her and sacrificing him, then holding his pulsing heart before her horror-stricken eyes.

At that very moment, a huge hurricane, the expression of the wrath of Father Hernandez's God, would strike the village and destroy it completely with wind and rain. The grieving Tashima and Father Hernandez would be the only survivors. Tashima would die of a broken heart. The priest, sensing his own imminent death, would record their history on a scroll of paper, seal it in a bottle and leave it on the bank of the Tashimee River, before exiting.

I had seen it so many times, and I could see it now in my memory. But I wouldn't be there to see it enacted this time, to watch the story they had fabricated for themselves and for the tourists. The Indians had been gone for hundreds of years, and now the land was completely tamed, the alligators fat on marshmallows, while here sat the Fiesta celebrants: a few descendants of the early settlers, some Italian families fresh from Queens, retired firemen from Detroit, and tourists on their way to Disney World.

But I gasped as the priest came in—Forrest Miller. He lifted his head and began to unroll his scroll. That was when I turned and slipped away through the dark.

I knew I was running out of time. I walked quickly over the uneven ground towards the river. I had expected to have to be careful, walking through the scrub in the dark. But I went easily, without a false step. Something in me knew the way. I had spent countless hours as a child playing there. The knowledge of every dip and marshy place, every tricky spot, was in my legs, and arms, and body, and some hidden part of my brain.

I followed the river to the bridge, climbed up the embankment, onto the sidewalk along Main Street. I hadn't borrowed a car, because everybody in town knew everyone else's and it might be remembered later. I knew I should walk, save my energy, but I couldn't. I couldn't wait any longer. I trotted, and I fought myself at every step to keep myself from going any faster. Quite apart from the consideration of avoiding fatigue, I was more likely to attract attention, running, and in boots, no less.

But there was no one on these quiet residential streets to see me. Almost everyone was at the pageant, or the carnival, or one of the parties in honor of the Fiesta. Then I started to run flat out, my boots pounding against the pavement, the sound of my blood pounding in my ears.

When I reached the corner to the Miller's house, I slowed down. I turned at the service alley that went behind the houses. The air was heavy with a sweet, almost cloying scent. Was that honeysuckle? I wasn't sure. I had spent so many warm nights at Susan's house, but I didn't remember this smell. And then I remembered, it had been twenty years. Twenty years is plenty of time for a small cutting to grow to a large plant, to cover a fence, to grow up a wall, to become the flourishing vine that could saturate the air with that overpowering scent.

My body still remembered the way. I crossed the large back yard, filled with rose gardens, and fruit trees, and patios, without even thinking about it. I found myself at the back door. I didn't remember pulling the key out of my pocket, but, somewhere along the way, I had. I looked at it for a moment, surprised, and then I slid it into the lock.

It turned easily, so smoothly. I took one last look behind me, to be sure no one was watching. I couldn't see anyone, but it was dark, and there were many trees, and dark, shadowed areas. Through the windows of the house across the back alley, I could see the strange blue flickering light of a TV.

I slipped through the door, closed it behind me. For good measure, I locked it.

I was standing in what Susan's mother called the "garden room." The floor was cool white ceramic tiles. A round table surrounded with white wicker chairs sat in front of the French doors, with a view of the rose garden. It could have appeared on the front cover of any house-decorating magazine.

I stood there for a moment, searched inside myself for any second thoughts, and I didn't find any. I might not learn the truth, it might be too late, the evidence might be gone. But this wasn't about the past. I had to know about myself. Was I really willing to make every effort to confront the truth?

Chapter Twenty-One

I went straight to Forrest's study. First, I made sure the curtains were completely closed. Then I put a small table lamp on the floor before turning it on. I cursed myself for not thinking of a flashlight.

The photograph albums were on the lower shelves, about two dozen of them. I sat down on the floor, and pulled them out at random, flipping through the pages. They were, just as Etta Mae had described them, monuments to Forrest's vanity. A photo of Forrest shaking a politician's hand, a yellowed newspaper clipping of the mayor naming the Little League field after its benefactor, Forrest Miller. At first I looked at each picture, but I soon got bored with the seemingly endless tributes to Forrest. I started skimming over each page quickly, then turning to the next. I was so intent on my search that I lost my awareness of my surroundings, and the danger, until I heard the unmistakable sound of the front door opening. I scrambled to my feet as fast I could and looked frantically around the room for a means of escape. I considered climbing out the window, but rejected it as too slow and too noisy.

On a hunch, I went as quickly and quietly as I could to slide open the top desk drawer. Bingo—there was a gun. I picked it up carefully. I did know, of course, that pulling the trigger was the way to make the thing fire, but that was the extent of my knowledge. I had heard of a safety, but had no idea what it looked like or where I would find it. I didn't know how to tell if the thing was loaded, either. Since I had no intention of shooting anyone anyway, I wrapped both my hands around the handle, fastidiously avoiding the trigger. I planned to rely only on its deterrent capacity, and that only if necessary. My favorite scenario would be to hide quietly, undiscovered, in the study until I could escape unnoticed—the use of the firearm never required.

I dropped to my knees and crawled under the desk awkwardly, with the gun still in my hands. I made myself as small as possible, pressing my knees up against my wildly thumping heart. The footsteps were fairly light. I hoped it was Mrs. Miller out there. Explaining to her what I was doing there was going to be a little rough, but it seemed infinitely preferable to attempting the explanation with Forrest or one of his thugs.

The footsteps stopped right outside the study door. I held my breath. The door opened slowly.

"Hey, Laurie, you in here?" It was Susan.

I tried to scramble out from under the desk, banging my back pretty good along the way.

"Susan?"

She stared at the gun in my hand which I put it down on the desk slowly.

"I was worried about you. I came to help."

"I love you, Susan." I didn't know why, but it seemed important to say that.

She looked uncomfortable. "Me, too. Uh, Laurie...?"

"Yeah?"

"I didn't tell you everything. I'm sorry. Don't be mad. I was so ashamed."

She looked so unhappy and I felt so bad for what I'd done to her. She'd done the best she could to make a life for herself under difficult circumstances, and I'd popped back into it just to make things worse. "Ah, Susan, don't be ashamed. It's not your fault. You didn't do anything wrong. Look, I know all about your sister. About Billie."

"You do? I don't even know all about Billie. But, Laurie, the photographs. They used to be in here."

"You knew all along? You've seen them?" That hadn't occurred to me. I was dumfounded.

"Yeah, I know. I'm sorry. I already said that." She stopped, for a moment, and then shrugged. "You know, I tried hard not to think about it. Ever. Like if I didn't think about it, then it didn't happen." Her expression started to break, the lines in her face sagging. "They all shot, at one time. So no one would know who did it. Then they mutilated his body. Then they threw him in the stream." Her voice was expressionless, like she was reciting a verse in a language she didn't understand.

"How do you know all this?"

She shrugged again. "I listened. When they thought I wasn't around, or that I wasn't paying attention. When I was a kid. When the men would get to drinking and talking. This was a big event to them—having their chance to kill a 'nigger' and get away with it. But then, things changed. By the time I was old enough to understand the implications, they didn't talk about it anymore. You could tell 'nigger' jokes, sure, and be dead set against integration, but what they did would have been called murder by then, and investigated by the state police, even the FBI. The Klan had dwindled down to almost nothing around here. Momma was after Daddy to get out. They fought about it a lot. But I think they were really fighting about my sister. My mother hated my father for what he did to my sister, and she hated herself for not being able to save her. But how could she save a daughter who did what Billie did?"

She sat down on the edge of the couch and looked up at me, intently, as if desperate to convince me of something. "I didn't really understand until I was a lot older. By then, I'd sneak in here and go through Daddy's stuff. And when I was, I don't know, eight, maybe, or nine, I saw the pictures. In a moment, I knew it. The whole thing. What happened. And at the same time, I didn't believe it. I was a lot younger when I heard about that stuff, and maybe I'd misunderstood. Maybe it was my over-active imagination. And I closed the album and walked out of this room, and made myself forget it. I forced myself never to think about it. Because there was nothing I could do about it, and to live with it would just be too much. How could I live knowing my father was a monster when I have to eat Sunday dinner at his house every other week. He pays my husband's salary. He's my children's grandfather." She shook her head as though answering a question someone else had asked her.

"I had enough to do, just to figure out how I could get to live my own life. Billie hadn't gotten away with it, and I was determined to. But then I kept letting myself get carried away by your crazy ideas. Skinny dipping at Deer Key. Skipping school. Smoking pot in the girls' room. Sometimes it felt really good. And sometimes, I couldn't quit thinking that one false step, and I'd end up like Billie. I knew I had to get away from him, but if I kept doing it your way, I'd lose. I'd never get out, never get away from him."

She started sniffling. I put my arms around her. She pushed me away. "We don't have time for this now. Let me show you where I think they are."

She got down on the floor and started looking at the albums, one after another. After she'd flipped through a half-dozen, she started to seem frantic.

"You know," I said, as gently as I could, "he may not have kept these particular pictures. Whatever else you have to say about your father, he's not stupid."

She didn't look up. She pulled out a few more albums, looked through them quickly, shoved them back on the shelves. Then she pulled out a beautiful, leather-bound one, looked at the cover, and handed it to me with an awful smile.

I took it out of her hands, and I was surprised that my own were shaking. You think you want to know something, and then you see that you really don't. But I took it from her anyway, and sat back, cross-legged on the floor. I opened the heavy covers slowly. I turned each page slowly.

Susan got impatient. She reached over and starting flipping quickly through the pages. Then suddenly, she stopped. She got up on her knees and studied the page before her for a moment. Then she sighed, sat back down, waved her hand over the page.

It was pretty dark, and I guess my eyes aren't as good as Susan's, because I had to take the album over to the lamp to really be able to see. I wanted the truth to be clear. Putting the album down on the floor in the circle of light made by the lamp, I crouched over the page. There were five pictures. Two in the top row, and two in the bottom, and one right in the middle of the page. They were black and white. The one in the middle was a bound, mutilated body hanging limp against a stake. The body was recognizably human only because of the clothes, and the hands. I was thankful the photograph was not in color, but black and white was plenty bad enough.

The other four were shots of the crowd standing around the body. Those appeared to have been taken after the shooting and before the mutilation. Every man had a gun in his arm or at his side. Some men were in all the photographs, and some were only in one. I had no way of knowing whether every man involved had been photographed. The first thing I did was study every face. The one I was looking for wasn't there, and I sat back on my heels for a moment, immensely relieved. My father was not in any of the pictures. I had looked, and I was sure of that. Some of the faces had been vaguely familiar, and, if I studied them again, I would probably recognize them as younger versions of men I had known all my life. Two I had recognized immediately. Mr. Johnson, the pharmacist, was one. And Mr. Berry, Johnny's father, was another.

I sat up again to lean into the light, and continued studying the photographs.

"You're right to do this," Susan said. "The Klan's getting so big again, much bigger and better organized than it ever was before. And they're smarter now. They even have a public relations consultant." She was sitting right beside me, and she ran the flat palm of her hand across the top edge of the album page. "I'm glad you're doing this."

I was still studying the photographs. "Susan, did he ever… abuse…you or Billie?"

I was shocked at her bitter laughter. "Not the way you mean. I was spanked as a little kid, sure, but nothing you'd call a beating. And he never tried anything sexual with me. I don't know if he tried anything with Billie, of course. I have no way to know. But don't you see, Laurie, he didn't have to beat us. He had complete power. He controlled us completely, and, if we were crazy enough to disobey, he could have us thrown in the looney bin. He didn't have to rape us. It was clear our bodies were his to control anyway. That's what killed him about me getting pregnant. I'd had sex without his permission. But then, of course, I was in Tom's power, and Tom was in my father's. So…"

I heard something right then, and I could tell Susan heard it, too. Two cars. They pulled up. One in the front driveway, one in the back alley. The engines were turned off. Car doors opened, and slammed shut. Voices and footsteps outside.

I hurriedly pulled the photographs off the page, and shoved them under a couch cushion. Susan hadn't moved. I whispered, "Maybe you can crawl out your old bedroom window."

It was too late. The front and the back doors were opened, and they were tramping through the house. With my one last calm thought, I pulled open the door to Forrest's bathroom and pushed Susan in. "This is silly," she protested. "This is my parents' house."

"Humor me," I whispered as forcefully as I could.

I closed the bathroom door. Just a few seconds later, the study door was pushed open. A group of men I'd never seen before was standing there. I want to say that they were big, ugly, stupid looking men. That's the picture I have in my mind when I think about it. But it's not true. They looked like everyone else. Just five regular guys. One of them yelled to let the others know they had found me.

"We found the intruder in here," is actually what one of the guys said.

"Intruder? Is that what I am?" I said. "Then why don't you call the cops?" Then I smiled, tried hard to smile cute and sweet and nonthreatening.

The one that appeared to be the leader said, "That's up to Mr. Miller. He's the lawful owner. We're just going to keep an eye on you until he gets here."

"Well, in that case," I said. "I'll call the cops." I moved toward the phone. One of the guys stepped forward, unplugged the phone from the wall, and stood there with the cord in his hand.

"No, Ma'am. You won't. This is Mr. Miller's phone and you don't have his permission to use it."

"Then I'm out of here. See you guys later." I took a couple of studiously nonchalant steps towards the door. One guy stepped in front of the door, wouldn't let me pass.

"You can't keep me here," I said. "This is imprisonment. You're not the police. You have to call the police, or let me go."

"Who are you to tell us what to do? You broke into someone else's house, and you're talking to us about your rights? Forget it. Wait here, and work it out with Mr. Miller."

Susan's voice behind me said, "She didn't break in. She's my guest."

I turned around. She was standing in the open door to the bathroom, holding herself every inch the daughter of the most powerful man in town.

"Excuse us, Mrs. Dalman, we didn't know you were here."

She nodded her head, graciously accepting his apology. "This is my old friend, Laurie Marie Coldwater."

"Yes, Ma'am," said one of the younger boys. "We know who she is. Coach Coldwater's little girl." I was both taller and older than he was.

"Well then, I'll see you gentlemen to the front door, unless you'd like a cold drink. I'm sorry that you were troubled for no reason." She was walking to the door. The man blocking it stood to one side to let her by. But no one made any move to follow her.

Susan looked back at them, puzzlement on her face.

"We can't leave, Ma'am. We have to wait here for Mr. Miller, just like he said."

Susan was trying not to show that she recognized her complete lack of power, but her face was white. "I'm going to have to ask you for that phone so I can make a call."

"No, Ma'am. I'm sorry." The kid talking did look sorry. "You can go wherever you want to make a phone call. But you can't use the phone here."

The look on Susan's face was empty and lonely and defeated. Being the daughter of the most powerful man in town didn't help much when he was the one she was up against.

We were all just standing there, in deadlock, when another car pulled up in the driveway. A car door opened, and then another. Two car doors shut.

Footsteps came up the driveway, and then the front door opened. One of the guys stepped around Susan to greet the newcomers in the foyer.

We heard Forrest Miller's hearty voice. "So, boys, you catch a fox in the henhouse?"

All the men laughed. I didn't think it was so funny.

"No, sir, Mr. Miller. Nothing so interesting. I'm sorry to say we have been annoying your daughter and her friend."

"Well, it won't do to have all these good-looking men in the house with your wife, will it Tom?"

"Lord, no, that wouldn't do at all." None other than Susan's husband, Tom, was with Forrest.

"Boys, I want to thank you for your assistance. You hurry, there might be some of that beer left down at the park."

"Yes, sir, Mr. Miller." And the guys were out of there.

I walked into the hallway after them. They went out through the front door, except for the oldest and fattest. He went through the French doors in the breakfast room. I was pretty sure that he wasn't leaving, that he was lurking out there in the dark.

Susan walked out of the study then, and stood beside her husband and her father. She looked like a little girl, ashamed and frightened.

"Hi there, Laurie. You sure are looking good after all these years." Tom didn't appear the least bit nonplussed by the situation. "Sorry we don't have time to sit and talk over old times."

I was speechless.

He took Susan's arm. "We've got to be going on home now. Mrs. Miller is baby sitting and Susan doesn't want to impose by keeping her too late."

Susan looked up at him beseechingly. "Why don't we drop Laurie off home on the way?"

Mr. Miller said, "No, no. You get home to my grandbabies. I'll make sure Laurie gets home safely."

"That's right, honey," said Tom, grasping Susan's upper arm, "your daddy will take care of her."

"I don't want to leave her," Susan said, almost begging.

"Don't be silly," Tom said sharply, and he opened the front door and pulled Susan out. She struggled to stay put, but it was no contest. He yanked her over the threshold, and then he yelped.

Forrest and I looked at each other in surprise.

"She bit me!" he yelled.

I laughed.

"Susan, what's going on here?" Forrest demanded in the iciest, blackest, hardest voice I'd heard in my life.

She stood straight in the porch light. "I hadn't finished saying good-bye," she answered in a voice that was trying hard for dignity, but was shaky from her trembling. "I just wanted to remind Laurie that I'll be giving her a call first thing in the morning. We're going on a shopping spree. I'll be holding you responsible, Daddy, if you forget your obligations as a host and keep Laurie up so late she gets over-tired."

I'd never seen or heard a less threatening threat than the one Susan had just made, but her bravery still took my breath away.

Forrest grumbled, "I know my manners, child, you just worry about your own. And don't go around biting your husband. Folks might say you're crazy."

Tom had her arm again, and was pulling her towards the car. I hated to think how Susan's husband and father were going to make her pay for her little rebellion on my behalf.

Then Forrest stepped toward the door with his arm extended to close it. Suddenly, I couldn't believe what was happening. It was a movie running in slow motion. It was swimming in cane syrup. It was one of those dreams you have, where you know you have to run, and you try and you try and you can't.

Then, just before the front door closed, my panic shocked me into action and I threw myself towards it, screaming, "He's going to kill me! He's going to kill me!"

The door slammed shut, and Forrest Miller stood in front of it. I was all over him like a wild cat, scratching and biting and kicking. He pushed me away and I ran like hell, like fire, like I'd never run before, like I was made of running, like running was what I'd been born for. Headed for the back yard, for freedom, for life, for Sammy, for the girls.

Chapter Twenty-Two

As I grabbed the latch, I saw the dark silhouette through the glass doors. The big guy was waiting for me. I'd never get by him.

I whirled around and Forrest was right behind me. I thought, he's going to kill me.

Forrest said, "Calm down. You never seemed the hysterical type before. I just want to talk to you."

"Let me go."

"I should think you would show a little gratitude. You broke into my home and I'm not even calling the police. The least you can do is have a little chat with me."

I screamed as loud as I could, a long and wailing scream like a siren. It hurt my own ears. I was hoping—I was actually praying—that the neighbors would hear.

The big guy stepped in through the doors, grabbed me from behind, and clapped his hand over my mouth. I could barely breath, and he was so strong and big I couldn't get any leeway to push or hit or struggle against him. Forrest just stood there in front of me, smiling.

I struggled with everything in me. The big man didn't budge, didn't even seem to notice. Within minutes, I was completely exhausted. I collapsed against my captor, deciding to rest and think of a new plan.

Forrest spoke then. "Jesus H. Christ, you're crazy. We won't hurt you. We're not in the business of hurting women. He's going to move his hand. If you scream again, we'll just let you go, and you'll never hear what I've got to say."

Let me go! They weren't going to murder me! For one second, I thought about getting the hell out of there as soon as the monster let me loose. Then I thought about the photographs. I could tell Johnny about them and he could get a warrant and come look for them. But by the time he got here, Forrest would have found where I'd hidden them. It wouldn't be hard. The album was still on the floor in Forrest's study, open to the page where I'd ripped them out.

Maybe I could still figure out some way to get the pictures out of there with me.

"Laurie," Forrest said in a patient voice, "as always, I admire your spunk. But you're barking up the wrong tree. There's no story here. You think you know something, but you really don't. You have no way of knowing how things were then. And you don't seem to appreciate who will get hurt if you keep on with this. Members of your own family, for instance."

"My father wasn't involved in this," I spat at him.

He smiled at me. "You have no way of knowing that. But this whole conversation is theoretical, because nothing happened. Except a nigger got drunk and drowned. But have it your way. Assume that something did happen. What makes you think your father wasn't involved?"

I didn't answer.

Forrest smiled.

I couldn't stand it. "He's not in the pictures!"

His smile didn't change, not one little bit. "So what does that prove? Supposing something happened, and supposing there were pictures, there's still no reason to suppose everyone present that night cared to pose for the pictures. Some folks are camera-shy, you know."

I stared at him. He went on. "This is all theoretical, you understand. Let's suppose that some men didn't have balls enough to do what had to be done. But they knew all about it, and never turned anyone in. And stayed here, lived here, didn't leave town. I'd say that was an admission on their part that the dirty job was necessary, wouldn't you?"

I started to interrupt, but he kept talking.

"And let's suppose some more. Suppose every man brought a gun that night and there were better than thirty men. But suppose the night ended with less than a dozen holes in the nigger? What does that lead us to suppose? That maybe some men came without ammunition, knowing from the beginning that they didn't intend to shoot? Maybe so.

"But would they be more or less responsible than the men who came with their weapons loaded? Since they let the others think they were shooting, too? Aren't they the truly despicable men, more so than the ones who actually shot, who thought they were doing a necessary and a painful task, defending their wives, their daughters?

"Do you think it could have been easy for these men? Keep in mind that these are the same men that sat in the pews of the First Baptist Church and the Riverside Methodist the very next Sunday morning. Who confront their souls' salvation every week. Unlike you, who I doubt has ever given your own soul a thought.

"And suppose some men came prepared with ammunition, but faltered at the last moment? Chickened out? When it was their turn, when their groups were called, they stepped forward and aimed, but never fired. What about their guilt?

"And finally, suppose that some of the men there that night had had relations with Belinda. Suppose that one of them had been the first. Whoever he was, after he took her, she was finished. It was that first step that eventually led to the nigger full of holes, and Belinda lost to me. What do you suppose about that man's guilt? Nothing is as simple as you seem to believe, Laurie Marie.

"While you're supposing, honey, think about this. If you keep on this way, it's your own family that will be hurt. You're going to end up making them the laughing stock of the town, running around half-cocked, making crazy accusations like this. And if I catch you trespassing on my property again, I'm afraid I'm going to have to call the police, in spite of our long friendship. Now, as I don't see a car outside, would you like for me to give you a ride home?"

"No place in this town is home to me, " I snapped. "I don't live here anymore." I was angry beyond bearing. I would almost rather he had killed me than to stand there and hear Forrest tell me calmly that they were going to get away with it and there was nothing I could do. And for me to stand there and listen, and realize the truth of what he said.

I'd write an article for *The Rag*, spill everything I knew about Forrest, every nasty, sordid, cruel detail. Since I had no proof, Forrest could sue me, and win. And he would find a way to make it look like my father was involved, I knew he would. If my story were believed, every man of a certain age in town would be smeared with the taint of a racial murder, but I'd never be sure who was guilty, and who was not. No respectable magazine would print it without solid proof, but I was willing to bet that Jerry would. To me it sounded like the sort of romantic gesture—going down in magnificent flames for a lost, but just, cause—that Jerry had been looking for ever since he got thrown out of Dalton.

I told Forrest that I'd take him up on his offer of a ride. We walked to the front door. When we reached it, I asked if I could use the bathroom. Forrest nodded, of course. I sauntered down the hall towards the bathroom, and then, when I reached the study, dashed in the door. I planned to grab the photographs and get out of the house however I could. Kicking them both in the balls, if it took that.

Okay, so I overestimated my abilities there.

I had just grabbed for the cushion when the big guy grabbed me and Forrest picked up the photos. I kicked and screamed with everything in me, but he just laid me out on the couch, held my arms with one hand and my legs with the other. I screamed louder and spit at him, but I might as well have been screaming in a hurricane and spitting in the Gulf.

Forrest tore the photographs into little pieces and put them in a little heap in the fireplace. Then he turned, and opened a drawer in his desk. As he did, he noticed his gun lying on top where I'd left it. He laughed and picked it up. "So you were playing with my firearm. I bet you don't even know how to use it."

I admitted as to how he was right.

"If you think you can behave now, I'll let you up."

I said I thought I could behave. The big guy let me up, but he kept a close eye on me as he moved toward the door and stood there with his arms folded.

I sat up on the couch, smoothed my hair, and grasped at that old crutch of mine. Sex as a weapon. I unbuttoned a button on my blouse. Forrest stood there watching me, still smiling. Then he turned back to the drawer he was looking through.

"You know," I said, "I've always wanted to touch your gun." So it wasn't subtle. I knew he'd know what I was up to, but I hoped he'd be so sure of himself that he'd want to play.

He looked up at me, poker faced, "Found them," he said, picking up a box of matches. "Is that right?" he asked. "You'd like to touch my gun?"

"Could I, please?" I asked.

He picked it up off the desk top and walked over to me. He sat down right beside me, his thigh against me. He held out the gun. I stroked it suggestively. He smiled, the way he'd been smiling all night, and I looked at his long yellow teeth and mentally flagellated myself for ever admiring the man. I glanced over at the big guy. He was still standing there, but he seemed to be enjoying the game.

"Tell me, how does the safety work?" I purred.

Forrest grinned, and the big guy was laughing. "You think I can't see what you're up to?" he said "But you can't shoot me, Laurie. First, you're not that kind of girl. Second, you don't want to spend time in prison. Just because you've got some ass-backward theory, you still don't have to go shoot a man in his own house. Here, I'll take off the safety and hand it to you. That's how sure I am you aren't going to do something stupid."

He handed me the gun. Then he turned, kneeled before the fireplace, and struck a match.

"Stop!" I screamed, half-crazy with impotent anger. "Stop right now or I'll shoot you!"

He put the match to the little pile of paper. "No, you won't."

"Yes I will!" I screamed, holding the gun out with both hands, trying my best to point it in his direction, but my arms were shaking.

The big guy dove at me. I went down on the floor, the gun still in my hands. From far off, I heard a shot and I felt something jump in my hand. There were two surprised yells, and some swearing. I don't know if I dropped the gun, or if it was taken from me. I just shut my eyes.

When I opened them, Forrest was on the floor cussing and groaning, holding his thigh. There was blood pooling on the carpet.

I jumped up and ran to the fireplace only to find a small, gray heap of ashes on the red brick.

The big guy had the phone, calling for an ambulance. He hung up hurriedly and went over to look at Forrest's leg. Forrest was still cursing. They ignored me. I picked up the phone and called the only local number I knew by heart. I called my Momma. Loud and clear I told her she'd better hurry on over as I watched Forrest's man applying pressure with a cushion to stop the bleeding.

First there was the sound of a car engine so revved up it sounded like a rocket coming down the street. Then a squeal of rubber as it swung into the driveway. A car door opened before the engine was off. Just about the time the front door burst open, I heard the sirens. Momma got there first, with Johnny a close second. She came into that study door like the Marines. For a moment I was wondering how I was going to explain what had happened.

Turned out I didn't need an explanation. It was enough for Momma that her daughter had found it necessary to shoot Forrest Miller. She lit into him, cussing him up one way and down the next. Problem was, apparently Momma hadn't had much experience with those words. She had the general rhythm and vocabulary right, but something was wrong in the translation. "You fuck-damned-shit piece! God asshole you mother!"

I burst out laughing. Forrest got this look on his face like Momma's diction was hurting him more than his leg.

When Johnny burst through the door, his gun in hand, he looked from me, hysterical with laughter, to my mother spouting twisted obscenities, to Forrest still writhing on the floor.

The rest of it went by fast forward. Forrest Miller claimed I'd broken into his house, was discovered by some of his friends, and when he'd tried to settle the matter quietly with me, I'd taken his gun from his own desk and shot him. The big guy said it had happened exactly like that. Then the ambulance arrived and took Forrest away. Johnny sent Momma home, too.

Then he sent a couple of officers over to the Dalman house to get Tom and Susan's statements. I didn't want to think about what Susan would be forced to say to back up Forrest and Tom.

I showed Johnny the tiny pile of ashes in the fireplace. I showed him the blank spots in the photo album filled with pictures of Klan rallies. I told him what I'd seen, and who I had recognized. Then I asked him, without any real hope, if he'd be able to get Forrest for murder.

Johnny shook his head. "Laurie, who got shot here tonight?"

I looked at him. "Forrest Miller."

"That's right. And where did he get shot?"

"In the leg."

"In his own *study*. And who shot him?"

"Me."

"So who is the most likely person to be charged with anything here?"

I sat in dumb silence for a few moments. I already knew this, but had been fighting not to admit it to myself. "But he planned and organized a man's murder."

"How are you going to prove it? The pictures are gone. No one's going to testify. Assuming anyone did talk, he would be testifying to attempted murder himself."

"You could offer immunity in exchange for testimony."

"But why would anyone do that? I don't have any evidence to hold over anyone. So why would anyone implicate himself in this?"

"Sammy's mother could testify."

"She has no real evidence."

"Susan...?"

"Do you really think she'd testify against her own father?"

I sat there quietly for a long time. After awhile, Johnny put his arm around my shoulders. I leaned my head against him, and then I found myself crying. We just sat there like that, for a long time. Every now and then, one of the other officers would stick his head in the door and Johnny would motion him away. And I just kept crying.

I don't cry much, as a rule, but I had been making up for lost time ever since I arrived in Port Mullet. Right then, I cried for Elijah Wilson, and for Billie. I cried for Sammy, growing up without a daddy. And for Etta Mae and Sapphire, spending their lives in their father's power. And for Susan, who, despite all her plans, still lived as a prisoner. I cried for my own daddy, who couldn't make peace with having a daughter who inherited his own lusty spirit, who insisted on the rights he thought were the privileges that came to him and his sons as a result of their maleness. And for Momma, who had struggled with me so because she had been afraid that I'd end up like Billie.

The sobs were getting louder and harder, and I felt out of control. Johnny's shirt was wet and smeared with snot. He didn't move, except to give me a handkerchief, which I demolished in no time. He didn't say anything at all. I cried for awhile about what Johnny and I had done to each other, things we would never be able to forget.

And then I'd finished crying. My eyes were red and swollen and my sinuses ached. My head hurt like hell.

When I'd been still for a few minutes, Johnny gently disentangled himself from me and got up. "Don't move," was all he said.

He went into the bathroom, and I heard the water running. He came back with a hand towel wrung out in cold water. He lifted my face with one hand, and with the other softly wiped my face clean. He went back, rinsed out the towel again. He told me to lie down on the couch, and I did. He folded the towel carefully, and laid the cool cloth across my swollen, ugly eyes.

He went away for awhile, to make phone calls and talk to his officers. Then he came back, took me out to his car and took me home.

Momma was in the kitchen. She started making coffee when we came in. He walked me to my bedroom door. I threw myself on the bed with all my clothes on. I think I went right to sleep, but in my dreams Momma and Daddy and Johnny were sitting at the kitchen table, drinking coffee and talking in a low murmur, and I couldn't hear what they were saying.

Chapter Twenty-Three

I got up about five in the afternoon. Dinnertime in that part of the world. Momma fixed me a plate, and I sat down to eat it. She sat down across from me.

"You got a couple of calls this afternoon."

"Did I?" I was buttering biscuits like there was no tomorrow.

"Johnny called to tell you that Forrest Miller isn't going to press charges."

I nodded, added fig preserves to one of my biscuits. One just butter and biscuit, austere, as it were. The other with the sweet richness of figs. I wasn't surprised by the news. I had woken up with several certainties right there in my mind, all orderly and ready, even before I opened my eyes.

One of them had been that Forrest wouldn't press charges. If he did, I would defend myself by dragging in Elijah's murder and the Klan. A lot of it wouldn't be admissible, of course, but Forrest wouldn't want to open himself up to any of the publicity and scandal.

The other certainty was that I was going to do my damnedest to tell the story I knew, about Billie and Elijah and the murder, and tell it the best I knew how, come hell or high water. I'd need to talk to Sapphire and Etta Mae, of course, because they might not want to stay in that isolated little house in Sheriff Pierre country once the shit hit the fan. On the other hand, they were two strong women, and they just might. There were others who were going to be hurt by what I was going to do—I thought of Johnny's face when I told him about his father in the photograph—and there were still others that were just going to be angry at me for making such a fuss and causing so much trouble. I hated to think I was risking the tentative connections I'd made with my parents. But I'd made up my mind to let the chips fall where they might. It wasn't the kind of carelessness I'd usually been guilty of, the not thinking things through kind. I'd thought it up one side and down the other, and I knew I was going to hurt for the folks I was hurting, but I was going to do it anyway.

Momma continued, "He had more to say, too, but, really, I think it best you hear it from the horse's mouth."

"Hear what, Momma?" A car pulled up in the driveway as I spoke.

"Look, here he is now, with little Susan Dalman. That poor child."

My appetite evaporated suddenly. Momma hurried to clear away my dishes and put up more coffee. She had it perking before they got to the kitchen door. She put out cups and fixings, and then discreetly floated away towards the back of the house.

Susan's face was pale; she wasn't wearing make-up, and she wasn't smiling. In spite of that, she didn't seem to be falling apart. There was a sense of serenity and composure about her that I'd never seen before.

Johnny was pale, too, and he did seem nervous. His hands trembled slightly and he had trouble with the cover to the sugar bowl.

Susan spoke first. "We're on our way to the station, Laurie, but I had to see you first."

I nodded, immensely lost and curious. Was she going to apologize to me for having to back up Tom and Forrest's stories? That wasn't something she'd say in front of Johnny, was it?

Johnny placed a thin folder on Momma's wood-grained formica table and pushed it toward me. Nobody said anything. The two of them just watched me as I flipped it open.

Inside was the photo of the armed men standing over Elijah's body. I looked up at them in bewilderment.

"But Forrest burned... Where did you... ?"

"I slipped it down the front of my shorts."

"What?"

"When Daddy and Tom got there. Remember, you stepped out into the foyer? I waited just long enough to get this before I followed you out of the study. I'm sorry. I was too frightened to get any more."

"Sorry?" In my excitement, I jumped up so quickly that my chair fell over on the floor with a clatter. Of the three of us, no one made a move to pick it up. "You're sorry? Is that what you have to say?" I ran around the table to Susan and pulled her from her chair, wrapping my arms around her and holding her tight against me.

"Oh, Susan, I always knew you had it in you, I swear I did. I'm damned proud of you, girl!"

When I finished my merciless hug, I pulled back, arm's distance away. She looked good and solid, but serious, and she gave me a slight, sad smile that was as real as smiles get.

I looked past her at Johnny, who was standing now and who

also looked serious. "So, Johnny, what does it mean? Can we get him?"

Johnny's voice was firm, but unusually quiet and slow. "Forrest? I hope so, eventually. He's not in this photo, obviously, and only a few of the other men are. It's a hell of a good place to start an investigation, though. I interview those guys, tell him I have the photo, and, believe me, some of them will start talking. We can offer some of them immunity in exchange for their testimony against Forrest and the others. We can exhume Elijah's body, too, and investigate the cover-up in the coroner's office. It'll be long and hard and messy, but there's a good chance we'll reel in Forrest in the end. The photo by itself is enough for you to publish one hell of an expose." He leaned over to the table and picked up his cup, took a sip of coffee, put down the cup, and stared in it. "And it's enough to ruin my father. Hell, it'll pull down the whole structure of this town, and I bet you anything everybody in the state will be making jokes about Port Mullet. Congratulations, Laurie. Not only did you burn your bridges behind you, you're gonna leave the whole damned town in flames."

I looked at Susan standing with her head bowed and I thought of what that photo meant to her marriage, to her mother, to her children's future, to her whole life as she had known it before last night. I knew no words powerful enough to help her with what she had to face.

I turned back to Johnny. "But you're going through with it?" I hadn't meant to, but I spoke it in a whisper.

"Hell, yes. I'm going through with it." He closed the folder, picked it up, and took Susan's arm. The color was coming back to his face.

I followed them to the door like I was sleepwalking, the magnitude of the implications only beginning to seep into my consciousness. Susan put her hand on my arm and looked in my eyes. "I didn't do it for you, Laurie. I did it for Billie. I owed it to Billie." We hugged again, this time lightly, as if we had already started to move apart. Then she walked down the sidewalk between Momma's hibiscus plants, leaving me alone with Johnny.

Through the fog and confusion wrapped around my heart, I felt a sharp stab of pain. I didn't want Johnny to hate me. I would still do what I had to do, but I deeply regretted all the sorrow I'd brought into his life.

"So, you're leaving me with the ashes again," he said.

I couldn't reply.

He extended his hand toward my face and I almost flinched. He touched my cheek gently, a sad tenderness in his eyes. I grabbed his hand with both of mine, pressed it hard against my lips and kissed it. Then I let it go. He turned and walked towards the car where Susan was waiting.

"Emma's a good woman," I called after him. "Be happy with her. I know you have it in you."

He gave no indication that he'd heard.

I walked back into the house. I didn't know where Momma had been hiding, but now she was back in the kitchen, already shoving the coffee cups in the dishwasher.

Then she turned to me. "Your daddy's gone to the airport."

That was a surprise. "What for?"

"Another one of your calls while you where asleep. Your nice friend, Sammy. She's coming to visit. Says she was worried about you. Makes me feel better, knowing someone is looking out for you like that."

I looked around the kitchen like I was looking for an escape. Sammy? Here? I was more than ready to leave this place, go back to my real life. Home. My home was in the city. Even Momma had said it like that.

I didn't want Sammy to see me at my parents' house. I didn't want her to see her lover as a trapped adolescent, acting like a jerk around her family, being treated like a child in return. And I wanted to tell her what I had found out about her father on our own territory. I didn't want to tell her in Port Mullet, where we were surrounded by the rednecks who had killed him.

I was relieved, grateful beyond belief, that my father had not been in those photographs. And I was grateful that he had tried to protect me from the ugliness of the Klan, by letting me grow up ignorant of its very existence. He had apparently raised my brothers to share his belief that the Klan was silly and pathetic. With a pang of anxiety, I wondered what he was doing that very minute. Was he treating Sammy with his patronizing Southern chivalry act? Would she know he treated all females like that, or would she think it was a matter of race?

My stomach was churning when the car pulled up. I felt as naked and vulnerable as I ever had. My major victory in leaving Port Mullet had been that I'd created a persona to hide behind, and, now, with my two separate worlds colliding in one place, I was afraid it was me who would suffer the damage. I might just disintegrate into bits of matter, flung out to float through the cold, empty distances of the universe.

They came in the kitchen door. Sammy first, looking great, looking wonderful, looking like sex and love and food and good times, just like I remembered. And Daddy right behind her, carrying her suitcase, smiling.

I hugged Sammy right there, before I said a word. I tried hard to make it the perfectly appropriate hug. When it was over, I was exhausted from the effort of trying to keep the balance right.

Momma had still more food ready, and she sat Sammy right down at the table, and fixed her a plate. To my surprise, instead of escaping to the living room to watch TV, Daddy sat down at the table, too. The two of them asked Sammy questions about her daughters and her profession. They seemed honestly interested in the answers. Sammy fished her picture album of the girls out of her purse, and handed it to Daddy. He and Momma oohed and aahed over them while Sammy finished her banana cream pie.

Afterwards, Sammy accepted my mother's suggestion that she "freshen up." After she left the room, Daddy said to me, "That's sure one fine-looking woman." I blushed. Then I worried that perhaps he was expressing his own interest in her, not complimenting my own. I hoped not. I'd made a lot of progress this trip to Port Mullet, but I wasn't yet ready to accept any suggestion that my father and I were turned on by the same woman.

I ran after Sammy and caught up with in the hallway right outside my bedroom. We kissed again, more passionately this time. I was carried away by the sweetness and familiarity of Sammy's lips and mouth and tongue, and yet I was aware of the tingle in my stomach, the danger. After all, this was my parents' house, and someone could walk in on us any minute. And I'm telling you, that added a fizzy kick to the kiss that made it that much better.

When I forced myself to pull away, I asked her how she'd been able to take a break. She told me she had arranged for another midwife to take her calls for a few days, so that we could spend some time alone together. She said that while I'd been gone, Rachel had finally been weaned. Sammy attributed that occurrence to the security Rachel had felt in not having to share her mother with me for a few days. Now it was my turn to have Sammy to myself. But should an emergency arise, with the patients or with the girls, we'd be on the first plane out.

While she was explaining, I pushed open the door to my bedroom. For a moment her face reflected the dissonance between the flowered and ruffled decorating scheme and what she knew of my taste. Then she said, "Your father must have put my suitcase somewhere else, it's not in here."

So much had happened since I woke up that morning that I hadn't even spotted the mine field that we now had to cross. "Uh. Well. I bet he put it in the guest room. Really Momma's sewing room. Next door."

I backed out of my room and opened the next door. Sammy followed me, a knowing grin slowly taking over her face. "Yep," I said, "here it is. Right here in the guest room. Next door to my room."

Sammy walked over, reached down and put her hand on the handle of the suitcase.

"Uh, Sammy…"

"Yes," she said, sweetly.

"I have something to tell you," I began.

"You didn't tell them," she said. She didn't look angry. She was still smiling.

"Nope. I meant to, you see, but—"

"You went and told my mother. *And* my aunt. But you didn't even tell your own parents. Who you've been staying with all this time. I tell you, you're one courageous girl detective, Laurie." But she was still smiling.

"Well, you see, it's like this…"

"No," she said, picking up the suitcase, and heading for my bedroom. "It's like this. You tell them now. Right now. Or I'm taking my suitcase right back to the airport and getting on the first plane north." She swung her suitcase up on my bed and snapped open the latches. She looked at her watch. "I need a shower and clean clothes. So you have, let's say, twenty minutes. That ought to be long enough. Have fun." Then she started pulling things out of her bag. I had clearly been dismissed.

I left Sammy and went back into the kitchen, determined to engage in mature conversation with my parents. I had a plan designed to prevent me from taking off on some piece of impulsive bad behavior, however momentarily satisfying it might be. My plan was to take Sammy down to Sanibel Island, for two days and nights of beautiful solitude. I figured we could leave in the morning for a holiday of swimming, and beachcombing, good seafood and wine, along with long, frantic nights of sex. I was going to keep this delightful prospect in mind, the carrot I dangled in front of myself to ensure my own good behavior.

Now was the time. I was a grown-up, wasn't I? I couldn't just hide my lover away in New York, and fail to acknowledge her in front of my family. If I did, I was still a kid, still running away from being Coach Coldwater's little girl, instead of moving towards who I wanted to be.

"That's one nice girl, that Sammy," said Daddy.

"I'm glad you like her." I stumbled on, opting for immediate disclosure instead of graceful build up. I was afraid that if I took my time, I might chicken out. "She's my girlfriend. My lover. And her little girls, Annie, Sarah, and Rachel, they're special to me, too."

Momma's expression was frozen. Daddy looked shocked for a long moment, and then he laughed. "Well, if that isn't the craziest thing I ever heard tell of. This has got to be another of those phases you keep going through." He shook his head, acting as if the whole prospect was amusing, but nothing he could take seriously. "Good Lord, Baby, that woman is a mother. What could you possibly be to her girls? You can't be their mother, and you damn sure can't be their daddy. It's no wonder Johnny Berry divorced you. You act like you don't have good sense a lot of the time."

The kitchen door opened and my brothers, without Walter, who had gone off on a camping trip, or so he had told Momma, came piling in with some of their friends. "Hi, Baby. Hi, Daddy. Momma, is there anything to eat around here?"

As the boys sat down, and Momma started carrying bowls and platters of food to the table. She still hadn't commented, but at least she hadn't cried or screamed or called Johnny. I started thinking about the girls' summer vacation. I ought to take them swimming in the Gulf. They should really know what that was like. And fishing, out in the Gulf, and down the river, too. Sammy might have a hard time getting away, but I could bring Annie and Sarah down for a visit, and maybe even Rachel, too. I had a feeling that Rachel and I were really going to get along now that we wouldn't be competing for Sammy's breasts. Hey, I thought, we could go visit Etta Mae and Sapphire, and then stop at Weeki Wachee on the way back. Those city girls had never seen anything like the underwater mermaid show, I was certain of that.

For a moment, I had a flash of what the girls would look like, sitting around the table while Momma brought them plate after plate of food. She had been awfully taken with the photos Sammy had shown her. Hadn't she said often enough how she wanted grandchildren? I was absolutely certain that her daughter's lover's black children was not at all what she had in mind, but I hoped I could win her over. After all, it looked like they might be the only grandchildren she was going to get from me, maybe from any of us.

Sammy walked back into the room then, swinging her hips in that wonderful way she does. Big brother Seth looked up in surprise. The others were concentrating on the food and the conversation, and hadn't noticed yet. Seth winked at me, and gave the thumbs up. I walked over to him, draped my arm around his shoulder, and ruffled his hair in gratitude.

My brother, Paul, said, "Baby, introduce us to your friend."

"Baby?" said Sammy.

We were up early the next morning. I hoped to avoid anymore discussions with my parents about Sammy and me. My emotions had been stretched in all directions the last few days, and I felt the need for some recovery time, first on Sanibel Island, and then back home in the city. I figured that the interval of time before my next visit would give my folks time to adjust their thinking. Here they'd always thought I was a man-crazy slut, and then they discovered that actually I was a woman-crazy slut, too.

It was no surprise that Daddy had gone fishing. But Momma was waiting with grits and eggs and bacon and a determined look in her eyes. She clearly meant to have one serious talk. After breakfast, Sammy gracefully excused herself, and there I was, alone with Momma.

"Now, I've got something to say, and for once, I don't want you interrupting or talking back until I've said my piece."

I nodded.

"I'm sorry, Baby. I know it's my fault. I failed you. I didn't give you enough guidance. Didn't manage to teach you all the things a girls should know, though Lord knows I tried. How to fix your hair, wear your clothes, get along with a man. If your daddy and I had been stricter on you about that kind of thing, you would have been able to keep a nice man. Like Johnny Berry. And you wouldn't have to fall back on this kind of thing."

I wanted to jump in right there, turn back the flood of misunderstanding and misplaced guilt, but it was too late. There was no stopping Momma.

"Now, I think right highly of your friend Sammy. She seems like a fine girl, and she's always welcome to visit here with you. But I have something real important to say, something I never want you to forget. You just say the word, anytime, and I'll send you the money to get the professional help you need."

Then she turned away and started packing an amazing number of sandwiches in the cooler for Sammy and me. It took a short while for me to catch her meaning. For just a second there, I thought she meant she'd pay for a professional hair styling. It hurt to know she thought my love for Sammy meant I was sick. There were a lot of things I wanted to set her straight about. But she had been good to Sammy, and she hadn't tried to stop us from sleeping together under her roof. I figured Momma and I had made enough progress for one visit. We'd already covered more emotional ground in the last few days than in all of my life up until then.

An hour and a half later, my love and I were headed south in a rented convertible. Sammy was driving, we had the top down, and the wind was in my hair, my feet up on the dash, and my left hand on Sammy's thigh.

Suddenly I pulled my feet down, sat up straight, took my hand off Sammy. Two signs had caught my eye at the same time. The first one was small, metal, rectangular. It said, "This section of the highway adopted by the Port Mullet Rotary Club." The second was a large, commercial billboard set back from the road. It read: Miller Groves Development, Beach Site Homes and Condominiums.

The image of Elijah Wilson's mutilated body, surrounded by smiling men with guns, flashed into my mind. And in the trees behind, a dark native girl, arms and legs covered with tattoos, watched me. Then they were both gone and the sun was bright, and the sky cloudless and blue. I touched Sammy's leg again. I knew that beyond the palm trees was the Gulf, warm and salty, that Sammy's flesh was sweet beneath my hand, and back in the city, three terrific little girls were waiting for us to come home.